"So you'll marry some man you hardly know?" Elijah asked, hearing the edge in his own voice.

"Maybe," she said.

"Don't." He sighed. "You're better than that. You always were. Wait for the right man, the one who will love you properly."

Tears rose in her eyes and she looked away. Her words were so quiet that he had to step closer still to catch them. "He wanted his food cooked like she used to cook it. . . . He wanted his shirts folded the way she used to fold them." She wiped at her eyes. "I didn't like coming second. Is that sinful of me?"

So he'd been right—Mervin wasn't the saintly older man after all. He'd sensed it, somehow. Elijah stepped closer and slid a hand around her waist. What had she been through? Had she really been stationed under a dead woman's shadow in her own home with her husband? What would that have done to her?

"You deserved better than him," Elijah murmured.

"I was vain and stupid." Her voice trembled. "I thought because I was young and . . . relatively attractive . . . that he would love me. I thought that I could be enough."

"You are enough," he retorted. "Sadie—"

She raised her gaze tentatively, and he dipped his head down, catching her lips with his.

Her eyes fluttered shut, and he pulled her against him in a slow kiss.

BOOK YOUR PLACE ON OUR WEBSITE AND MAKE THE READING CONNECTION!

We've created a customized website just for our very special readers, where you can get the inside scoop on everything that's going on with Zebra, Pinnacle and Kensington books.

When you come online, you'll have the exciting opportunity to:

- View covers of upcoming books
- Read sample chapters
- Learn about our future publishing schedule (listed by publication month and author)
- Find out when your favorite authors will be visiting a city near you
- Search for and order backlist books from our online catalog
- Check out author bios and background information
- Send e-mail to your favorite authors
- Meet the Kensington staff online
- Join us in weekly chats with authors, readers and other guests
- Get writing guidelines
- AND MUCH MORE!

**Visit our website at
http://www.kensingtonbooks.com**

The Bishop's Daughter

PATRICIA JOHNS

ZEBRA BOOKS
KENSINGTON PUBLISHING CORP.

www.kensingtonbooks.com

ZEBRA BOOKS are published by

Kensington Publishing Corp.
119 West 40th Street
New York, NY 10018

All Kensington titles, imprints, and distributed lines are available at special quantity discounts for bulk purchases for sales promotion, premiums, fund-raising, educational, or institutional use.

Special book excerpts or customized printings can also be created to fit specific needs. For details, write or phone the office of the Kensington Sales Manager: Attn.: Sales Department. Kensington Publishing Corp., 119 West 40th Street, New York, NY 10018. Phone: 1-800-221-2647.

Zebra and the Z logo Reg. U.S. Pat. & TM Off.
BOUQUET Reg. U.S. Pat. & TM Off.

First Printing: May 2019
ISBN-13: 978-1-4201-4911-1
ISBN-10: 1-4201-4911-3

ISBN-13: 978-1-4201-4914-2 (eBook)
ISBN-10: 1-4201-4914-8 (eBook)

10 9 8 7 6 5 4 3 2 1

Printed in the United States of America

Prologue

A fly bounced against the kitchen window as Sadie Hochstetler hung the gas lantern on a hook in the center of the ceiling. The morning was still dark, the days shortening on this end of August in Morinville, Indiana, but the outdoor early morning chill hadn't done anything for the kitchen. It was still hot indoors. Sadie was up earlier than she usually rose for the day, and the rest of the family was still asleep—Mamm and Daet, her younger sister Rosmanda, and Sadie's own three-year-old boy, Samuel, who slept in a little bed beside her own . . . for most of the night. He usually ended up crawling into hers sometime in the darkest hours, and she pretended not to notice.

Her son crawling into her bed couldn't go on forever. She'd have to put a stop to it. But with her husband, Mervin, passed on, there was that vast empty space of clean white sheet next to her, and a little boy with rosebud lips and wispy blond curls whose daet had died before any of them even knew that Sadie was expecting.

Golden lamplight spilled over the kitchen tabletop that had been scrubbed down to a dull sheen. Sadie pushed open the window, waiting for a moment to see if she'd be rewarded with a puff of breeze. She wasn't. The fly bounced twice more against the glass, and then escaped.

Sadie opened a cupboard and pulled a stool closer to let her reach the highest shelf. Deep at the back was a small tin box, and this was why she'd come down so early— sacrificing a few more minutes of sleep—to get a peek at the letters from her brother, Absolom, when she could read them alone. He'd been gone from them for nine years now, and she'd been left with only the memories of her brother's lopsided grin and ready jokes behind Daet's back. But he'd written over the years—a few times. Not often. Mamm's letters outlining the church's reasons for the Ordnung had mostly gone unanswered. Until a few months ago, when his letter arrived in the mailbox at the end of the drive.

Sadie pulled down the tin box and pried it open with a soft creak. She took the top letter, then glanced toward the ceiling, listening. There was still silence from above. She didn't read these letters often, but some mornings she missed her brother more than others, and she'd come to see his words on paper, as if they could bring him back in some way. She opened the letter and scanned the now-familiar words . . .

Dear Mamm and Daet,

I know it's been a long time since I wrote to you, and I wanted to tell you that I haven't forgotten. I just didn't know how to answer. But things have changed around here, and I wanted to tell you about it. You should know.

My girlfriend, Sharon, is pregnant. We haven't been together all that long, but the baby is mine, and I've got to stand by her. I'm going to be a daet now. She's due in August, and I'm real excited. I thought you should know that you'll have another grandchild.

*But this also means I can't come back and join
the church. I'm sure you can see that. Sharon
wouldn't make a good Amish wife. She's not like
our girls. She's loud and fun and hates rules. It just
couldn't fit, and if I came home, I'd have to come
back without her and the baby. I can't do that. I've
got to work and support her.*

*We've moved to a different apartment, and we're
living together. So I'm going to give you my
address, so you can reach me if you want to. I want
to hear from you, but you've got to stop asking me
to come back. It can't happen.*

*I know I've disappointed you—especially you,
Daet. I know I'm not what you wanted or hoped
for in a son, but I'm doing my best here with the
Englishers. And I'm okay. You don't need to worry
about that.*

I miss you.

Absolom

It had been nine years now since Absolom had left
home, and Sadie's heart still ached at his absence. He'd
missed so much—Sadie's wedding, Samuel's birth, Mervin's
death. . . . If he'd stayed, he'd have been married long ago,
with a houseful of children and a smiling wife, just like
their older brothers had. But he'd given it up for . . . what?
A life with the Englishers, out there where the rules no
longer applied, and life made no sense.

This being August, Absolom's child would be born soon.
If it hadn't been born already. Would he write when the
baby arrived? Or would he stay silent? Sadie wanted to
know about Absolom's child—if it were a boy or a girl, and
if it resembled him at all. But Mamm and Daet hadn't
replied to that letter. It had sounded too final, and perhaps
they'd seen the same thing Absolom had talked about—the

impossibility of his return. He'd have to walk away from a father's duties to do so, and while they hadn't raised him well enough to stay Amish, they'd certainly raised him well enough to stand by his parental responsibilities. For what it was worth.

Sadie refolded the letter and returned it to the pile. She stretched to push the box into the back of the cupboard again just as the floorboards above her head creaked. That would be Mamm and Daet, up for the day. Mamm would join her in the kitchen preparing breakfast, and Daet would go out for morning chores. Rosmanda always had to be woken by Mamm with a tap on her bedroom door, and three-year-old Samuel would sleep another hour before Sadie went to fetch him for breakfast.

Sadie reached for the kindling and bent to start the fire in the belly of the stove. Babies, absent brothers, even dead husbands—they didn't change anything. The day began the same way, with a fire in the stove and breakfast to cook. Solace was in the work.

Chapter One

Sadie looked out the window, watching as Daet trudged out toward the barn. She smoothed her hands over her apron, but her expression was grim. Daet wasn't well. He'd been to the doctor in town, and he'd been diagnosed with a heart problem, prescribed several different bottles of medication, and told he needed to take a break. But Amish men didn't take breaks—they worked, just like the women. Breaks felt sinful somehow, unless it was a Sunday, and Daet was both a farmer and the bishop of their local church. A break from one job meant time for the other. Besides, there were three hundred head of cattle getting ready for market, and the sale of those meat cows was a big chunk of yearly income.

Sadie, Mamm, and Rosmanda worked on breakfast. This was their domain, and while Sadie and Rosmanda had been helping out Daet with the cattle, he didn't like having them forced into men's labor. He was hiring a hand, he said. Someone to take care of the extra work until Sadie's brothers and nephews would come to help with the haying.

"I wonder when Jonathan Yoder and Mary Beiler will finally get married," Mamm commented.

"They aren't that serious," Rosmanda said as she filled a pot with water.

Sadie passed Mamm the corn meal for the fritters they'd soon be frying up. She glanced over at her sister. Rosmanda's hair was rolled up underneath her white kapp, a single tendril falling loose down her neck.

"They've been courting for almost a year," Sadie said with a short laugh. "That's serious. Besides, the Beilers planted three extra rows of celery this year . . ."

Celery—the main ingredient for wedding soup. That was as much as Sadie could say without betraying her friendship to Mary. Jonathan had already proposed, and Daet would be announcing their banns in a matter of weeks.

"How many times did Mervin take you home from singing before he proposed?" Rosmanda asked.

"Four," Sadie replied. "And I knew how to keep a secret until the banns."

Rosmanda muttered something, and Sadie and her mother exchanged a look. While Mamm patted the corn dough into a soft patty, Sadie tossed some thick lard into the pan where it slowly melted into a puddle. What was with her sister's moodiness over Jonathan and Mary? Their relationship was well known—those banns wouldn't exactly be a shock.

"You're not old enough to worry about eligible bachelors, Rosie," Sadie teased. "Keep your eyes to the boys your own age. I don't think Mary will be giving Jonathan up without a fight."

"Well, maybe I don't want to have to marry an old man like you did," Rosmanda snapped, and Sadie froze for a moment, the barb sinking in.

Old man. Yes, she'd thought the same at her age, but at twenty and having the Stoltfuz sisters with their blond hair and sparkling complexions as her competition, she wasn't in a position to be choosy. Besides, like other farmers,

Mervin had been in good shape—long limbs and tight muscle.

"He was a kind husband," Mamm cut in. "Rosmanda, you could do far worse than a decent man like Mervin."

"Kind?" Rosmanda turned. "He didn't leave her anything!"

"He had grown children." Sadie was tired of explaining this, pretending that it hadn't cut her as deeply as it had when she'd seen the will. "And he did leave me some money. If he'd known I was pregnant—"

"You were his wife!" Rosmanda shook her head.

There had been a full farm, which he'd left to his youngest son, who'd been working the land with Mervin. The older boys had married and already gotten mortgages for their pieces of land farther away from the family. And then there was the boy who'd opened a woodworking shop in town for the tourists, and made a more regular income than his farming brothers.

"There were other considerations." His children, who'd never quite accepted her.

"You deserved—" Rosmanda started.

"And you're questioning a man's authority," Mamm snapped. "Watch your mouth, Rosmanda. Your sister married a good man who provided for her comfortably. A young widow can marry again. And a woman who can't hold her tongue won't get married at all."

The thought of another marriage brought a heaviness to Sadie's chest, though, and it wasn't rooted in her love for her late husband. She knew how hard marriage was now that she'd experienced it, and a decent man and a woman who could cook might look like a successful match to the outside world, but Sadie had never been lonelier than in her marriage. She'd missed her parents and her sister, and while her husband's grown children who had stayed in the area were kind to her, there was always an awkward distance. It wasn't an easy family life to navigate.

"Enjoy this time," Sadie said. "You're under your father's roof, and you'll miss these days. I guarantee it."

Even Absolom seemed to miss those simpler days before life became complicated and difficult. These times were not to be taken for granted. And Sadie was keeping her own advice. She couldn't stay a burden to her parents forever, either, and she knew she'd have to get married again. It was the proper thing to do. But she'd miss this time, this rest between husbands. Maybe the next one could be younger . . . but a younger husband came with younger children from his first marriage, and she'd be raising a houseful of kinner that would never truly see her as their mamm. There'd be sidelong glances and insolent silences— anger at the one person they could blame because everything was heartbreakingly different.

Mamm passed the corn patties, and Sadie slipped them into the pan, the lard popping and spattering. She stepped back to avoid being burned. The women worked in silence for the next few minutes, getting breakfast finished and put on the table. And while she worked, Sadie attempted to tamp down the annoyance she felt toward her sister. So she was the example in life to avoid, was she? She wished she felt more indignant, and a little less exposed. How much had Sadie let slip during her short marriage? How much of her unhappiness had been obvious to others?

They covered the dishes with lids and plates to keep them warm so that Daet would have a hot breakfast when he came back in. Sadie headed upstairs to get Samuel up, relieved to leave her sister behind her for a few minutes. Rosmanda was getting more and more irritable—which was normal enough at her age—but her barbs were too well aimed. Sadie wiped her hands on her apron as she climbed the staircase, and when she opened her bedroom door, she couldn't help but smile when she saw her son lying spread eagle in the center of her bed, the sheet kicked off so that his little legs were bare to the morning cool.

"Sammie," she said softly. "It's time to get up."

Samuel stirred, then blinked open his eyes. He yawned and blinked a few times more.

"Good morning, sugar," she said with a smile. "Come on. We'll get you dressed and wash your face. Are you hungry?"

Samuel nodded. "I want breakfast."

"Me, too." She grabbed his clothes that sat folded on a chair, waiting for the day. She peeled off his night shirt and had him dressed in no time. He used the chamber pot—little boys didn't have the bladder control to make it out to the outhouse. She'd take care of this later when she made beds and cleaned the upstairs.

"Now let's pray to start the day," she said, and he obediently clasped his hands together. "Lord, we thank You for this day. Guide our steps and bless our ways. Amen."

It was a simple prayer, and Samuel liked the rhyming. As a good mother, Sadie taught her son a simple faith—that there was right and there was wrong, and God blessed the righteous. Except Sadie knew that it was infinitely more complicated than that. It was possible to do everything right, to be a pillar of female virtue, and still not earn her own husband's love . . .

As she and Samuel came downstairs, Daet was just coming in from the mudroom in sock feet. His shoulders were stooped, and he paused at the door to rest against the jamb.

"Benjamin?" Mamm said, hurrying toward him, but he waved her off.

"I'm fine, Sarah. Just a bit tired." Daet came all the way

inside the kitchen and looked at the table with a weary smile. "Now that's a beautiful sight."

Rosmanda pulled the lids and plates off the bowls of food, and steam rose from each dish. Samuel crawled up into his booster seat, and he stared hungrily at the corn fritters, his particular favorite. Sammie wouldn't dare touch the food before they prayed, but she spotted his fingers inching toward the table, and she shot him a warning look. At three, he was old enough to follow the rules.

The family sat around the table, and they bowed their heads in silent prayer. When Daet raised his head, they all followed his example, and the meal began.

"Your mamm and I talked about hiring some help around here," Daet said, filling his plate with corn fritters, bacon, and fried eggs. "Here, Samuel. A fritter for you."

Daet dropped a cake in the center of Samuel's plate, and the boy beamed up at his grandfather.

"You all know what the doctor said," Daet went on. "So I've hired a young man who will be sharing meals with us during the work day, so you'll be needing to take him into account in the cooking."

"Who is it, Daet?" Rosmanda asked, her eyes lighting up. She was hoping for someone handsome and close to her age, Sadie knew, and she smothered a smile.

"Elijah Fisher," he replied.

Silence descended on the table, and Sadie's heart stalled, then jolted to catch up. Elijah Fisher had been Absolom's best friend—*her* best friend. They'd played together as kids, then grown up together. Elijah Fisher had been her first kiss, and many more kisses afterward. He'd been her first love, a part of her coming of age, and in one fell swoop of betrayal, he'd lured Absolom with him to the Englisher world, leaving her behind without even a good-bye.

"But Daet—" Sadie began, sounding more breathless than she intended.

"It's already done, and your mother was fully in agreement," Daet replied.

"Mamm?" The sisters turned to their mother, who had just put food into her mouth. She chewed slowly, showing no signs of hurry.

"He's a part of our community now," Daet went on. "Coming home again isn't easy. Some grace is necessary."

"We are all sinners," Mamm murmured once she'd swallowed.

Sadie wasn't in disagreement with the theology here, but she hadn't forgiven Elijah, either. Elijah had been exciting and daring—an intoxicating combination when she was young and naïve enough to think that nothing could change. She'd felt like his whole world when he'd looked down into her eyes, but his promises that he'd never look at another girl obviously had been nothing more than words, because he'd left, taken Absolom with him, and she'd never heard from him again. As for Absolom, he'd never have gone if it weren't for Elijah, and then once he was outside of their community, he'd never returned. But Elijah had—a few weeks ago, visibly defiant and still sporting that strange, short-cropped Englisher hairstyle.

And Absolom had stayed away.

"He needs work," Mamm said. "His parents told us, and it isn't easy to find a job, especially when he's been away for so long. We are obliged to care for our neighbors."

"There aren't other farms?" Rosmanda asked woodenly.

"When the Lord puts a needy person in our path, He doesn't ask us to send them to someone else," Daet said. "We are obliged to help."

"And your daet needs the help, too," Mamm reminded them. "You know what the doctor said."

Sadie put some oatmeal, sugar, and cream into a small bowl for Samuel, and passed it to him with a spoon. Daet had made a decision, and there would be no changing it. This might be her home, but it wasn't her farm, and she had no right to tell her father how to run it. That was a man's work, not hers.

And while Elijah Fisher might have been their play-mate in years past, he was no longer just a rambunctious boy who liked to fish and run. He was no longer a gangly teen who told her that she was pretty and held her hand when no one else could see. He was now a grown man who'd spent a significant amount of time with Englishers and had lured Absolom away. He was trouble, and Sadie was firmly of the opinion that someone else should give him a job.

But her daet was the bishop, and they must be an example in public forgiveness of the one man who'd caused their deepest grief.

"He's arriving any time now," Daet said, pushing back his chair. "So I'd best get out to meet him. He'll be eating with us for lunch."

Elijah followed Bishop Graber from the buggy barn where his horses were now lodged for the day, and toward a farm wagon, already hitched and ready to take them to the cattle barn farther ahead. He glanced around at the fa-miliar farm. Nothing had changed since he'd last been here as a teenager. The last time he'd been on this land, he and Absolom had been sneaking away in the dead of night with bags over their shoulders.

It had been cowardly, and he'd regretted it later. Not the leaving, but the way he'd done it. His parents had deserved a good-bye, and so had Sadie.

Sadie lived with her parents again, too. Now that her husband had died, she'd come back to the family home to raise her son, and he glanced toward the house automatically. Some towels flapped on the clothesline, but that was the only movement.

"I need to ride," the bishop said, drawing Elijah's attention back. "My ticker isn't doing what it's supposed to do anymore, and it leaves me winded. It's a blow to a man's ego when this happens."

The bishop hoisted himself up onto the wagon bench with a grunt.

"Yah." Elijah wasn't sure how to answer that. A blow to the ego—wasn't that what the Amish aimed to do, crush the ego? They worked as a group, worshiped as a group, disciplined the likes of Elijah and Absolom as a group. Elijah's father had done what he'd expected—he'd followed the church decrees and had never once gone out to visit his son in the city, to see what had become of him. Not because his daet didn't love him, but because the community was more important than one rebellious son. Elijah had hated that part of the faith—the pressure to conform—which had been a big push toward his exit from the community. He'd wanted to be more, and that wasn't lauded here among the plain people.

Elijah hopped up into the front of the wagon next to the older man. The bishop's face was red splotched, and he breathed shallowly, leaning back like a man who'd run a mile in boots.

"You might as well drive the horses," the bishop said. "It'll be part of the job."

Elijah took the reins, then flicked them to get the horses moving.

"Are you alright?" Elijah asked.

"Fine. Fine. Drive on to the barn."

Elijah didn't want this job, but Bishop Graber was offering a fair wage and then some, so he couldn't be picky. He wouldn't be back at all if it weren't for his father's letter confessing that he couldn't even afford new rubber boots, let alone the fabric for his mother to make herself a new dress to replace the ones that were so worn, she'd hemmed up the frayed bottoms almost past the length of decency. It was the first letter that had actually sounded like his father's voice, instead of the constant flood of religious arguments. Elijah had been torn at that point—his daet had never bothered to come see his life in Chicago, and he'd obstinately frozen Elijah out of the family business until he'd had nowhere else to turn. And Elijah was supposed to dump the life he'd been building on his own and return now?

In the end, his duty as his father's only son had won out. And Elijah didn't make enough in Chicago as a common laborer with a road works team to both pay his share of the rent with Absolom and send money home. Yet. Absolom and Sharon needed the help in making ends meet, so they'd offered him a bedroom in their apartment. He and Absolom were close to opening their own lawn care and snow removal business, and the prospects were good. But Daet needed help now, so coming back was his only option in the short term. Even so, he wasn't staying for long.

Abram Fisher, Elijah's daet, made rolls of barbed-wire fencing to sell to local farmers, as well as pressed nails and spun twine. It was a fine and honorable Amish livelihood, but the Englishers could do it all cheaper and faster, so when Elijah's father bought a new barbed-wire machine that sped up the process considerably in order to keep himself in the market, that hadn't gone over well with their plain neighbors. It didn't take long for the elders and the bishop to come do an inspection. This machine required electricity, and could not be hooked up to a gas engine—

and that was a problem. If the Fishers wanted to remain in good standing with the church, the machine had to go. Even if it was Abram's last hope of competing with the Englishers.

Farmers could use electricity in their barns, but the Fishers couldn't use it for their machinery in the shop. It was a double standard, and Elijah knew that the elders' vote was heavily guided by the bishop's hard-nosed views—and Elijah wasn't convinced that the bishop didn't hold a secret grudge against the Fisher family for Elijah's role in Absolom leaving Morinville.

This job working on the bishop's farm was a miracle, his mother said. The Lord moving, his father said. Elijah wasn't so sure about that.

"I'll need you to help me tend to a lame cow in the barn." Bishop Graber interrupted his thoughts as they approached the barn. "And there's the milking to be done every day, filling the feeders in the fields, the watering troughs, mucking out the stalls, tending to the horses . . ." The older man eyed him.

The last time they'd spoken was the day before Elijah and Absolom left Morinville for Chicago. Was he remembering what he'd told Elijah then?

"All right," Elijah said.

"The pay is fair for the amount of work," the bishop went on. "But it's a lot of work. I'll be doing what I can, but I've been ordered to slow down by my doctor."

The bishop was a relatively wealthy man, owning his farm free and clear. He could afford to hire help, to slow down as the doctor ordered. There were men, like Abram Fisher, who weren't so blessed.

"I can do the work," Elijah said. "I'll need some direction at first, but I'll pick it up."

"You'll do fine," the bishop said. Elijah reined in the

horses at the barn, and the older man turned toward him. "I've been meaning to ask . . . have you heard from Absolom?"

When Elijah left for Morinville, Absolom had already moved into a new apartment with Sharon. Moving in. Shacking up. Absolom had been both excited and guilty— a combination that Elijah had gotten used to over the years.

"No. I haven't."

The bishop sucked in a breath, and for all his stoic facial expression, Elijah saw deep sadness in the old man's eyes. He nodded. "Let's get to work."

Was that part of why the bishop had searched him out in particular for this job? Because before Elijah left for the city, the bishop had had some pretty strong words for him. *Know your place, and stay away from Sadie. You'll never marry her. I never suspected that you'd be foolish enough to lay a finger on her, but seeing as you are, you are no longer welcome on this farm. Ever. If you step foot on this farm again without my express permission . . .* How the bishop ever found out about Elijah and Sadie, he had no idea. The bishop didn't say—but he also hadn't been wrong.

And then, after being gone for nine years and back for two weeks, the bishop showed up at his parents' door and offered him a job. Elijah had assumed it was linked to his father's financial decline—a guilt offering of some sort— because he had no idea why he'd bring Elijah back to his farm at this point in time. His daughter was single again, after all—and hadn't their relationship been the original problem? But perhaps the bishop's guilt was more complicated.

Elijah worked hard all morning, seeing to the cattle, mucking out stalls. He even noticed a calf that didn't seem to be thriving and might need to be bottle fed. He might not like the bishop much, but he'd do his job properly. A man wasn't much if he couldn't be trusted at the plow. That's what his daet had always said, anyway.

When lunchtime came around, Elijah was sweaty and hungry, and he drove the wagon back toward the house. He took the horses into the buggy barn to let them rest, cool down, and eat, while he would head to the house to do the same. But his stomach clenched into a nervous knot.

The family would be there. And that included Sadie. She was a boyhood love when he was young enough to think that it was only about the boy and the girl, and the rest of the family didn't matter. It was laughable now, that level of optimism, and nine years should have been enough to wipe her out of his heart.

When the horses were stabled, he headed over to the house. The side door was open, as if waiting on him, and when he stepped inside, he noticed the bishop had taken off his boots already and gestured toward the kitchen. The smell of beef stew and fragrant bread met his nose, and his stomach rumbled in response.

"A good morning's work, Elijah," the bishop said with an encouraging nod. "I'm grateful."

Elijah didn't know how to answer that. He was being paid for the privilege. So he opted for silence—an Amish man's best resort. He bent to take off his boots, and then followed the bishop into the kitchen.

The women were there. He saw the bishop's wife with her back to them as she bent over the oven to pull out another rack of bread. Rosmanda wouldn't look at him, but Sadie stared him straight in the face. No Amish bashfulness for her. Her son was at the table, already sitting up on his knees and waiting for the food. He'd heard about the boy's birth after her husband's death, and it felt strange to see the kid in person.

"Welcome," Sarah Graber said, turning toward him with

a smile. "Sit, sit. You men need filling and fast. Rosmanda, get the lemonade. They must be parched."

The girl did as she was told and started filling tin cups, and Sadie pulled the lid off the stew in the center of the table and began dishing up steaming bowls. It smelled delicious, and Elijah didn't wait upon ceremony. He was here as a hired hand, and lunch was his due. He eased into a chair opposite Samuel, and Rosmanda sat next to him with Sadie across, next to her son.

They bowed their heads in silent prayer, and when the bishop cleared his throat, they all dug in.

"And how did you find the work this morning?" Sarah asked.

"Fine, fine," Elijah said.

"We'll need to order more fencing from your daet," the bishop added. "Remind me to place the order."

"Yah. He'll be happy to supply it," Elijah replied. Orders—that was what his father needed. He glanced toward Sadie to find her glittering eyes fixed on him. She dropped her gaze to her bowl and took another bite.

"How have you been, Sadie?" Elijah asked, looking up from his bowl.

"I'm well." Her words were overly formal, clipped.

"You look . . . happy." He couldn't exactly say what he was thinking—that she looked more than happy, she looked beautiful. The last nine years had refined her, deepened her somehow.

"How is my brother?" she asked, and the table went silent.

"He's doing pretty well," Elijah replied, wondering what he could say at this table—what Absolom wouldn't object to. "He's excited about the baby."

He'd have said more if he weren't surrounded by her family on all sides, and he felt heat creeping up into his face. "A tree fell across the creek," Elijah added. "Down by the edge of your property." Down where they used to walk together, where he used to steal kisses. Blast it. He wasn't trying to remind her of that . . . or was he? He'd only meant to change the subject.

"You were there today?" Sadie asked, and when her gaze flickered up toward him, he could see by the pink in her cheeks that she was remembering the same thing he was.

"Checking on the fence." A lie. He'd just wanted to see it again, see if anything had changed . . . hoping it hadn't.

"I haven't been there since I was a child," she said, and she looked away from him. A child—she'd been considerably more than that. But she was right that she hadn't been a woman yet. Neither of them had been old enough for the way they'd felt.

"Yah. Of course. It's been a long time."

The bishop cleared his throat loudly, and Sadie nudged a bowl of sliced bread toward Elijah.

"Bread," she said.

Sarah shot her daughter a look of warning and murmured, "Sadie."

It had been borderline rude, but at least she'd offered it.

"Thank you," Elijah said quickly, taking a thick slice of bread and folding it in half to dip into his stew. Back in the day, Sadie had been funny and quick witted, but she was also stubborn as a mule when she got offended, and from what he could see, not a whole lot had changed about her. Even back then, she'd been the bishop's daughter, haughtily warning the boys when she thought they were overstepping appropriate play. *My father, the bishop . . .*

Elijah looked across the table at the pale-faced beauty. He held a whole lot against her father, but his issue with Sadie was a different one entirely. She had been fifteen when he left, and by the time she was twenty, she was married to some old man whose best days were behind him. As her father had pointed out, she'd been too good for the likes of Elijah, and he knew for a fact that she'd been worth more than Mervin Hochstetler, too. She didn't have to throw herself away like that, marry a man old enough to be her father. Whose idea had that been, anyway?

"What?" Sadie asked, meeting his gaze, and he quickly looked away.

"Nothing," he said. "May I have more stew?"

Sadie rose from her chair to serve two more heaping ladlefuls of stew into his bowl, and in so many ways he could see the youth in her still—the shape of her hands, the glitter in her eye. But he was disappointed to see that she'd never gotten past her cautious ways.

Sadie didn't take risks; she calculated instead. And by refusing to leap, she'd stayed very firmly on the ground. And he was a man who liked a heart-soaring leap. The sky had always held more for him than the dirt ever had. Even now.

Chapter Two

After the men went back to work, Mamm took Samuel out with her to pick the green beans that were ready to be harvested from the long, straight rows of the garden. Apple and cherry trees flanked the garden, the apples not yet ripe, but hanging heavily on the limbs, promising a good harvest. They grew all their own produce—beets, lettuce, tomatoes, cucumbers, carrots, radishes, three different types of string beans, potatoes, onions, garlic, celery, herbs. . . . If they didn't grow it and can it, they didn't eat it that year. Down in the cool basement, there were rows of labeled shelves, now nearly empty that the canning season was upon them again.

But Sadie's attention didn't stay fixed on the garden through the kitchen window. Farther in the distance, Daet and Elijah trudged back toward the buggy barn. Her father looked frailer than he ever had before, and Elijah was definitely a bigger man than he'd been at seventeen. He'd filled out, his shoulders had broadened, and where he'd once been lanky and thin, he was now muscled. He'd been "cute" before, and now that he'd solidified into manhood, he could draw her eye in spite of her better judgment. His eyes hadn't changed, though. She'd noticed that from across the table. His dark gaze was just the same. . . . It hardly seemed fair. Nine years with the Englishers should have softened him, ruined him a little, made him easier to dismiss.

The men disappeared out of her field of view, and she turned from the window.

Elijah made Sadie uncomfortable. He took too many liberties because of a childhood friendship, and he didn't back down and look away like he should. She didn't like that. It was probably the result of his years spent with the Englishers, and this grated at her, too.

Absolom would be different now also, and she wondered if she would even recognize him. But more than that, he was living with a girl, like man and wife, but he hadn't married her. That was unheard of in Amish society. A woman was worthy of marriage—commitment. Children conceived outside of wedlock were certainly born to married parents—the elders saw to that. And her brother had said that his girlfriend would never fit into Amish life, so this Sharon must be very different from the women in their community. Sadie had trouble even picturing what she might look like. Was she like the Englishers who frequented the farmer's market?

Elijah would know. And that was even more disconcerting. She wanted to be able to dismiss Elijah completely, but he was the only one who could tell them about Absolom's Englisher life.

Sadie pushed a plug into the sink and turned on the water to wash the dishes.

"What's the matter?" Rosmanda asked, bringing bowls to the counter.

"Nothing." Sadie sighed. "Thinking about Absolom. That's all."

Rosmanda didn't answer. There was nothing to say.

They'd said it all before, over and over again. They'd tried to imagine why he'd left and situations that might push him back to them. But all they really had was a hole where their brother used to be. Absolom had made a choice, and they couldn't undo it.

"I wouldn't do what Absolom did," Rosmanda said.

"Good." Sadie glanced over her shoulder at her sister who was clearing the table. "It wouldn't be a happy life. I'm sure Absolom regrets it. He just can't undo it now."

"I don't even want a Rumspringa," Rosmanda went on.

"You'll have a decent one," Sadie replied. "Like mine. It's possible to explore a little bit without launching yourself past the church's boundaries."

"No, I mean I don't want one at all," she replied.

Sadie wondered if Rosmanda would have said this in front of their mother. How serious was she?

"Rumspringa is important," Sadie said. "It helps you to not regret anything, to make an informed decision."

"My decision *is* informed," she replied with a shake of her head. "I've watched what happened to our brother. I've seen other girls get into trouble. I don't need to go to movies and stay out too late in order to know what I want. And I want to be a wife and a mother."

"You're too young for both," Sadie replied with a short laugh. "You might as well enjoy a little freedom for a year."

"Who says I'm too young?" Rosmanda shot back. "Mamm got married at sixteen."

"So what are you suggesting?" Sadie asked. "That you skip your Rumspringa and join the church now?"

"Yes."

It was ridiculous. Sadie turned off the water and reached for the first stack of dishes. Rosmanda was still a kid in so many ways. Yes, she'd seen the worst that could happen with their brother, but that didn't mean she had the maturity to face starting a family.

"Marriage isn't as easy as you think," Sadie said.

"I can keep house. I can cook, clean, keep a garden. I can sew better than you can!"

"It isn't only about the work, Rosie," Sadie sighed. "It's the marriage part."

"I know about that."

"You know how babies are made," Sadie shot back. "And that is a very small part of marriage, might I add. I'm talking about caring for a man, getting along with him, anticipating him. It's not easy, and while you might imagine a husband being tender and intuitive to your feelings, they, quite frankly, aren't."

"Because you married an old man!" Rosmanda retorted.

"He'd been married before," Sadie replied. "He had four sons and five daughters. He knew about women already. He was better than most in that respect."

"Maybe you weren't very nice to him," her sister retorted, and Sadie felt anger simmer. She knew her sister had no idea what she was talking about, but it still stung.

Nice. She'd been sweet and attentive. She'd been up fifteen minutes earlier than necessary to start breakfast. She'd smiled and nodded and kept her mouth firmly shut when she disagreed with him.

"That's the thing," Sadie said. "It isn't about being nice and cooking well. It's about connecting with him in a way that satisfies your heart. And his. If you have that connection, it doesn't matter if you burn a pie, because he'd still rather eat the middle of the pie with you than have a perfect pie with someone else. Finding that place with a husband . . . that's the tricky part. And without it—"

She didn't finish that thought, because there were things she wouldn't speak out loud. Like her loneliness in her marriage, and how working her heart out in that kitchen, cooking the best meals and scrubbing every inch of it to a shine, hadn't made any difference, because there was still that gulf between them that made Sadie's heart ache. It wasn't supposed to be that way.

"Other women have done it," Rosmanda said. "I can, too."

"You could," Sadie said quietly. "But being a little older might make it easier."

Rosmanda shot Sadie an irritated look and picked up the first plate to dry. "I'm not immature."

Her sister wouldn't hear her. Rosmanda hadn't been married before, and the example of marriage she'd grown up with was their parents. Mamm and Daet were a happy couple who had lived contentedly together for more than forty years. But they'd also found their rhythm already, and they had shorthand in communicating with each other in front of the children. Rosmanda wasn't seeing a marriage forged in their own kitchen; she was seeing one polished. Those were two very different stages in a marriage.

"Mamm will tell you the same thing," Sadie said. "You might not need your Rumspringa to know what you want, but it will certainly give you time to grow into it. Is there a boy you've got your eye on, or something?"

"No. I just don't want to be left over."

A lie? Sadie wasn't sure. But to be one of the girls who didn't find a husband—that was a valid fear. It was better to be widowed than never married, and Sadie had made a choice in husband for similar reasons. She'd wanted to start her life, and Mervin had qualities she wanted in a husband— he was God fearing, serious, and kind. He would have made an excellent father for Samuel, too—given firm guidance to keep him from making Absolom's mistakes.

"You're too pretty for that," Sadie said, nudging her sister with her elbow. "I hardly think you need to worry."

Outside the kitchen window, Mamm slowly rose to her feet and shaded her eyes with one dirt-darkened hand. Sadie slowed in her washing, and suddenly Mamm dropped her hand, hitched up her skirt, and jumped over the row of bean plants at a run.

"Benjamin!"

Sadie leaned forward. She couldn't see her father, but she'd seen her mother's face, and her stomach dropped. Something was very wrong!

Sadie and Rosmanda both ran to the side door in time to see Elijah half carrying Daet away from the buggy barn and toward the house. Daet leaned heavily on the younger man's shoulder, and his flesh looked gray, his hat askew. Mamm dashed across the grass to help support him on the other side as they brought him to the house.

"Get some wet cloths," Sadie ordered, and Rosmanda did as she was told, rushing to the cupboard for dish towels.

Sadie held the screen door open as Mamm and Elijah helped her father through. They squeezed past her, and she flattened herself against the door to make more room.

"I'm fine, I'm fine," her father was muttering, but Mamm flatly ignored him.

"What happened?" Sadie asked, as Elijah let Mamm take over. She looked toward her parents who were moving into the kitchen, then up into Elijah's dust-streaked face. Elijah licked his lips. He looked a little shaken.

"He passed out," Elijah said. "I don't know."

Mamm got Daet to a kitchen chair, and Rosmanda brought a cold cloth to put on his head. Daet took the cloth out of his daughter's hands to mop his brow himself.

"I got a little dizzy, that's all," Daet said. "I'm fine."

"The doctor said you should be taking it easy," Mamm said. "So maybe it's time you took his advice, don't you think?"

Daet smiled ruefully. "For a couple of hours, maybe. But there's cattle to check and a goat that gave birth, and—"

"I can take care of it," Elijah said. "I'll come ask you if I have any problems."

Elijah caught Sadie's eye and moved back toward the door. He wanted to speak to her, she could tell, and she followed him, stepping outside into the bright sunlight of the step. She blinked, then shaded her eyes to look up at him. Elijah stood closer than was entirely proper, and he kept his voice low.

"He's really not well, is he?" he asked quietly.

This was not something she wanted to talk about in Daet's hearing right now. She let the screen door swing shut behind her, and it closed with a clatter.

"No," she admitted. "The doctor said he has a problem with his heart, and he'd better take a break so that he doesn't have a heart attack. But Daet hasn't liked the idea of not working—"

"It's not our way," Elijah finished for her. "I get that."

Our way. She wasn't sure that Elijah had a right to that phrase now.

"He says he'd rather die on his feet," Sadie said bitterly. "We'd rather he not die at all."

"I thought he had," Elijah said with a shake of his head. "He turned this awful color, and he just dropped."

Elijah lifted his straw hat, scrubbed a hand through his hair—still awkwardly short in the Englisher style—then replaced it.

"We'll do our best to keep him resting," Sadie said, "but if he comes back out, try to keep him from overexerting himself."

"That's on me?" he asked bitterly.

"Yes, it's on you. We do the job we must," she shot back. Was he going to quibble now over what should rightfully be asked of him? Her father was ill, and he didn't know how to rest, just like every other Amish man. They might aim to humbly accept their lot in life, but hard work was the key in that—the great equalizer.

"He was mucking out a stall," Elijah said, adjusting his tone. "It was work, but hardly exertion."

No, Sadie could see that, and the realization wasn't comforting. Daet wasn't just working too hard—he was sick. His heart wasn't doing what it was supposed to do. Emotion closed off her throat.

"Look, I'll try," Elijah said. "I just can't promise I'll be successful. The bishop is not a flexible man."

She caught something in his tone there, but she didn't have the will to dig into it. Her father was not a flexible man—what Amish man was? They were determined to stay separate from the world, to be distinct, to be removed. Flexibility wasn't a lauded trait in the men of leadership.

"No, he isn't," she agreed curtly. "So be diplomatic."

Elijah shot her a flat stare that reminded her of years past. She and Elijah had always butted heads. The boys wanted fun, and she insisted on propriety. Her father was the bishop, after all. And somehow, against all her better instincts, she'd find herself alone with him again, his fingers twining with hers. . . . She pushed back the memories.

"If you want your father to rest, then maybe you should come and see the new kid your goat just gave birth to. I think your goat must have gotten out of your regular barn, because I found them both in a horse stall. The goat seems to have rejected the baby."

Sadie sighed. "I'll come."

Her father was ill, and nothing would be the same again. She'd already lost a husband. Please God, let her father be with them for a long time yet.

Side by side, Sadie and Elijah headed out toward the buggy

barn. They all had to do their part to keep Daet resting, and her part, it seemed, was to deal with Elijah Fisher.

Elijah jogged down the steps and strode toward the buggy barn with Sadie a step behind him. The sun felt warm on his shoulders, sweat inching down his back. Sadie ran a few steps to catch up, and he slowed slightly to match her pace. This was the first chance he'd had to be alone with her since his return, and he could feel her reluctance.

Did she really resent him so much?

"You wouldn't talk to me after Sunday service," Elijah said, glancing over at Sadie.

He wasn't sure what he expected from her. But she wasn't just an Amish woman. Not to him, at least. She'd been a friend once upon a time, more than friends, if he was utterly honest. He'd been head over heels in love with a girl whom he'd never be good enough to court, and as stupid as it was, he missed what he'd had with her. His time away from the community had put a mark on him, though. While his neighbors might forgive, they wouldn't forget, and he found himself missing the old days, before he was tainted.

That was the thing with Amish life—a man couldn't escape being known. All his mistakes, unless he hid them well enough, were up for public view. With the Englishers, they shrugged it off. *Nobody's perfect. Could be worse.* The Amish had a different perspective: if he'd abandoned the community once, he was a walking risk.

"You should be talking to the young men at service," Sadie said.

"I'm the only man my age who isn't married, and the younger men keep their distance," he replied.

"I don't know what to say. Maybe you scare them."

"Are you scared, too?" He heard the annoyance in his tone.

"I'm not afraid of you. I'm angry."

That was direct—he hadn't really expected that. They reached the barn. He pushed the door open for her, then stepped back to allow her to enter first. She paused and looked up at him, meeting his eyes squarely.

"I know I should forgive you, Elijah, and I pray daily for the strength to do it, but I haven't yet."

He was surprised both by her words, and that direct stare. Amish women looked down, looked away, bit their tongues. Sadie wasn't acting the part of a single woman with a single man. There was no deference to his masculinity, no acknowledgment of how things might look. He'd tried explaining this before to an Englisher friend—how appearances mattered—but Sadie wasn't giving appearances a second thought.

"You're more like the Englishers than you think," he said after a moment.

Sadie moved past him into the barn and he followed.

"Don't be cruel," she said curtly.

"Look at you!" he retorted. "Staring me in the eye like any Englisher girl would do . . . telling me straight that you don't like me. That's not Amish."

Sadie whirled around to face him. "Not Amish?" Fury snapped in her blue eyes. "I'm not the one who *left*! Don't you judge me on my Amish demeanor. I'm no girl anymore. I've been married, and I'm now a mother. Time has marched on, Elijah Fisher, and I'm not your playmate." She scanned the stalls, squinting in the dim light. "Where is the goat?"

She didn't wait for him to point it out, and she scanned the barn, stopping at the white and brown goat in a far stall, beside the stall the bishop had been shoveling out when he'd collapsed. She headed toward the goat and squatted down to inspect the situation. Elijah stood back. She obviously didn't require his input. She was right—she wasn't a girl waiting to be chosen by a man who fancied her any longer. She'd *been* chosen, and that lent her a certain sense of accomplishment. She was a mamm, too, and perhaps that had changed her most of all.

The baby goat had been cleaned off by the mother, and it bleated weakly. It needed milk. He'd have carried it to the house if he hadn't been carrying Sadie's daet.

"Come on . . ." Sadie murmured, and Elijah stepped closer to see her nudging the baby toward the mother's teat. The goat side-stepped away.

Elijah sighed and slipped into the stall with Sadie, taking hold of the goat between his legs to hold it still while Sadie brought the baby back to the mother's milk. The goat jerked forward, but Elijah held it firm.

"You've got a job to do," Sadie murmured, and for a moment, Elijah wasn't sure if she was talking to him or to the goat.

"I can see that you hate having me here," he said, as she pushed the baby's mouth toward the mother's milk once more. The baby latched on, and the mother kicked. Sadie let go of the baby and looked up at Elijah.

"Do you want me to be a good, quiet woman, or do you want the truth?"

Elijah released the goat from his grip, irritation simmering inside of him. "I value honesty," he said. "It might be all I have left."

"Then I'll be honest," she replied. "You're the reason my brother left our community."

He left a beat of silence, waiting for her to continue, and when she didn't, he said, "So this isn't about you and me—"

"Whatever we were is in the past, Elijah," she retorted. "But my brother is still gone, isn't he?"

"There is only so much you can blame on me," he said with a bitter laugh.

"Really?" Her eyebrows crept upward. "Because he said as much in his note to us. He was leaving with you so that he could bring you back. That was all. It was his Rumspringa, too, after all, and he had no issue with us. That was you."

And then neither had returned. Until now. Elijah rolled her words over in his mind. "I can't believe he wrote that . . ."

It wasn't the truth—not as Elijah knew it. Absolom had wanted to leave, too. He'd been cramped under his father's dominion. The bishop expected higher purity from his own children since they were examples to the rest of the community. The bishop's position was chosen by lot, and guided by the Almighty. And God never gave more than a family could bear. Absolom had resented those crushing rules, the lengthy list of things he must not even think, and he'd complained about it at length. He was frustrated, angry, and more than once he'd said how much he hated his father. And yet, Elijah still carried around a nagging sense of guilt that Absolom might have reconciled with his father if it weren't for Elijah's dreams for a better life in the city . . . and his pressure to bring his friend along.

"He'd have stayed home if it weren't for you," Sadie said. "He didn't want you to go alone."

"That's true. I don't deny it. But he stayed with the Englishers," Elijah pointed out. "If this were only because of me, he'd have come back. So why didn't he?"

"You tell me!" Her eyes flashed, and he watched her visibly compose herself, hide the sparking emotion back under a veneer of calm. Maybe he should give her more credit—

the chilliness he received from her might be a step above her actual feelings.

Sadie nodded to the goat again, and he pulled the mother goat closer to her kid once more and restrained her as before. Sadie brought the baby closer to the milk, and this time the kid managed to latch on and start to drink without the mother lurching away.

"I asked Absolom to come back with me a couple of years after we left, but he'd changed too much. His life had changed too much," Elijah said. Sharon had changed him most of all—she was different from the others, at least for Absolom. She'd been Absolom's first real love.

"And you hadn't?" Sadie asked pointedly.

"I've changed, too, but I have my own reasons for being here," he retorted. He wasn't here to fit back in and be a good Amish man. He was here to help his parents, for as long as that took, and then head back to the city where he had plans to grow a business without Amish leadership cutting him off at the knees.

"What's Absolom's girlfriend like?"

He struggled for words. "She's an Englisher." He shrugged. How else to say it? She was as foreign to this way of life as it was possible to be.

"I see," Sadie said with that tight disapproval he'd learned to expect from anyone who asked him questions about the outside world. But she didn't see—that was the problem. Sadie had no idea what was out there in the Englisher world, the loneliness he and Absolom faced on their own. You could take a man out of the Amish community, but you couldn't change where he'd come from. The Englishers acted like the Amish had hatched from eggs, and they could cut off family without much problem if they got into an argument. But the Amish knew where they came from—the parents who'd loved and protected them mattered. And Absolom was no different. He missed his family desperately, but what was a man to do when he'd changed too much to fit back in, and his family wouldn't take him back unless he did? He couldn't slice off the new growth any easier than he could carve a pound of flesh from his own body.

"Why won't he marry the girl?" Sadie asked, her voice low.

"I don't know. Maybe it wouldn't feel like marriage without a bishop for the vows and a plain girl with her wedding apron."

"The child won't know who it is like this," Sadie said.

"Would you rather he marry her?" Elijah asked. He was actually curious about what she thought was a good solution. "She'd never fit in here. She'll never make an Amish wife."

"I don't know. What's worse?" She sighed.

"Englishers are different, Sadie," he said. "The children make their peace with their parents' arrangements. They can grow up to do things differently if they want to. Englishers want freedom, not obligation. They want love without the demands."

In contrast, an Amish life was full of limitations, love packed into boundaries. Instead of width, there was depth, and while width could feel free and easy, depth could be painful in the plunge, and that narrow way could grow incredibly cramped.

"Love is full of obligations . . . demands, as you put it," she said with a shake of her head. "Love is more than a feeling. You might not see that, but I do."

"And why wouldn't I see that?" he asked.

"Weren't you the one who told me how you loved me, and then left?"

Sadie released the kid and it suckled noisily without her

support. Elijah loosened his grip on the mother goat, and eased away. They watched the two doing what nature required to feed an infant. Sometimes what was natural and right needed a little enforced structure to keep it going— duty, obligation. She was angry that he'd left her without saying anything, but she didn't know the whole story, either.

"You should never have come back without Absolom," Sadie said.

"Then I'd still be out there," Elijah said, his throat thick with emotion. "Because Absolom wasn't coming back . . ."

Sadie met his gaze, then looked away, but she didn't answer. Maybe she would have preferred it that way.

"Do you hate me that much?" he asked.

Sadie opened her mouth, closed it, then said, "I don't know."

Fair enough. He'd expected some religious deference about Christians not being permitted to hate, and she'd surprised him there.

"I'm sorry," he added.

"For which part? For leaving? For bringing Absolom with you? For claiming to love me and then disappearing one day?"

"We were *both* young," Elijah said quietly. "You were fifteen, Sadie . . ."

And she'd been under her father's dominion. He'd had every right to tell Elijah to shove off.

"Very young," she agreed. "And now I am older and wiser." She rose to her feet. "I'll check on the goats again. Are you leaving them here for now? Or are you bringing them back to the cow barn?"

"Sadie, your father told me to leave you alone."

She froze, then turned back toward him. "So you left Morinville completely?"

"It was the way he said it." Elijah sighed. "And the other

frustrations. I wanted to be more than a farmer. I wanted a chance at more. But he's the one who told me to stay away from you. I wasn't welcome back on this land. I wanted to say good-bye, but he wouldn't allow it."

Sadie shook her head. "You could have stayed in Morinville and proven yourself. You could have seen me on service Sundays."

"Sadie, I was seventeen. My pride had been bruised, I was filled with doubts and anger. . . . We had three years until you were eighteen, and at that age, three years felt like an eternity."

"You didn't write."

"I was trying to get over you." He might have been young, but he'd seen the writing on the wall. He'd never be good enough for her, and three years wouldn't have changed that. In Morinville, there was a slot waiting for him—the place where he'd fit into the community. He'd work alongside his daet in a business that didn't interest Elijah in the least, and he'd stay in his place. For the rest of his life. The thought was enough to choke him.

"Obviously, you managed to get over me." She nodded toward the goats. "Where will I find them?"

So that was it? She didn't want to hear his side of things—all she seemed to want was to have someone to blame besides her beloved daet.

"I'll bring them back to the other barn," Elijah said woodenly, idly picking up the shovel the bishop had been using. "After I finish in here."

Sadie met his gaze for a moment, her blue eyes swimming with conflicting emotion. Then she turned and strode back through the stable and pushed open the outside door, sunlight bathing her.

"Sadie, I did love you," he called after her, and she turned back, shooting him a sharp look.

"That wasn't love, Elijah," she said curtly. "It was lust. Now, if there are things I can take care of, tell me first, so that Daet can rest."

It wasn't love? Maybe he hadn't had anything to offer her or her family, but he'd most certainly loved that woman.

"Yah. Sure."

And she stepped outside, leaving him in silence. He didn't deserve her anger—not as much as she thought he did.

But regardless, whatever relationship he and Sadie had once shared had only given Sadie new liberties in making her resentment of him known. Whatever it was between them—love or lust, depending on who was doing the remembering—was safely in the past.

Chapter Three

Sadie had just finished hanging the laundry out to dry in the summer heat. It wouldn't take long until the fluttering shirts and dresses smelled of sunlight and fresh air. Samuel liked to hand her the clothespins—his favorite part of the job—and he'd stand next to her with a cloth bag of pins clutched in his pudgy little hands, beaming up at her every time he lifted the bag and she reached inside. Now the laundry was all hung, swinging in the warm gusts of wind, and Sammie was upstairs lying down for his nap.

She hadn't seen Elijah since breakfast. She packed him a lunch at his request so that he could eat out in the fields while he worked. Avoiding her? Perhaps. She should have been relieved to be free of him for a day, and she was . . . except she'd thought about him regardless.

Rosmanda was in the kitchen, with Mamm to supervise. She was still learning, too. The clatter of pans, and the voices of her mother and sister filtered out into the hall. The house was quieter now with only two daughters and a grandchild in the home, but it was still full of life, as a house should be.

Sadie paused in the doorway to the sitting room to look

at her father. He sat completely still on the rocking chair, his brow furrowed. An open Bible lay on one knee, and his black suspenders contrasted with his white, button-up shirt. His long gray beard fell down his chest, and, as Sadie looked at him, the memory of being a little girl on his lap, and the tickle of his beard against her face, brought a smile to her lips.

And Daet had been the one to tell Elijah to go away? If that were so, then her daet knew what she'd been doing with Elijah . . . the kisses, the hand-holding. She'd been too young to court, and too young for whatever they'd been playing at. All these years, she'd thought it was her secret, but the thought of her father knowing all of it embarrassed her. Still, Daet had never breathed a word about that.

"Come in, Sadie," Daet said quietly.

"I didn't mean to disturb you, Daet," she said. "I still need to gather the eggs—"

"All the same." He raised his gaze to meet hers with a solemn expression.

Overhead, Sadie heard the creak of the springs on her bed and she sighed. Samuel was jumping on the bed again, thinking his mother wouldn't notice.

"That boy—" She turned back toward the stairs and called up to her son. "I want you lying down. You obey your mamm, or I'll come up there!" The creaking stopped and she shook her head. "He's getting more willful."

"They do that." Daet nodded. "It doesn't stop, either."

Was he thinking of Absolom? Strange how a family of seven children could feel so bereft when one was missing, like it would never be whole again.

Sadie came into the sitting room and sank onto the couch opposite her father. She smoothed her apron over her knees. He looked wan, and she was glad he was inside today, instead of out at the barn. They had enough financial comfort that hiring more employees was a possibility. God had blessed them, and perhaps it was for such a time as this, when illness threatened.

"Are you working on your sermon?" she asked.

"I'm trying to," he said. "It's not coming easily, though."

"What will it be about?" she asked.

"Dying to self," her father replied. "He must increase, but I must decrease."

It was a common Amish theme, one that had been preached again and again.

"How are you feeling, Daet?" she asked.

"Fine." He paused, glanced toward the window. "Perhaps that isn't entirely honest. I want to feel fine, Sadie. I feel more tired than I've ever felt. Not the kind of tired after a long day of work. Something deeper, and that frightens me."

Her father had never been this open with her before, and she looked away, suddenly embarrassed. As she did, she saw her son's little form in the doorway. For all his noise on the bed, he'd crept down the stairs silently enough.

"Sammie," she sighed, and Daet looked toward his grandson, too.

"Samuel, what are you doing down here?" Daet demanded, his voice deep and authoritarian. Sadie knew that tone from her own childhood—the kind of bark that used to make her jump.

Samuel was silent, staring at his grandfather with round eyes.

"Answer me, young man," Daet said. "Why are you not in bed?"

"I'm lonely," the boy whispered, and Sadie's heart melted. He wasn't very old, and he hated being alone.

"Oh—" Sadie rose to her feet.

"No, Sadie," Daet said. "He must learn."

Sadie's breath caught. It was the same line Daet had used

when she was a girl, when he'd decided it was time to cut a switch and bring his point home. *The child must learn*. And learn they must. There was the right way, and there was sin. There was obedience, and there was defiance. If the rod was spared, the child was spoiled.

"Come here, Samuel," Daet ordered.

Samuel trembled slightly, but approached all the same, pale bare feet pressed against the wooden floorboards.

"So you will not lie in bed and rest?" Daet asked solemnly.

Samuel didn't say anything.

"Samuel, go upstairs and lie down," Sadie said. She was giving him a last chance to obey.

"I'm lonely," the boy whispered.

"So you will not obey your mamm?" Daet asked, his voice quiet.

Samuel's eyes flickered up toward Sadie, then back to his grandfather. Did he know what he was risking for a cuddle with his mother?

"Well then." Daet reached down and picked the boy up, but instead of turning him over a knee, he settled him on his lap, on the leg free of the Bible. "If you will not rest in your bed as your mamm has asked you, then you must learn."

"Daet—" Sadie's heart jumped in her chest. She didn't let Samuel run wild—she certainly did discipline, but she could take care of this herself. She was his mamm, after all. Her father flatly ignored her.

"Samuel, you will listen to the word of God." Daet raised the Bible in one hand, the other cradling the boy against his chest. Samuel fiddled with the crinkly end of Daet's gray beard between two tiny fingers, and Daet began to read aloud from his German Bible. It was high German, and Samuel wouldn't understand the words, but the import in his grandfather's tone of voice seemed to mean something to the boy. Samuel looked at Sadie pleadingly. He wanted to be held by his mother.

"Mamm—" Samuel whimpered.

"No." Daet's voice grew firm again. "If you will not rest, then you will listen as I read. That is all, Samuel."

The boy leaned back into his grandfather's embrace once more and Sadie rose to her feet. She had expected something more disciplinary from Daet than this gentle scene, and she wondered if his illness had softened him. Perhaps he was too tired now to be the wall between right and wrong for his grandchildren. And maybe this approach was what Samuel needed—time with his grandfather, time with a *man*. Samuel tended to cling to Sadie, and perhaps if Mervin were still with them, her son would be more confident away from her. She could be a loving mother to her boy, and she could dote on him, feed him, discipline him . . . but the one thing she could never give him was a father's touch. She couldn't teach Samuel how to be a man.

She took one last look at her son on Daet's knee, and she wondered why her father had never said anything to her if he knew that she'd been playing with dangerous boundaries with an older boy. Why hadn't he disciplined her then? Unless there was something to what Elijah had said . . . her father's dismissal of Absolom's best friend. Perhaps Daet felt more responsible for what had happened than she realized. She wouldn't ask him about it—it was too humiliating. Leaving the sitting room, she headed out toward the mudroom where her rubber boots waited.

"I'm going for the eggs, Mamm," Sadie called into the kitchen.

"Oh, good," Mamm replied. "We'll need more eggs for the lemon meringue pies we're making next."

Rosmanda was kneading a heap of dough, and she

looked up at Sadie, her face flushed in the August heat. Sadie chuckled and turned toward the door. Just yesterday, Rosmanda said she wanted to be married right away, and Sadie had informed their mother of it. It looked like Mamm was about to give her youngest daughter an introduction to doing all the hard jobs herself. If Rosmanda thought the work was hard now, she could try it all again at eight months pregnant.

The screen door banged shut behind her, and Sadie headed across the yard and down toward the chicken house. The afternoon sunlight blazed overhead, and down the path, coming from the cow barn, she could see Elijah walking, a toolbelt full of tools slung over one shoulder. She felt a rush of frustration. They hired several seasonal employees for harvest and planting, as well as calving and branding . . . but to have Elijah walking this farm like he belonged here. . . . He had been almost like family once, but those days were long past. While the hole her brother left behind had never healed over, she'd stopped missing Elijah.

At least, she'd thought she had until she saw him again, and she found her heart speeding up when she saw him from across the barn yard. She'd been a stupid girl nine years ago, allowing herself to toy with emotions she had no business playing with, and she wouldn't do that again.

"Good afternoon," Elijah called as he approached. His sleeves were pushed up past his elbows, revealing strong forearms. He had certainly hardened into a man in the years he'd been gone, and she hated that she was noticing that.

"Hello." She slowed as they approached each other. They stopped on the path, and Elijah looked down at her in a way that made her feel self-conscious.

"You okay?" he asked, narrowing his eyes. He'd always been rather intuitive when it came to her feelings.

"I'm fine. I'm getting the eggs."

"About yesterday—" he began.

"Elijah, I don't want to talk about that," she cut in. "It was a long time ago—a lifetime. I was fifteen, and my father got protective. I hardly blame him. You weren't so mature yourself. Let's just leave it."

"Okay." Those dark eyes met hers, and a small smile came to his lips. "If that makes you happy."

"It doesn't make me happy," she snapped. "It makes having you here less awkward if we don't have to rehash a childhood mistake."

"We weren't exactly kinder," he replied.

"We weren't old enough to court, either," she retorted. "It was . . . playing with fire. Let's just let it go."

Elijah lifted his hat, wiped his forehead with a hand-kerchief. "Fair enough. I'm going to fix those loose rails on the fence by the house."

"Did Daet ask you to?" she asked.

"I saw it and decided to get it done," he replied. "Is there a reason I shouldn't?"

She paused, eyeing him irritably. *Because this isn't your home*, she wanted to say. *Because going above and beyond won't change what you did to us.* But she couldn't say those things, so instead she said, "I can do it myself later."

"It's a man's job, Sadie." He caught her eye. Was that reproach she saw? Was he sensitive about a woman staying in her place? How about a man staying in his—and keeping to the Amish world?

"It's *my* family's farm," she retorted. "With Daet ill, I do what I must."

"Then give me a hand with it," he said, heading past her and shooting her a wry look. "I wouldn't turn you down."

So English of him, these quips. Elijah didn't talk between the lines like the Amish tended to do, and it left her feeling uncomfortable. Distanced language gave people a

sense of personal space, and his direct way of talking felt . . .
invasive. He may have come back to his people, but he was
still different from his time with the Englishers.

Sadie wasn't about to shout anything after him, even if
she could think of how to answer that, so she strode on
toward the chicken house instead. She had other things to
worry about besides Elijah Fisher's return to their community. If only he could find some other place to belong—
somewhere far away from her—so that she could let the
past rest more easily. Some memories, sweet as they had
been, were only an embarrassment when exposed to the
light of day.

Elijah dropped his toolbelt onto the grass and gave the
first loose rail a shake. The rail beneath had already fallen
on one side, and it wouldn't take much for a half-grown
cow to push through. This wasn't a field—this was the
fence that blocked off the barn and chicken coop from
the house, but still, a solid fence was a necessity. As much
as he hated working on the bishop's farm, he was honor
bound to work for the hours he was paid.

He glanced in the direction Sadie had gone. She was in
the chicken house. When he'd seen her on the porch, he'd
felt the resentment radiating off of her like heat from a coal.
He shouldn't care—not this much, at least. And he wasn't
about to explain to her exactly why her father's words had
cut as deep as they had. Her father was right, and he'd been
wounded when he saw it, but his feelings didn't change
facts. Sadie would never have been for him. He'd been a
foolish kid sneaking off to kiss a girl he had no right to, and
stupider still to fall in love with her.

But where it came to Absolom, perhaps he did still owe
her a guilt offering. Elijah had pressured his friend to come

with him—pointed out that they could finally have a bit of freedom, reminded Absolom of all the irritations he'd complained about. It was their Rumspringa, so it was forgivable. That had been his argument, at least. He'd never counted on Absolom changing so much once he was out in the Englisher world. Still—Absolom had made the choice to stay with the Englishers, and for that, Elijah couldn't blame himself. Every man had to choose his path.

Elijah picked up his hammer and started prying loose nails out of the post. For the next half hour, he pulled loose rails from the fence, putting his own frustration into the work.

The side door to the house opened, and Elijah ignored it. The family had their own jobs to do around here, and he had his. He was fairly paid, and that was why he was here—the money, crude as that sounded, even in his own mind. The Englishers admitted to that more easily than the Amish. Money wasn't supposed to matter for the plain people. It was a stumbling block. But it also bought food and paid bills, so it was only the well-off, like the bishop, who got to piously think of other things.

"Elijah!" It was Rosmanda's voice, and he looked up to see her standing on the step with a tall glass of lemonade in her hand. "Are you thirsty?"

"Yah." He was, actually, and he put down his hammer and met Rosmanda halfway across the grass to accept the glass. Sadie's little boy followed after his aunt, and Elijah smiled down at the boy.

"Hi there," Elijah said. The boy looked a lot like Sadie, the same blue eyes, the same shape to his lips. Samuel blinked up at him in silence, so Elijah accepted the drink, downed it, then wiped his mouth with the back of his hand and gave the glass back.

"Thank you," he said.

Rosmanda nodded, and turned back toward the house. Duty done, apparently, but Samuel didn't follow her.

"Sammie," Rosmanda called. "Come on."

Instead, the boy headed toward the fence and clambered up the half-dismantled rungs. It wouldn't hold the boy's weight—and Elijah reached out and caught Samuel just as the board gave way. The boy blinked into Elijah's face in surprise.

"Careful," Elijah said.

"Sammie!" Rosmanda swept back across the grass and held out her arms for her nephew. "I'll take him."

Samuel was looking in the other direction, toward the barn, and sure enough, striding down the path with a plastic bucket of eggs in each hand, was Sadie. When she arrived at the fence, she put down the eggs and rubbed her hands where the handles had bit into her flesh.

"Daet's sleeping," Rosmanda said. "Mamm says it's the pills the doctor gave him, and we need to let him rest."

"Yah, of course," Sadie replied. "I'll keep Sammie out here for a bit."

"I'll take the eggs in to Mamm," Rosmanda said. She exchanged a look with her sister, then picked up the buckets and headed back toward the house. Sadie's gaze followed Rosmanda's retreat.

"So, are you going to give me a hand?" he asked.

Sadie looked toward the house once more, then back at him. "I suppose I'd better."

Samuel headed off for the garden—a safer direction by far—and Elijah picked up a rail and held it against the post where it needed to be nailed.

"Hold this, would you?"

Sadie grasped the board and held it in place while Elijah hammered. She was strong, and she put her back into the work, but she wouldn't look at him. When the board was nailed into place with one nail, he headed over to the other side and pulled the board level.

"And here . . ." he said. Sadie came over and held the board as he asked.

"Do you miss it?" she asked after a moment.

"Miss what?" With four hard thwacks, the nail bit deep into the post.

"Life with the Englishers."

"Yah, I guess I do. There's a certain amount of freedom out there. No one cares what you wear, or what kind of hoe you buy. There's no judgment about the stuff we get judged on here. Things are faster, too. Cooking, shopping, traveling. Everything is so quick. A man has a chance at building something for himself—putting some money away, getting ahead."

"A man can do well in Morinville," she replied.

"Not all of us."

Absolom had adjusted to Englisher life better than Elijah had. He'd figured out the Englisher ways to slow things down, like staying in and watching TV for hours in the evenings after work. It took the place of farming, in a way. It used up the time.

"Did you have a girlfriend?" Sadie asked, looking over at him directly for the first time, and he felt heat rise in his cheeks.

"Yah. I dated a bit." Elijah picked up another nail and set back to work securing the rail.

"Anyone special?" Sadie asked after a moment.

"No one I married," he shot back, and color tinged her cheeks—not in a bashful way, though. She looked more annoyed.

"And my brother doesn't feel guilty for . . . for . . . living in sin like an Englisher?"

"What do you mean, *like an Englisher*?" He straightened and fixed her with a stare.

"You should know." She looked less sure of herself now, however. "No self-discipline."

He spun a nail between his fingers. "Do you really know what the Englishers do?"

"I've heard the stories. They have no morals," she shot back. "They have no rudder."

He was tired of her haughtiness. She was only spouting back what she'd been taught all her life, but he'd lived with Englishers who had shown more Christian charity than he'd encountered in Morinville. His own daet had never come out to see him—to find out what had entangled him outside of their community. In the city, at least parents had the freedom to do as they thought right with their own children. The fact that his parents had done nothing but write religious letters had hurt on a deeper level than he admitted to anyone.

"When we first arrived in the city, we slept on a park bench," Elijah said. "Volunteers in a church van came by and brought us food. They brought us back to their church and set us up with a Mennonite family who helped us figure things out. Those people had morals. They had a rudder. You have no idea what you're talking about."

"Maybe I don't know any Englishers," she said, lowering her voice. "But I can see what that life did to my brother. He's on his own out there. I don't know why he chose that woman over his family, but—"

"Like your marriage." Elijah crossed his arms over his chest. "To Mervin Hochstetler. That was a better choice?"

"Mervin was a good man."

"Old enough to be your daet," he added. "I still don't get it, Sadie. You weren't some homely girl with a good heart who would need to settle like that. You were the bishop's daughter, and you had both looks and intelligence. You didn't need to marry him."

"Is it impossible to believe that I loved him?" she demanded.

Elijah looked her over. She didn't meet his eye, then she glanced away irritably.

"Did you?" he asked.

"I learned to. At least I knew he'd never go English on me."

Like Elijah and Absolom had. He winced, but he wouldn't be put off, either.

"You had men you knew a whole lot better than Mervin Hochstetler," Elijah replied. "*I* knew you better than he did!"

After years of hanging out with her brother, afternoons at the creek, evenings in the Graber front yard, meals eaten with her family, and teasing her like he teased his own sisters . . . and then when his feelings changed, and he saw her as much less of a sister . . . Elijah knew Sadie rather well.

"And you weren't here, were you?"

"I'm not saying your father would have allowed it," he muttered, picking up another rail.

"Don't flatter yourself, Elijah Fisher," she interrupted curtly. "All I'm saying is that a girl has to wait to be courted. Yes, I knew other men, but they weren't stepping up. Mervin did, and he was a decent man and a kind husband. I could have done worse."

"Yah," he agreed reluctantly. "You could have."

"And you're right—my father did approve of that match," she went on. "He knew Mervin well, and he said that he would be a good husband—loyal and honest. He'd been very attentive to his first wife."

Something crossed her face then, a flicker of irritation, and Elijah couldn't help but wonder what that was.

"*Was* he as good to you as your father promised?" Elijah asked.

"That isn't your business," she retorted. "It isn't right to ask about private matters between a man and wife."

He dropped his gaze and gave a quick nod. It *was* an inappropriate question, but he wanted to know. Her reaction was too defensive to reassure him.

"You wrote to Absolom when you got engaged," Elijah said. "He was worried about you. He thought you deserved a younger man—someone where you could be the first."

Sadie was silent for a moment. "Absolom was worried?"

"Yah. You're his sister. He wanted you to be happy."

So had Elijah, for that matter, but they were too far away to ensure any of it themselves. Elijah had gotten himself his high school diploma, and he was starting to feel in control of his life at long last, but he felt utterly helpless when it came to Sadie. She was out of reach.

"I don't need protecting, Elijah. I'm safer here in Morinville than either of you ever were out there."

Who was he to argue? He was checking in to make sure she was okay. That was all. Absolom had asked that much of him.

"Hold this," he said gruffly, and Sadie complied, holding the rail against the post as he pounded the nail through the wood.

In a way, his time with the Englishers had ruined him. There had been a time when he'd been as sure of himself as Sadie seemed to be—as confident in his own rightness. But he'd seen too much, and he was left with more questions than answers. So while Sadie's naivety annoyed him, he was also a little envious. She'd stayed at home, kept the community's respect, and had never been faced with the confusing world outside of their farm life.

"Elijah, I don't know why my father hired you," Sadie said, as he hammered another nail into place. "It makes no sense to me. But here you are. I could continue to fight this, but my displeasure isn't about to change my daet's mind. Here's the truth—we need you here to keep my daet from working himself into a heart attack."

Elijah positioned the last nail and sent it through the wood with two hard thwacks. "Yah. He told me."

"So, is it possible for us to set aside our differences and work together to keep this farm running without burdening my father?" Sadie asked.

Elijah nodded slowly. "Sure. I'll do the job, Sadie."

"No, I want more than that." She fixed him with that direct stare of hers. "When he says something harsh, or pushes you too far, I want you to stay on. Don't quit."

Perhaps she knew her father's capabilities better than she'd been letting on.

"He could find someone else," Elijah said. "He probably should, for that matter."

"In the time it would take, Daet would go out there and push it too hard. He's not well, Elijah. I'm worried. If you can't do it for Daet, do it for my brother."

For Absolom. Yes, he could put up with punishment for his friend, but he could also do it for Sadie—the woman he'd loved back when they were barely more than kinder, according to her.

"All right," he said cautiously.

"Promise me, Elijah. I've lost a husband, a brother . . . I can't lose my daet." She was no longer the angry woman in control—she looked almost desperate, and he felt a wave of protectiveness. She was scared.

"Yah, Sadie. I promise. For as long as I'm here in Morinville, or until your daet finds another worker. I can promise that much."

"What do you mean, for as long as you're here in Morinville?" she asked, a frown creasing her brow.

She hadn't put it all together yet—and he hadn't been

terribly forthcoming about his reasons for returning. He wasn't a contrite man returning to the faith—he was a son who couldn't let his parents sink into poverty.

"I'm here to help out my daet. I'm not staying. Once he's on his feet again, I'm going back to Chicago."

"You're—" The color drained from her face, then she licked her lips. "What's wrong with your daet? I thought you were back for good."

So no one had noticed? His daet had been working himself ragged. His mother had been hemming up the same three dresses for two years, and not one woman had noticed? It was frustrating, because his mamm had always been vigilant for the needy in their community. She'd notice some small detail—threadbare dresses, some lost weight—and she'd deftly put together a basket of food, or a roll of fabric, and leave it on a doorstep. But when his mamm was going without, no one noticed or intervened.

"Business has been rough. He wrote and asked me to come help him. I'm doing what I can, but this isn't permanent."

"I didn't know . . ."

"He doesn't want people to know. We'll sort out our own problems. There's no need for the community to gather support. And once I'm sure they'll be okay without me, I'm going back to Chicago. Absolom and I are starting up our own business."

At least his parents would be provided for with him here to contribute to the household, and he wouldn't just walk out on them. But that didn't change the fact that Absolom was waiting on him.

"Okay," Sadie said. "I understand. For as long as you're here, or until my father finds someone else. Just . . . help me run the farm."

"I can do that."

Elijah had obligations on all sides—his parents' financial

concerns, Absolom waiting for him to return to start up the business, and now Sadie's request that he help keep her daet from overexerting himself. He could tell Sadie to find someone else, but he still felt that sense of duty toward her.

She was right. His discontent had started all of this, and he owed her something. He just wished he knew what would make them even so he could put her out of his heart. His life was not in Morinville any longer.

Chapter Four

The next morning when Sadie arrived in the main barn, she found Elijah already mucking out the milking stalls. She let the door bang shut behind her, and he looked up.

"Morning," he said.

She gave him a nod and grabbed a shovel from the corner. She was tired, and she missed the days when she'd wake up and start the fire in the stove instead of coming out to the barn. But this was for her father, and she didn't want to make her daet feel bad. So why had her father made this more difficult for all of them by hiring Elijah Fisher? She still couldn't figure that out.

Elijah heaved a shovelful of hay into the wheelbarrow, then straightened as she entered the stall next to him.

"You're here early," she said.

"The earlier we start, the earlier we're done," he replied.

She began shoveling, uncomfortably aware of this muscular man in the stall next to her. He worked steadily, too, and before long Sadie had cleared out the stall. She knocked her shovel against the side of the barrow, dropping the last of the hay fragments onto the pile, then she bent to lift the wheelbarrow. It was heavy, and as she straightened, she felt a warm hand on her waist, and she sucked in a breath of surprise.

"Hey." She felt a tingle go up her spine at that low, soft voice. Why couldn't that part have changed—the way he made her feel with just a word? And he shouldn't be touching her so familiarly, either, but his touch was confident, sure. As if sliding a hand over a woman's waist was nothing out of the ordinary for him.

Elijah nudged her out of the way and picked up the handles of the wheelbarrow himself, wheeling it toward the side door without a backward glance. She watched him go—and she was struck by how different he was after nine years. He certainly wasn't the lithe teen he used to be. He was stronger now, and more sure of himself.

Sadie opened a bag of oats and poured some into the feeders to prepare for the milking—and she couldn't help but look up as Elijah came back inside. He headed for the pile of hay bales and hoisted one in front of him, his muscles bulging.

"Elijah, I was thinking," Sadie said. "You say you only came back to help your daet, but you didn't need to come. You could have just sent him money."

Elijah dropped the bale with a grunt. "How much do you think I made out there?"

She hadn't really considered that. "I don't know. Enough?" she said.

"Hardly." He pulled a knife from his pocket and cut the twine on the bale, the straw springing forward once released. "With the Englishers, education counts. And I had what every other Amish man has by way of schooling— eighth grade. I got paid a pittance. That's why I got my high school diploma in the evenings, and I get paid a bit more, but not enough to send money to Daet."

"But you always said you'd make more money with the Englishers," she said. "Wasn't that your mantra?"

"I was a kid. I had no idea. Anyway, for the time being at least, my best chance at helping my daet was to come home."

"Do you think that was your father's hope, that you'd have to come back?" Sadie asked.

Elijah looked over and caught her eye. Then he smiled that old boyish grin of his. "Probably. But it doesn't change anything."

"Like what?" she asked.

"Like where I can make something of myself."

He'd belonged here in Morinville once, and it sounded strange for him to talk this way, as if belonging anywhere else were even a possibility.

"So you're just going to leave after this," she clarified. "You'll help out your daet for a while, and then go back to . . . to . . ." She couldn't even bring herself to say it.

"Yah. That's the plan." He plunged a pitchfork into the hay and tossed it into the empty stalls.

"Did you know that you'd stay away forever when you left the first time?" She heard the quiver in her own voice. Had he *planned* on never seeing her again?

He heaved a sigh. "I was actually all set to come back when you married Mervin"—he shrugged, then plunged the fork back into the hay again—"and I couldn't come back and see that."

"See me married," she clarified.

"See you with some other man." He didn't look up as he worked. "And it was probably for the best. It gave me the kick in the pants that I needed to get some education, and to start a plan for a business that could really go somewhere."

"So you're happy now—with the Englishers," she said.

"Yah." He looked up with that quirky smile of his. "I am."

That was a strange relief, to not be the sole reason he'd stayed away, and yet it made it worse somehow, too. It was harder to fix, and for some reason she wanted to fix this for him. She wanted to find the answer, the comfort, whatever it was he was missing in their community, and show him that he'd made a mistake by leaving. Because, if she could fix this for Elijah, then she could fix it for her brother—and she could put up a protective hedge around her own child.

Elijah finished spreading the hay and straightened. "I'm going to check on the cattle water troughs. You can finish up here alone?"

Just like that, he was heading off without her, moving on to the next stage. This seemed to be a bit of a theme with them, but she understood. They'd have to work together, but he didn't have to stay by her side the whole time, either.

"I'll be fine," she said.

Elijah headed for the door. He looked back at her just once, and for a split second, he was the old Elijah again, those dark eyes always drawn toward her, no matter where they were, and she felt that tingle move up her spine once more.

He was right—maintaining some distance between them was probably wise. He most certainly wasn't staying in Morinville.

Later that morning, Sadie and Elijah clomped back up the steps to the mudroom after the chores were complete. The sun had already risen in a splash of gold, betraying how long they'd taken at the work. Daet wouldn't have taken half as long as they did, but Sadie had done her best, and when she and Elijah returned for breakfast forty minutes late, she was both exhausted and starving.

"Don't let Daet know that we're struggling," Sadie murmured as they stood on the porch before they went indoors. "We don't want him to worry. We'll figure this out."

Elijah looked down at her, and she felt his hand brush the side of hers. The touch might have been accidental, but she pulled her hand away regardless. It felt oddly intimate.

"I know," he said. "Trust me. I'd rather be working with you than your daet."

She wasn't sure if that was a compliment for her, or a stab at her father. But she didn't have time to get into it. She was hungry, and breakfast would be in the oven keeping warm for them.

Sadie and Elijah washed up, then went straight to the table where Mamm and Rosmanda had breakfast ready— oatmeal, fried eggs, bacon, and corn bread. Samuel was waiting for her, and she slipped into her spot next to her son, who crawled straight into her lap. This was the first time anyone but Sadie had woken him, and she felt a rush of guilt. She ran her fingers through Sammie's honey blond curls and pressed a kiss into his hair.

"Good morning, sugar," she whispered.

"Morning, Mamm."

Sadie felt Elijah's gaze on her, and when she looked up, she saw an oddly tender look on his face, which irritated her for some reason. He shouldn't have an inside view of her life like this. He shouldn't be able to watch a moment between her and her little boy when she was awash with maternal guilt over not having been there to wake him for breakfast.

Daet sat down at the head of the table like usual, and he gave Sadie a peculiar look before he bowed his head for grace. Breakfast was still warm, but the corn bread had toughened in the oven. Samuel took some coaxing to get back into his own chair so that she could eat, and the meal was consumed in record time. Everyone was hungry.

When they finished eating, Daet rose to his feet. "I'll

go out with you this morning, Elijah," he said. "Sadie has women's work to do."

Any other time, Sadie would have been grateful. Sadie looked to Mamm, who refused to make eye contact.

"Daet, the doctor—" Sadie began.

"Sadie." Her father's voice was low and powerful, and she sank into silence. Daet was the man of this home, and he'd spoken.

Daet gave her one last meaningful look before he and Elijah went out to the mudroom and got on their rubber boots. The women stood in silence until the outside door banged shut. Then Sadie turned to Mamm.

"What was that?" Sadie asked.

"He doesn't want you spending too much time with the Fisher boy," Mamm replied. *Boy.* He was in his mid-twenties, but any unmarried man was a "boy."

"I'm keeping up the farm, Mamm," Sadie said tiredly. "Daet has nothing to worry about between Elijah and me. With Daet's heart and the medicine, and—"

"I know. I told him the same thing," Mamm replied, reaching for a plate and beginning to stack them. "He's concerned for appearances."

"And I'm concerned for Daet's heart," Sadie retorted.

Rosmanda snorted out a laugh, then sobered when Mamm shot her a scathing look.

"If you are to ever marry again, Sadie, you'd better worry about appearances, too," Mamm retorted. "Your father rested yesterday and this morning. He needs to see how things are going out there. He's the only one who will notice if something goes wrong."

Sadie knew her mother was right, but her father's collapse still hung fresh in her memory.

"Rosmanda, go get the mail," Mamm said, turning to

her youngest daughter. "Sadie will help me with the dishes until you get back."

The mail truck came early, passing through their community in the wee hours of the morning, so if there was any letter to be had, it would be there already. Sadie picked up the greasy platter that had held the eggs, and the screen door clattered shut behind them as Rosmanda headed out.

Samuel was playing "clean up" with a little broom that Sadie used to play with at his age. It was good for the little ones to learn to do chores. Soon enough Samuel would be a big boy, tramping out to the barn with his grandfather to learn a man's work.

"You spent a good while outside with Elijah yesterday," Mamm said, her voice a little too controlled to be casual.

"Fixing the fence and keeping Sammie outside so Daet could sleep," Sadie replied.

"Yes, and I know your reasoning," Mamm said. "But Elijah might be thinking something else."

Her waist warmed where Elijah's hand had pressed against her, and she felt heat flood her cheeks. Sadie shook her head. "He's not, Mamm. We bicker more than anything."

"You're single and the daughter of the bishop." Mamm headed to the sink and turned on the water. "While I hate to be the one to point it out to you, you are an attractive woman, too. He might have plans to stop bickering some time soon."

"It isn't that. I'm sure of it. He's not staying in Morinville, Mamm. He's not back to stay."

Mamm turned abruptly. "He isn't?"

"He's helping his daet," Sadie replied. "His daet told him that he wasn't doing well, and he needed a hand."

"Are they struggling?" Mamm asked uncertainly. "I didn't realize . . ."

"And besides that, I think he feels like he's doing Absolom a favor. Absolom asked him to look in on me, to make sure I was okay."

There was a beat of silence, and Mamm planted a stack of plates heavily on the counter.

"Absolom did that?" Mamm's voice grew breathy.

"That's what Elijah said."

"So Absolom's still thinking of *you*, at least. You always were his favorite—"

"I'm sure he's thinking of all of us," Sadie broke in. "You're his mamm. There is no erasing that fact."

As if on cue, Samuel came over to where Sadie stood and leaned his cheek against her leg. She ruffled his blond curls lovingly. There was a bond between a mother and her son, and she refused to believe it could be so easily snapped. She wouldn't allow it to happen. Her son moved off again with his broom.

Mamm nodded then sucked in a stabilizing breath. "Did Elijah say anything else about Absolom?"

"Not really," Sadie replied. She wished he had now, seeing the longing etched in her mother's face. "I'd tell you if he did. I promise."

Mamm swallowed twice, then wiped her hands on her apron. "So what is Elijah doing then?"

"Working to help his daet with the money." Sadie shook her head. "Mamm, why did you hire him, anyway? This isn't easy having him around."

"Your father wanted to," Mamm replied. "He wanted to prove to the community that Elijah deserved to be accepted again."

"He isn't looking for acceptance here."

"I think your father wants to make sure that if Absolom comes back, there will be a place for him, too."

"Can Absolom come back?" Sadie asked. "He has a family now, Mamm. It changes things."

"The Englishers break up sometimes," Mamm said, looking over at Sadie with a half-guilty expression.

Sadie didn't answer, because she had thought it several times in the past, too. What if the relationship with Sharon didn't work out? What if they broke up, and Absolom could come home and start fresh? Except a child changed that—a child with their blood.

"You know how much you love Sammie," Mamm went on. "It's the same for me and Absolom. All of you children. I know I shouldn't wish heartbreak on my son, but if it's the only thing to bring him back from damnation . . ."

Sadie glanced over her shoulder to where Samuel dragged the child-sized broom across the floor. She'd do anything for her son, and if Mamm loved Absolom half as much as Sadie loved Samuel, then Mamm's heart would be shredded by Absolom's defection. There was no spiritual salvation outside of the community. Not for those born and raised in the Amish life. Absolom's choice hadn't been one of simple geography; it was an eternal one. How would Sadie feel if Sammie ran off to some Englisher girl and left his family and his chance at Heaven behind?

"God is the Good Shepherd, Mamm," Sadie said woodenly. "He's not done yet."

God couldn't be done with Absolom yet . . . because Absolom wasn't *home*.

The side door opened once more, and Rosmanda came back in. She held a white envelope in one hand.

"It's for Sadie," she said.

Sadie dried her hands on a towel and came to retrieve the letter. The return address was in Pennsylvania—where Mervin's parents lived. She'd written to them a few weeks ago asking if they'd like to come visit, but that was before

Daet's diagnosis, and she'd completely forgotten. Now, she felt a rush of anxiety as she tore open the envelope. Mamm and Rosmanda both watched her curiously as she scanned the page.

"They say they'd love to accept our gracious invitation," Sadie said with a weak smile.

"Oh . . ." Mamm sighed. The timing wasn't great—not anymore, at least. But these were Samuel's grandparents, and they deserved to keep a relationship with their newest grandson. Sadie glanced at the date at the top of the letter.

"It looks like the mail took its time getting here," Sadie said. "They'll arrive in two days."

"What?" Mamm closed her eyes, then took a deep breath and opened them again. "Alright, then we have to get busy to be ready for guests. Rosmanda, you'll clean the upstairs thoroughly this morning. They'll stay in the boys' old bedroom—that bed is in the best shape for older people. We'll need to pick up some new pillows in town, though. The ones we have are too used. We also need another two large bags of flour. It won't wait. And sugar, the biggest bag—"

Sadie nodded. "I'll go to town this morning and get what we need. Then we can start baking this afternoon, and spend the rest of tomorrow making bread, finishing the last of the washing, and making pies. Mervin used to like my cinnamon buns. They reminded him of his mother's. We could make a batch or two of those."

Samuel stared at them mutely, his little broom forgotten, but still clutched in one pudgy hand.

"Would you like to come to town with your mamm?" Sadie asked with a smile, and a grin broke over the boy's face.

Her boy . . . her precious baby boy. She couldn't even imagine him as a grown man at this point, but she knew she'd never forget those glittering blue eyes or the tousled curls, or the way he looked up at her with such love in that little face. She was his mamm—his whole world right now, and while Sadie's world was bigger than Sammie's, he was at the very center of hers.

Boys didn't forget this, did they? The mother who raised them, snuggled them, and poured her whole self into the loving of them? Because mothers never forgot, no matter how big their children got or how far they roamed.

Oh, dear God, let Samuel never leave them like Absolom had.

Elijah shoved the pitchfork deep into the hay bale, then pulled it upward, loosening hay before he tossed it into the horse's stall. The buggy barn would be the last stop for this morning's work. After this, he'd have earned himself a break. It had been a long morning with Bishop Graber along for the work.

Bishop Graber was a hard man. He stood by the traditions with the fixedness of a tree stump. He guarded the Ordnung with blind fervor, and if the old bishop could only hold his own in the barn, Elijah might carry his resentment a little more easily, but it was difficult to stir that stew of anger and resentment while the older man seemed to be withering before his eyes.

The bishop leaned against his shovel, breathing deeply.

"I can finish this alone," Elijah said. The bishop was shoveling out the last stall, but he'd slowed down to a crawl. He'd promised Sadie that he'd help her to protect her father from the workload, but that didn't take her daet's stubbornness into account. He'd offered twice already.

"No, no . . ." The bishop's dismissal was weaker this time, though. He pulled out a handkerchief and wiped his brow. "This is my farm, and I'm not about to let go of the reins completely."

"I'll be able to finish alone," Elijah repeated. It was better than pointing out that the bishop's womenfolk would be furious with Elijah for not handling the bishop better.

Bishop Graber leaned against a stall rung, resting. "Fine. I could use the rest, I suppose, but before I go inside, I have something to ask of you, Elijah."

Elijah straightened, his nose tickling from the dust. He rubbed at it with the back of his hand. "Yes?"

"I want you to write a letter to Absolom."

Elijah repressed a sigh. He knew the reason the bishop had hired him to begin with had to do with his son, but now would begin the uncomfortable demands on top of the workload.

"I don't know if that is wise," Elijah said.

"I disagree." The older man's tone held stubborn authority. "He needs to hear from you—his partner in rebellion. You might be able to appeal to his better nature, explain your reasons for return. You could expound upon the beauty of our simple life."

Elijah shot the bishop a quick look from beneath the dark brim of his hat. His daughter obviously hadn't told him that he wasn't staying.

"Family matters more than anything else," the bishop went on when Elijah had not answered. "What do we have if we don't have our loved ones?"

"He knows all that," Elijah replied. How often had Elijah and Absolom hashed through all of this together? No one walked away from the Amish world without some deep introspection.

"My son might not be thinking about God right now," the bishop went on. "I've tried to remind him of his Maker over and over again, and he's gone deaf to me. But if you were to remind him of his duties to God—"

"It's not so simple." Elijah turned back to forking hay. Was it his place to tell the bishop about his son's spiritual defection? He was tired of holding it all back—it felt too close to a lie by omission. "Absolom has gone Mennonite."

Silence sank around them, all but the scrape of metal tongs against the concrete floor and the rasp of the bishop's breath.

"But the Ordnung—" the older man said faintly.

Going Mennonite was worse than simple rebellion—it gave that rebellion a home, a church where the Ordnung was ignored and faith was enough.

"I cannot write to him about the Ordnung," Elijah replied. "He knows it all already. You have written to him about it several times yourself, and he read every letter. He no longer sees things the same way."

And that was something that the old bishop could never fathom—the other way of seeing things. The Englishers didn't live in sinful chaos as the Amish assumed. They had reasons for their choices, as did Absolom.

Bishop Graber leaned his shovel against the stall, but it slipped and clattered to the ground.

"Bishop—" Elijah sprung forward, but the older man was fine—still on his feet and staring emptily down at the stall floor.

"I believe I will go inside and pray on this," the bishop murmured, and walked woodenly toward the door. Elijah bent and picked up the fallen shovel, his heart thudding almost audibly in his chest. The bishop should not be out here—it was dangerous, and the next time he collapsed, there might not be time enough to get him the medical care he needed. That was a selfish load to leave on another man's shoulders.

Elijah followed him to the door and watched him walk slowly across the scrub grass toward the house just as Sadie opened the door and stepped outside.

"Daet?" Her voice filtered toward him, and Sarah, the bishop's wife, appeared on the step behind her daughter. There was a bustle of activity as the bishop was ushered inside. Elijah expected the family to stay indoors, but a few minutes later, the screen door at the house banged again, and Elijah went to the door to see Sadie coming back out. But this time, her son was in tow behind her.

She wore a bonnet over her kapp, and as she walked, she tied the strings beneath her chin. Elijah crossed his arms over his chest as she approached the covered overhang that housed the buggy in summer months, before it required more protection from the elements.

"Elijah—" She startled. "Hello."

"Hello." He uncrossed his arms. "Hitching up?"

"Yes, I'm going to town." She headed into the barn toward the draft horses' stalls. Sammie hung back, waiting.

"For the doctor?" Elijah asked, following her.

"He's just tired. We've seen him worse." Sadie turned toward him, then shook her head. "Daet says he just needs his pills. I'm going to town for flour and sugar and a few other things." She turned back. "Sammie, stand back, son!"

"I'll hitch you up," Elijah said.

Sadie paused, then regarded Elijah for a moment. "What happened out here? Is he upset about something?" Sadie took a bridle and blinders off the wall and headed for the first stall.

Elijah took the second bridle and blinders and headed for the other horse. "He asked about Absolom."

"And?" Her voice came to him slightly distantly as she approached the large horse.

"I told him that Absolom went Mennonite," he replied. "That's all."

They emerged from the stables a few minutes later, each leading a draft horse toward the buggy. Samuel stood obediently next to one of the buggy's big wheels.

"If he's gone Mennonite, then he won't come back. Ever." The words came out in a breathy rush. "They'd give him the easy path—tell him it's truth."

"It's not exactly like that." Elijah slung the harness over the first horse and began tugging at straps and doing up buckles. "It's different out there. It's hard to explain."

"What does that mean?" Her voice was pinched as she worked next to him, harnessing up the other horse. "Mervin always believed that he would come back. . . . Mervin's son had left for a little while. He met an Englisher girl, but he came home after a few months. He missed his family. No girl could take the place of a whole life—"

"Sadie, what am I supposed to say? I can't predict the future." He came around the front of the horse and stopped short in front of her. She straightened, and looking down into her face, he could see her faint freckles across her nose, her lips slightly parted. She looked up at him, eyes clouded with emotion, and he found himself ever so tempted to duck his head down and catch those pink lips with his. But he wouldn't—obviously. He cleared his throat and took a step back. Her cheeks pinked.

"I know. It's just . . . Mervin's parents are coming to visit." Sadie backed the horse in front of the buggy. "They're coming in two days."

"To see Sammie," Elijah concluded.

"And to see me," she replied primly. "I'm their daughter-in-law. I'm part of the family."

Of course—her in-laws. Stupid of him not to think of them that way. She had a family associated with Mervin, a whole heap of connections. He didn't know why that made him feel irritable, but it did.

And suddenly, as he attached the shafts to the harness, the full realization struck him so forcibly that he let out a huff of breath. She'd been a married woman. She had in-laws, a husband, a whole life while he'd been gone. It was easy to imagine that the slower life out here with the Amish had simply ground to a stop while he was away, but that hadn't been true. She may have accepted a man beneath her, but she'd indeed married him, and while she was now a widow, Elijah—two years her senior—still wore the fresh-shaven face of a single man. More than that, Mervin's death didn't erase those connections.

Elijah crossed in front of the horses and took the shaft from her hands to finish hitching up for her. Sadie took a step back, and Sammie slipped a small hand into hers.

Why was it that Elijah could see her with her little boy at her side, and he still hadn't been able to picture her properly wed? He'd known it for a fact, but his heart had never given him a picture of what that might look like. Maybe it was because he'd never seen her in that role of wife. Or perhaps something inside of him wanted to keep her down at his level—single, free, still learning.

"I'm going to see Dawdy and Mammi," Samuel lisped. "They're coming to visit, and Mamm will make pie to eat. They will rock in the chairs on the porch with my other Dawdy."

Elijah finished the last buckle and slipped his hands over the reins to straighten them all the way up the front of the buggy. Then he stopped and looked down at Samuel.

"He's excited." Sadie shrugged faintly. "The timing is difficult, but it will be good to see them, all the same."

"I never knew how to picture you married," he admitted quietly. "When I knew you, you were the girl who used to tell me off when you thought I was being stupid, and you never wore your shoes often enough. You kept getting your dress dirty when you kneeled on it in the garden—"

"I'm not a girl anymore," she said.

"I know, I just . . . in my mind I see you catching minnows in the creek, and I haven't caught up."

The creek was his most powerful memory of her, the place

they'd escape to to be alone. He could vividly remember how she'd leaned into his arms, the taste of her lips, the way his heart would pound in his head as he pulled her ever closer. . . . They'd thought too little about the future, and too much about the moment. All he'd been able to think about in those long summer days was getting her back into his arms. He'd been young and stupid, and figured maybe he could court her one day when they were both older. . . . But he hadn't been thinking anything through then, just following his youthful passion.

"You missed a lot." Sadie lifted her son up into the carriage, and the boy disappeared into its depths, giving them a sense of false privacy. She turned toward him. "You *both* should have been here, Elijah."

Her tone seemed to tremble with meaning, but if there was more to her words besides resentment, he had no way of knowing. Neither of them should have left— Rumspringa wasn't for that level of disobedience. And if he had been here in Morinville, what would he have done? She'd never have gone for the likes of him, even if he'd been stupidly in love with her as a heady teen. He was as far beneath her as Mervin had been.

"I can't change it, Sadie," he said quietly.

"I know." Sadie lifted her skirts to the knees to hoist herself up into the buggy. She settled on the front seat and accepted the reins he handed up to her. Samuel planted himself next to his mother, his legs sticking out straight in front of him.

"You be good for your mamm," Elijah said, slapping the side of the carriage and stepping back.

"I'm going to get a stick of candy!" Samuel shouted out the window as Sadie flicked the reins and the horses started forward.

"Hush."

He heard her remonstrance to her child as the horses

pulled out of the shelter and struck a rhythm as they headed toward the drive. Elijah stood there in the shade of the overhang, thumbs in the front of his pants and his gaze locked on the back of that buggy.

Life in Morinville hadn't stopped when he'd left, and neither had his. He hadn't been married, but in place of that, he'd experienced a world of computers, cell phones, cars, and gas stations. He'd worked construction with Absolom and they'd inhaled the scent of oil and gasoline as roads were pressed out in front of them like dough on a countertop. He'd met women who treated him like a baby animal to be coddled, and he'd met other women who'd had holes in their hearts as big as his. He liked the wounded women better because they didn't shrink away from him when he talked in his slow and halting way, working his mouth around the English phrases he wasn't used to.

Never once when he was away was he able to describe to anyone that feeling of belonging that he got here with his own people. There weren't enough English words for it. In Chicago, he'd been a number at best—so many different numbers had clung to him. Here, he was a full person—a man to some, a boy to others. He might be a burden or a reminder of unpleasantness. Some might like him, and others might not, but all the same he was Elijah Fisher, son of Abram and Nettie Fisher. He'd been born to fence making, quite solidly below the likes of Absolom and Sadie. He knew who he was here, and a social security number couldn't give that kind of identity.

And even so, Morinville could not be his home again. Elijah told people that he'd changed too much, but the truth of the matter went deeper. He'd always trusted in his parents' love and support, and when he went to the city as a teenager, he'd been terrified. He wrote his daet a letter, pouring it all out onto paper. He was scared, angry, heartbroken. He wanted a conversation, a discussion; he wanted to be heard. His father's reply had been brief: *The bishop advises us not to talk to you about such things unless you come home.* The rest of the letter had been religious discussion about the strength of community. His father's choice was clear.

The betrayal had been as shocking as a slap to the face. The feeling of security that had surrounded Morinville in his mind evaporated upon reading that letter. He was no longer Abram's son, at least on a heart level, if he moved away. There was a limit to his father's love, and that limit had been determined by the bishop.

Boys hardened into men, whether they did it at home or away. Manhood had found Elijah, and he decided that he would have to build a life for himself. He wanted financial security and a business that thrived and grew under his leadership, unfettered by a church's restrictions. He wanted a chance to see how far he could go.

The community of Morinville might know him better than Chicago ever would, but he couldn't trust them. The group always came first—even before confused sons who needed their daet's support. That wasn't a place Elijah could ever call home again. He preferred the Englishers. At least with them, he knew where he stood.

Chapter Five

Elijah clomped into his home later that evening, his body aching from the day's labor. He wasn't used to farm work anymore, and it would take some time to build up his stamina. Besides, he'd never worked more than the family plot before he left for the city. He'd spent long hours with his daet in the back of the store, guiding barbed wire into the machine that wove the fencing together. He'd lifted and stacked heavy rolls of wire. He'd helped to load up customers' trailers, and then he'd gone home and helped his mamm with the family's chickens and milk cow. So he was no stranger to hard work, but all of that work, including construction, had been nothing compared to the demands of another man's farm.

"Are you hungry, son?" his mother called from the kitchen.

"Yah, Mamm." He pulled off his boots and hung his hat on a peg. The house smelled of fresh baking—bread and shoofly pie.

"How was it today?" his father called from the kitchen. Elijah emerged to see his daet at the table with a mug of tea in front of him, and his mamm at the counter, buttering two thick slices of bread.

"The same as usual," Elijah replied. "Lots of work. The bishop isn't doing well."

"How sick is he?" His mother cast a concerned look over her shoulder.

"He needs to rest a lot," Elijah said. "And he keeps trying to work like he used to, but he can't keep up."

Elijah could barely keep up with the work, either. He had blisters on his feet and hands to attest to that, but at least his heart wasn't going to give out.

"It was kind of the bishop to give you this job," his father said.

"Kind?" Elijah dropped into a kitchen chair. "I'm doing the work of two men and getting paid for one. Besides, after what he did to your business, he owes us."

"Owes?" Daet raised his eyebrows. "Don't let pride get the best of you, boy. The community voted on the machinery. This wasn't the bishop's fault."

"The elders voted, yes," Elijah conceded. "But that isn't to say that the bishop's views didn't factor in. He's an influential man, Daet. You know where that decision came from."

"Money is not everything," his father replied curtly.

"No? Then why am I here?" Elijah heard his voice rising, and he bit off the words and looked away. His father wanted it both ways—Elijah's help, and to keep his idealized view of their community.

Elijah's mother handed him the buttered bread, casting him a look of warning.

"Thanks, Mamm."

She smiled in response, and her eyes looked tired. She'd been up since before dawn, and it was nearly ten now. She nudged a jam jar toward him, and he dipped a spoon into it, daubing lumps of strawberry preserves on top of the creamy butter.

"We need the money you make there, son," Daet said after a moment. "Now is not the time to cause waves."

That concession wouldn't have been easy on his father, and Elijah could see his point. They did need the money. Elijah swallowed a bite of bread before answering.

"We'll figure it out, Daet. One of the things the Englishers say is that nothing stays the same. Even the bishop's influence. You can always count on change."

"They can also count on hellfire," Daet retorted, and Elijah shook his head. Arguing religion with his father was about as effective as arguing the bishop's undue influence. His father saw things the way he saw them, and he could not be swayed.

"What I'm trying to say is—"

"Don't tell me what the Englishers think." His father's expression was tight, and he pushed back from the table with a noisy scrape.

His parents were glad he was back, but there was still the scent of bitterness surrounding anything to do with the Englisher world. His daet wanted him to sink back into place here as if he'd never left, but Elijah was no teenager anymore, and while there were aspects of the Amish life he missed on a bone-deep level, he wasn't about to be smoothed over and put into his place like his father had been.

"Eat," his mother murmured. "Do you want some milk?"

Elijah nodded. "Thanks, yah."

She rose to her feet again and headed for the gas-fueled refrigerator.

"Have you been speaking to Absolom?" his father asked after a moment.

Elijah shook his head. "No."

"He wrote you a letter." Mamm's voice was quiet, but it

cut through the tension and Elijah stopped chewing, tucking the food into his cheek.

"What?"

"Eat, dear." She poured a glass of frothy milk and slid it across the table toward him. He took a gulp of milk to wash down the rest of the food, but it felt like it stuck halfway down, a painful lump in his chest.

"He wrote to me? Where is the letter?"

Mamm pulled it out of her apron pocket and put the envelope face down on the table, then turned away.

Elijah picked up the envelope. It was still sealed, and his name and address had been printed in those childish block letters Absolom always used when he was trying to write neatly. Elijah tore open the envelope and scanned the contents of the letter. It was short and to the point, his friend's voice coming through the words.

Dear Elijah,
It isn't the same around here without you, and Sharon says to tell you that you're missing out on the best season yet of Mystery Hunters—*that show you were watching with her on TV. . . .*

Already, the flickering commercials and the heavy-handed stories from the television felt like a thousand miles away. They'd had a numbing effect on him, though, and let him forget his feelings for a little while. It was easier to center his emotions around fiction than it was to face reality most times. In that respect, he couldn't really judge the Englishers. He was no better. And sitting with Absolom's girlfriend on the sofa, he used to think about how he'd explain all of this to Sadie . . .

"What does it say?" Mamm asked impatiently.

Elijah scanned the last of the letter.

"Absolom is a daet now." Elijah scrubbed his hand through his hair. "His girlfriend had her baby."

"Oh . . ." His mother didn't seem to know how to respond to that, and she didn't say anything more.

"Girlfriend," his father muttered. "Those Englishers. Not even a wife, and he's having children with her. Backwards. All of it."

Elijah scanned the words again from beginning to end. A father . . . his friend. It seemed so impossible, even though he'd seen Sharon large with child. Nothing would be the same for Absolom ever again.

"Was it a boy or a girl?" his mother asked at last.

"A girl." And as the words came out, he heard the tremble in his own voice. Absolom now had a daughter. Elijah didn't know what that would feel like, but he could imagine the swell of paternal protectiveness that Absolom would be feeling as his emotions grew into this new responsibility.

"He also wants me to hurry back," Elijah said. "He's eager to get started on the new business."

"A new business," his daet said bitterly. "There's a business right here that needs you!"

"Daet, I don't mean to offend you," Elijah said. "But I want more than this. I can't do it. You know that."

His parents fell into silence for a few beats, and then his father said, "You'll have to tell the bishop."

"My business doesn't concern the bishop anymore," Elijah said curtly.

"His son does, though," Daet replied. "You'll have to tell him about his granddaughter."

Elijah looked up, then heaved a sigh. He'd rather tell Sadie, and let her pass the news along.

"I'm sure Absolom will tell his family," Elijah replied. "They likely received their own letter. Or will soon."

"Still—you have to tell him what you know," his mother

agreed. "We can't keep Absolom's secrets. What would the bishop *think*?"

"I'll—" Elijah cast about, looking for a solution. He'd promised the bishop he'd tell him if he had any news, but marching up and announcing this . . . he wasn't even thinking of the bishop's health. He was thinking of Absolom and his duty to his friend. "I'll take care of it."

"You'll tell him, though," his mother clarified. "Yourself."

"Nettie, let him be. He's a grown man now. He knows what needs to be done."

Elijah was grateful for his father's support, and he rose from the table and tucked the letter into his pocket. He'd had more autonomy living his life with the Englishers. There was less at stake in his choices, fewer people who cared either way. It was the soaring freedom of a sparrow in a hurricane.

"I'll go to bed now," Elijah said.

"Have you had enough to eat?" his mother asked.

"I'm fine, Mamm. I need to think. I'll see you in the morning."

"Good night, son." His father picked up his mug and took a sip of tea.

Once Elijah's foot hit the creaky stairs, he could hear the murmur of their voices starting up again. He couldn't make out the words, and he climbed the stairs that led to his bedroom. Even his younger sisters had all married and moved on. It was awkward to be here—the last remaining child under his parents' roof at this age. But he was their only son—their last hope.

He touched the letter in his pocket, and his mind went back to the room he'd rented in a Chicago apartment—four people living together with as much polite distance as possible. That's where Absolom had met Sharon—they'd been housemates. And while Absolom crept into Sharon's room at night, Elijah had been so desperately lonely that he'd lain in bed thinking about the only girl he'd ever loved. The rope swing and the little silver fish that flashed through the slow-moving water—he and Sadie used to try to catch them together—Sadie with her dress tucked up to keep dry, biting her bottom lip in concentration. Absolom would laugh at them and make jokes. Elijah always hid how he felt about his buddy's sister when Absolom was around, because otherwise it would have been awkward between them. And Elijah would imagine what it would be like to see her again once he was successful. Even if she never loved him again, for her to see he'd done well for himself . . . that was the fantasy.

But Sadie hadn't slipped into the past quite so easily. Seeing her again, he'd hoped that he'd feel differently about her, recognize how very young they'd been back when she'd made his breath catch in his throat at the very sight of her. She was harder to rinse out of his heart than he'd thought, but that didn't make it impossible, either.

He'd leave Morinville again, and when he did, he'd have to leave Sadie's memory firmly in the past. He couldn't carry her with him anymore—his heart couldn't take it.

Tomorrow he'd give this letter to Sadie, and maybe it would comfort her, too. Because while Elijah had thought of Sadie for the last nine years, she hadn't been thinking of him. She needed her brother, and this letter would be a connection to him.

Elijah had never been her answer.

Sadie worked hard all that day, and the next. Her in-laws would arrive the very next day, and there was still so much to do. They'd baked since sunup, whipping up pies, bread, and racks filled with thimble cookies. The food wasn't just for Mamm and Daet Hochstetler, but for the people who would come to visit them here at the house, too.

Rosmanda was currently scrubbing every square inch of the upstairs, and Mamm had been called away by an elderly neighbor who'd hurt her leg and needed Mamm to help get some cooking done to feed them for a few days. That's what neighbors were for. Here at home, Sadie had finally gotten Sammie down for his naptime this afternoon so that she could hang up the laundry before lunch. Her son would be dressed in crisp, clean clothes when he saw his grandparents, or she would collapse in the attempt.

Sadie put down the hamper, overflowing with wet clothes, on the hallway floor while she glanced into the sitting room where Daet dozed in his rocking chair. He was fully asleep, his hands limp on top of the Bible in his lap. Was he really going to try to preach that Sunday?

Sadie sighed and hoisted the hamper again. It was heavy, and her arms trembled under the weight of it. She angled her steps out the side door, bumping the screen door open with her hip on her way through. She dropped the hamper onto the porch with a grunt, then straightened, putting her hands into the small of her back. As she did so, she caught herself scanning the yard, her gaze trailing over the familiar places she normally saw Elijah working.

What was she doing? She felt her face heat at the realization of her thoughts. But she'd been noticing things about him lately—his muscular arms, that direct dark gaze, the way his lips turned up when he was about to say something smart-alecky. Maybe it was because he was young, and her husband had not been. She'd been willing to adjust her marital expectations for Mervin, knowing that he was twenty-odd years her senior, but she was no longer married, was she? And for all of Elijah's many faults, he was still an attractive man. Too attractive, maybe.

Last night, she'd dreamed an uncomfortable dream where she and Elijah were back at the creek, except they were no longer children, and Elijah had been standing on

a rock midstream, holding his hand out to her, saying,
"Jump! I'll catch you!" He'd been so handsome, the sun
shining on his hair where his hat had fallen off, and his
sparkling gaze had met hers so directly that it took her
breath away. She'd hesitated, and the moment she'd made
up her mind to jump and let those strong arms catch her, he
suddenly turned away and walked off—although it made no
sense to think of it now. Walked where? He was in the
middle of the stream. How? But he'd left her perched on
the edge of the bank, her heart aching with emptiness.
She'd awoken feeling frustrated, and she'd started her day
an hour early just to escape that clinging dream feeling.

And here she was, scanning the yard for him.

It was funny what the mind did when it was resting at
night. Untangling memories. But it was more than that.
She'd been attracted to him in that dream, and she'd wanted
to feel his arms pulling her close so desperately that when
he walked away from her, she'd nearly cried. She was no
naïve girl—she'd been married, after all. She knew *exactly*
what she was missing, and it was the physical connection.
To be held close in strong arms, to be desired . . .

Sadie picked up the first item of clothing—one of
Samuel's shirts—and shook it out. Then she pinned it to the
line and reached for another shirt, her hands doing the work
automatically.

One aunt had given her some very sage advice the day
before her wedding. *Sadie*, she'd said. *When the lamp is
turned off and the sun is set, the arms around you feel the
same, whether he's young and strapping, or older, like
Mervin. In the dark, a man is a man.* Her aunt had been
trying to tell her not to let her eyes wander as the years
went by, and Sadie had taken that advice to heart. But now,
standing in the sunlight with a pile of wet laundry at her feet,
she was thinking about strong arms and long nights. . . .

Was she missing a man's touch that badly, that she'd inserted Elijah Fisher into her dreams?

The side door to the buggy stable opened, and a wheelbarrow came out first, followed by Elijah. He rolled the load of manure over to the dump pile, then tipped the barrow forward, giving it a clanking shake before he turned back again. It was then that he saw her, and gave her a nod. He left the wheelbarrow beside the barn and headed in her direction. Sadie didn't slow in her work, but she watched him cross the grass, trying to calm the flutter in her stomach.

He didn't know about her dream, so she had no reason to be uncomfortable . . . and yet that dream had made her look at him a little differently today, noticing the way he walked and the way his shirt clung to his muscular biceps, much as she tried not to.

"Sadie." Elijah pulled off his hat and wiped his forehead, then replaced it, squinting up at her from where she stood a couple of feet above him on the porch.

"Good morning, Elijah." Prim and proper was probably the best approach.

"How are you doing?" he asked.

"Fine." She bent to grab another item of clothing and came up with her own dress. She shook it out twice, the wet fabric snapping.

"You upset about something?" He frowned slightly. "What's wrong?"

"Nothing." She softened her tone. "I'm busy, is all. My in-laws arrive tomorrow."

And truthfully, she wasn't looking forward to this visit. Her in-laws hadn't loved her quite so well as she'd implied. They'd thought she was too young of a choice, and they'd never hidden it well.

"Ah." Elijah nodded a couple of times. "I've been waiting to catch you alone."

Sadie's breath caught, images of her dream slipping in past her defenses, and she shot him a cautious look. "Why?"

"Have you gotten the mail yet today?" he asked instead.

"Yes."

"Have you gotten anything from Absolom lately?"

Her mouth went dry, and she licked her lips. "No. Have you?"

"Yes. Yesterday, a letter arrived. I only got it last night when I got home."

Sadie's heart sped up at those words. There was news. The baby? It had to be. She'd been hoping that his child's birth would make him write again . . . but he hadn't written to them. He'd written to Elijah.

"What did he say?"

"I've got it here." He fished around in his shirt pocket and pulled out a folded piece of paper. She finished pinning her dress to the clothesline, then trotted down the steps and came around to where he stood. He held out the paper to her, and she eagerly snatched it up and opened it.

Dear Elijah,

It isn't the same around here without you, and Sharon says to tell you that you're missing out on the best season yet of Mystery Hunters—*that show you were watching with her on TV. She wants to know when you're coming back.*

She's had the baby. A girl. She's a healthy little thing—lots of squirming and crying and diapers and such. We named her Sarah—after Mamm. She's a beautiful baby, Eli. I don't even know how to explain it, but when that baby is your own kinner, you see it differently. And that cry sounds different, too. It makes you want to fix the problem right quick.

"He named the baby after Mamm," Sadie said with a misty smile. "That will mean the world to her."

Mamm was convinced her son had forgotten her, but this was proof that he hadn't, and never would. Elijah was silent, staring down at his boots, so she kept reading.

> *Sharon's cooped up in the apartment, and it isn't like at home where the women all help each other out. She's by herself a lot, and she's been getting sadder and sadder. You know how she always struggled with that, and with the baby it's a lot worse. Chase helps his mamm out the best he can, but with me working all the time, it isn't easy. . . . When I get home, Sharon and Chase are already asleep, so I sit on the couch and hold my daughter. Sarah looks me in the face, and I'm sure she knows me.*

"Who's Chase?" Sadie asked, looking up again.

"That's Sharon's son from another relationship," Elijah said. "He's about four now."

"Oh . . ." There was another child in that home? She hadn't realized that her brother was a stepfather, too. And the boy was only a little older than her Sammie. There was so much they didn't know.

> *I'm waiting on you to start up our company. I'm sick of this job, man. I can't wait to quit and be my own boss. Don't take too long. I have three customers lined up for lawn care, and I can't start without you.*

> *Absolom*

Sadie folded the page again, her mind working over her brother's words. Would there be a letter for them in a few days? Or had he decided not to tell them about his child at all? She licked her lips and looked down at the folded page in her hand.

"May I keep it?" Her voice was choked, and she cleared her throat.

"Yes," Elijah said. "It's fine."

"Mamm will want to see it." She tried to smile, but it fell short, and she looked away again.

"I'm sure he'll write to you," Elijah said, but she could hear the lie in his voice. He couldn't be any surer of that than she could be.

"I didn't know he had a stepchild," she said.

"Yeah, Chase is a sweet kid. Your brother is good with him, but he's not exactly a daet to him. He's more a buddy, I guess. The mother's boyfriend. It's different."

Different . . . that was an understatement.

"What does the boy call him?" she asked.

"He just calls him Abe." Elijah leaned against the side of the porch next to Sadie, and the warmth from his arm next to hers emanated against her comfortingly.

"I can't talk about my brother here in Morinville," she murmured.

"The shame," he said, understanding in his voice, and she felt a wave of relief at being able to say anything about her brother at all.

"We can't say that we miss him," she went on. "If we talk too much about him, we'd be a bad influence on others who might be questioning or confused. We can't let our personal grief shake someone who might be in a weak place."

"You could always talk to me."

"You're the one who lured him off," she said, bitterness oozing out of her tone.

"Maybe so." His voice stayed low. "And maybe even because of that, I'm strong enough to shoulder it."

That was something. He was a part of this mess, and she had no obligation to protect him from it.

"I know you resent me," he went on. "I understand that. But I'm also the only one who knows all about Absolom and what this has done to you. So, I'm . . . safe, I guess."

"You aren't safe," she replied ruefully.

"No?" She heard the smile in his voice and she refused to look at him. "Still?"

She felt a surge of annoyance. She couldn't let him know how he'd been making her feel. It wasn't his fault. It was hers—and she had to stop this.

"Don't tease me, Elijah," she said. "You don't get to do that. We might have been young, but you broke my heart back then."

Elijah's smile slipped. "I'm sorry, Sadie. If I could undo it, I would."

"Undo what? The kisses and promises? Or leaving?"

Because Elijah and Absolom had plans in the city—and even in this letter, Absolom was calling him back.

"I'd still have kissed you, Sadie."

Her cheeks heated. It was pain for nothing. And if she hadn't learned that early lesson about these fluttering feelings and fragile hopes, she would never have chosen the husband she did. But Elijah didn't regret leaving like he had. Elijah's feelings for her hadn't been strong enough to alter that course.

"Absolom should have told *us* about his daughter." Tears welled in her eyes. "He should have told *me*."

"He does miss you," Elijah said. "He says it all the time."

"But he doesn't write." She sucked in a wavering breath. "And neither did you."

"I missed you, too," he said after a moment. "More than you know. But I couldn't write to you. What would be the point?"

Sadie eyed him uncertainly. "You could have said that you were okay."

"You wouldn't have written back." He raised his eyebrows. "Would you?"

"No," she conceded.

"And I had feelings, too, Sadie. To write you, and get nothing back—" He shrugged faintly. "That would have hurt."

She'd been thinking of his rejection of them, not of his feelings of rejection from her. She didn't know what to say, and so she looked down at the folded letter in her hands instead.

"I've got work to do," Elijah said. He didn't wait for a good-bye. He started walking back toward the buggy barn and the abandoned wheelbarrow. His broad shoulders swayed with his natural gait, and she couldn't help but notice the way his body moved, the way he kicked out his boots when he walked, the way he tugged at his suspenders.

He said that he wouldn't have undone those kisses they'd shared. She breathed out a sigh.

Given the chance, she would, though. Because she hadn't bounced back.

Chapter Six

Amos and Elizabeth Hochstetler arrived the next afternoon, and, for all of Samuel's excitement about seeing his grandparents, he suddenly realized that he didn't really remember them, and he became shy, clinging to his mother's skirts.

Mammi and Dawdy, as Sadie called them for her son's benefit, were an older couple with white hair and veined hands. Elizabeth was as neatly pressed as she might be on a Sunday at service, and Amos glowered down at Samuel with his sternest expression.

"Hello, young man," he said. "And how are you?"

Sammie stared up at his grandfather, silent and stricken.

"I have something for you," Amos declared, and turned away with the same wrathful look as if he were reaching for a switch, but, after rummaging in his bag for a moment, he pulled out a wooden pair of horses, and Samuel's face lit up.

"For me?" he whispered, one hand still clutching Sadie's apron.

"Yes." The old man nodded decisively. "For my grandson. That's you, isn't it? Speak up now."

"Yes," Samuel said, braver now.

"Good. Come here and get them."

Samuel sidled closer and reached for the horses. Amos placed them in his hands somberly.

"Your daet liked horses, too," he said. "You will call me Dawdy."

"Dawdy," Sammie whispered.

Amos looked up at Sadie's father. "Shall we go sit, then?"

Rosmanda and Sadie brought the bags upstairs, and the men retired to the sitting room, leaving Sammie in the kitchen with his new horses. When Sadie got back down again, she found Rosmanda and Mamm in the kitchen. Elizabeth sat at the table next to Samuel, looking at him with soft eyes.

"He doesn't look like his father at this age," she said, glancing toward Sadie. "I can see Mervin in his ears, and in that curly blond hair . . . but his face must come from your people."

"It must," Sadie admitted. "I wish Mervin could have seen him."

She wished Mervin had even known she was pregnant in time . . .

"How have you been keeping?" Elizabeth asked, folding her hands.

"Would you like some tea?" Rosmanda asked to one side, and the old woman nodded.

"Samuel is growing," Sadie said. "I'm constantly sewing him new clothes as he outgrows everything, or wears them down to threads."

"Yes, they do that." Elizabeth smiled, but with less warmth this time. "I ask about you, though."

Sadie blinked. "Oh. Yes. I'm . . . fine, I suppose. I'm managing."

"You see, we—I mean our side of the family—are concerned about you," Elizabeth went on. "I know this is a rather abrupt way to bring this up, but, as you know, I don't believe in avoiding difficult discussions. We think it's time you married again."

Sadie shot her mother a look of alarm, but Mamm didn't return it. What was happening here? Did that "we" include her own parents?

"Mammi, with all due respect," Sadie said, "I'm raising my son, and I don't want to simply hand over his upbringing to just any man. Mervin was a good, strong husband who could have guided Samuel well, and it's my responsibility—"

"Do you know why Mervin didn't leave you any money?" Elizabeth interrupted.

Sadie looked toward her mother and sister. Mamm was studying the countertop, and Rosmanda was watching in undisguised curiosity.

"Because he didn't know I was pregnant," Sadie replied, her voice tight. That had to be it . . . added to the fact that he hadn't loved her as much as he'd thought he would. These things happened sometimes.

"It was because he had other grown children who needed to inherit," Elizabeth said, and gave Rosmanda a brief smile as she accepted a cup of tea from her. "You were young enough to remarry should something happen to him, and he expected you to do just that."

This was all very likely true, but Mervin had never breathed a word of it to her, and his death had certainly not been expected. Suddenly, Elizabeth's tender hand smoothing down Samuel's curls seemed less loving, and a little more demanding. They expected her to marry again so that they could assuage their own guilt about how their son had left her unprovided for.

"I will give it some thought," Sadie said numbly.

"There are some men in our district," Elizabeth said. "We would be happy to make introductions."

Sadie attempted to smile. This was the life of a woman— always obeying someone. Mamm brushed a hand across

Sadie's shoulder as she passed, a silent connection between mother and daughter. They'd discuss her mother-in-law later, alone.

"I realize that my son was not easy to be married to," Elizabeth went on. "He was a hard man who knew what he wanted."

"That isn't a bad thing," Mamm interjected. "He was kind to her. None of us complained about your Mervin. I can promise you that."

"Kind, yes," Elizabeth agreed, lifting a hand, then dropping it back to her lap. "But they were only married for a year."

"Not much time for . . ." Mamm glanced at Rosmanda, and she didn't finish the thought.

"It takes longer, normally," Elizabeth said.

The older women exchanged a knowing look, then both nodded as if in agreement with something over Sadie's head. It was irritating, because Sadie was no longer a girl—she'd been a married woman. She'd birthed a child in the very bedroom over their heads. She deserved the respect of being treated like the adult she was, but here they were with their veiled looks and unfinished thoughts hanging incomprehensibly in front of her, that mother-daughter connection of just moments earlier evaporating.

"*What* takes longer?" Sadie asked irritably.

"The smoothing out," Mamm replied, turning back to Sadie. "The first few years can be a challenge, and you never did get out of that phase. You don't know what marriage is like on the other side of getting to know a man."

What were they assuming about her marriage? And if they'd had concerns about her happiness, perhaps they could have given her some advice when the man was still alive.

"It wasn't difficult," Sadie countered stubbornly. She

wouldn't give them the satisfaction. "Mervin was a good man, and I loved him."

"And no one admits to it," Elizabeth said with a low laugh.

Anger sparked inside of Sadie, and she turned toward the counter where a pie sat, waiting to be sliced. Her marriage had not been easy. A happy wife was a successful wife. If a woman was unhappy in her marriage, then she was doing something wrong. And Sadie had been most certainly unhappy.

"Would you like some pie, Mammi?" Sadie asked primly.

"Please."

"Rosmanda will serve the men," Mamm said quietly, and Sadie began to slice the shoofly pie. Samuel came to Sadie's knees, small hands clutching at her skirt while she worked, and she felt a wave of maternal protectiveness. This was *her* son, and with Mervin gone, that didn't give her in-laws the right to choose Sammie's next daet.

They wanted her married again—safely provided for. And that was all well and good, but Sadie would have to hand her boy over to a man for discipline, and she would have difficulty doing that. Even having her own daet spank him was more than she liked. She'd be choosing not only a husband for herself, but a father for her son—a man to cherish and love Sammie like she did, but who could also provide a man's influence and guidance. Elizabeth was right in one thing—Sadie had been married before, and she knew how hard it was. She was no romantic girl anymore.

The pie was served, and Sammie was thrilled to get his plate, too. Rosmanda was wisely keeping her mouth shut, lest Mamm send her out of the kitchen to do some chore to get her out of earshot. But these conversations were good for younger women to overhear. How else were they supposed to learn about marriage, if not by listening to women talk? Still, there'd been gossip enough about Sadie's marriage that she wouldn't have minded a little more privacy. She cast her younger sister an annoyed look.

"Was it bad?" Rosmanda whispered. "Being married?"

"No!" Sadie retorted. "I was happy."

The poor man was dead. There was no time to sort out any of their differences anymore, and now her mother-in-law was soiling the last thing she had of her marriage—her pride. She'd been a wife, and whatever issues she and Mervin had had, those were private, behind closed doors. No one else deserved a view into that part of their relationship. She'd been a *wife*.

"Now, my son was a good man," Elizabeth said after she scraped the last bit of treacle from the plate. "But I wasn't blind to his faults, either."

Sadie turned toward the window, wishing herself outside, away from this scene. She'd rather be anywhere right now—in the barn, perhaps.

"We mothers know our sons," Mamm agreed with warmth in her tone. "You're a fair woman, Elizabeth."

"I do try to be." She pushed her plate away. "But my Mervin wasn't always fair. He judged every woman against his first wife, and she wasn't perfection, either. But he'd loved her so much that he figured her ways of doing things were the right ways."

Sadie clenched her teeth together. Mervin had never told her that "his way" was actually his late wife's way. But he'd had certain requirements in the kitchen—ways that things should be served, or how they ought to be cooked. His dead wife's influence had seeped into the very cracks of that house.

"They were married for twenty years," Mamm said. "It's to be expected."

"Yes, but he could have been a little more flexible after her passing," Elizabeth replied. "And he wasn't. But given time, he'd have seen the wisdom in allowing Sadie to do things her way, too. He'd have softened. But it would be enough to scare a young widow off of marriage again. It certainly would for me."

"Mervin was a good husband," Sadie repeated, trying to keep the tartness from her tone. "Our home was a happy one, and I am not leaping into another marriage, because I'm wiser than that. I'm not holding back because Mervin was a taskmaster. I'm holding back because not all men are as good as he was!"

A lie, and she'd harbor some guilt about it later, but right now, she was tired of the whole discussion. The older women both turned toward Sadie in mild surprise, as if they'd forgotten about her presence at the table. There was silence for a moment, and for the first time, Sadie saw a flicker of embarrassment on her mother's face. Sadie had been a good wife, and even after his death, she knew how to protect a man.

"It would be natural to be afraid," Elizabeth said, her tone softening. She fixed Sadie with a sympathetic look. "Every married woman knows that being a wife isn't easy."

Sadie *was* afraid, but she wouldn't admit it—not here, like this. Marriage had been so much harder than she'd anticipated, and she was in no rush to jump back into it again unless she was sure she'd have an easier time of it the second time around. But in this kitchen, staring down her mother-in-law, she couldn't admit that.

"Your son was the kind of husband every woman dreams of marrying." Sadie tried to keep the tremor from her voice. "I'm not afraid."

Elizabeth and Mamm exchanged another look.

"Samuel needs a father to provide a man's guidance," Elizabeth said quietly. "And you will need to provide that father for him, my dear. It's the Lord's will. A father gives a boy an influence that a mother cannot provide. If you neglect it too long, he will be too old to embrace a father's authority in his life, and he'll follow in your brother's footsteps."

The color drained from Mamm's face. "Absolom's shortcomings are not because of Benjamin," she said curtly. "Our son was raised with a firm hand and much love."

"No, no, I don't judge," Elizabeth replied with a shake of her head. "I only say that a boy without a father stands to take the wrong path, especially since his uncle did the same, and that won't stay a secret. The idea is already planted. Besides, Sadie here might have been young when she married my son, but she isn't getting any younger, is she?"

This from a wrinkled old woman! Sadie shut her eyes, looking for control.

"The wrong father could be equally detrimental to a child," Sadie said at last.

Her mother-in-law nodded her agreement with that, then she turned to Samuel with an indulgent smile.

"Do you think I could have a hug yet, Samuel?" Elizabeth asked gently.

Elizabeth had always been an opinionated woman, and even her gentle mothering seemed manipulative now. Who were any of them to tell her to marry again? They'd never approved of Mervin's choice in wife to begin with.

Samuel regarded his grandmother for a moment, then opened his arms to accept a snuggle. He had no idea how many ways his grandmother had just insulted his own mamm. Mammies were loving and indulgent. That's all he knew. And his dawdy had brought him a present. His love was successfully purchased.

But Sadie was not only their dead son's widow, she was the mother of their youngest grandchild. Death might sever the ties between husband and wife, but there were still strings attached between herself and her in-laws.

A wise woman would look closely at the family before she married the man. If Rosmanda wanted to learn, she might start with that.

The cows broke two fences that afternoon, and instead of calling his boss for assistance, Elijah had taken care of it himself. That had slowed down the regular chores, and the sun had set by the time he tramped wearily toward the buggy barn to ready his own ride home.

The sky was dark gray, and the wisps of cloud on the western horizon glowed crimson and burnt orange. Crickets chirped from the long grass he passed, and he slapped at a mosquito, then flicked it from his arm. He liked this time of day—the solitude, the peacefulness. His work was done for the day, and there was certain satisfaction in that knowledge. He missed this—the quiet, the connection to the natural world around him. He wouldn't have this when he went back to the city. He'd find his own apartment, too. Absolom and Sharon were happy to share rent with him again, but his buddy would need space if he was to grow into his role as a family man.

Elijah glanced toward the house—silent and dark except for a flickering light in the kitchen. He'd been avoiding the house today because he knew that Sadie's in-laws were there. He didn't want to interrupt. That was her life, so it felt inappropriate for him to come too close. He'd eaten quickly with his head down when he'd come in for meals, and then he'd quietly excused himself again.

But he'd gotten a good look at the older folks, and they looked like regular Amish—quiet, respectable, neat. They were from Pennsylvania, so he didn't know them personally, but he did catch the old woman eyeing him skeptically. They must have already heard about his recent history with the Englishers, and even if they hadn't, his Englisher hair gave him away.

As Elijah passed the side of the house, the creak of a rocking chair filtered toward him from the porch. Someone was up, and if they heard rummaging in the buggy barn, they might send up the alarm. It was best to go around and announce his presence so he could leave without a kerfuffle.

He cleared his throat in order to make a bit of noise and let his footsteps land more noisily than before. The creaking stopped, and, as he came around the side of the house, he spotted Sadie sitting on the rocker. She heaved a sigh when she saw him.

"Didn't mean to scare you," Elijah said quietly. "The cows got through a fence, so it took longer to finish up tonight."

"Oh . . ." She nodded, then brushed a stray strand of hair away from her face and back under her kapp. "No, it's okay. I was just getting some time alone."

She looked wan, tired. She belonged upstairs in her bed getting some proper sleep, but here she was outside on her own. Something was nagging at her.

"You okay?" he asked.

"I still haven't forgiven you," she said, meeting his gaze, but her tone didn't sound dismissive, exactly. The darkness seemed to soften the moment, and it sucked the barb out of her words.

"That's okay," he said. "But given your options around here, I'm the one person who won't judge you."

She smiled faintly. "How do I know that?"

"Because nothing you could do could match what I did." He crossed his arms. He'd be branded from now on—the one who went English.

"I hate it when you have a good point," she said finally.

"I know." He chuckled. "So how are you . . . really?"

That seemed to be the right question, because she rose from the chair, glancing back toward the house, then came down the front steps to his level.

"It's harder than I thought," she admitted, her voice low. "It's . . . I don't even know. It's different without Mervin, I suppose."

"I could see that," he replied. "How come you're out here? You only used to come out to the porch when you were upset about something."

"Maybe I am." She shook her head. "I'm the problem to be solved around here."

"You aren't a problem."

"I am to them. I'm the widow, and their son didn't provide for me. I make them uncomfortable."

"He didn't—" Elijah dug a toe into the dirt. "Wait, he didn't leave you anything?"

Elijah hadn't realized that. For a man to leave his new wife out of his will completely . . . how much had Mervin valued his young bride? She'd stepped down for him, and he didn't seem to acknowledge that. She'd not only deserved better than a man twenty years older than her, but if she was to marry him, the least he could do was to provide for her financially in the case of his death. Elijah and Absolom had discussed it at length when they'd received news of the wedding. They'd agreed on one thing—at least Sadie would be provided for. It could have been worse.

Except the old codger hadn't even done that much, and Elijah felt his ire rise.

"I didn't even know I was pregnant when he died," she replied, but her tone didn't sound convinced. She'd known she'd been treated shabbily. Had that embarrassed her?

"You were worth provision, with or without a child," he retorted.

She angled her head to the side in acceptance of that, but didn't answer. The moon hadn't risen yet, and only a sprinkling of stars had pierced the twilight. Still, there was enough light to make out the gleam of her eyes in the semi-darkness. She glanced toward him, and their eyes met. She was so beautiful . . . what had Mervin missed?

"So they're going to make sure you have something?" Elijah asked. How else could they fix their son's mistake?

"No, they want me to get married again," she replied. "Then I'd have a man to provide for me and help me with Samuel."

"You have your family," he said.

"I'm a burden on my family. My father is sick."

"So who are you supposed to marry?" he asked.

"No idea." She sucked in a deep breath, then let it out slowly. "I'm sure they have some prospects, but I'm not interested."

"Good."

"No, it isn't," she countered. "I have a son to worry about. And my mother-in-law is right. What if he goes Mennonite like my brother? He needs a father who can guide him. If my little boy did what *you* did . . ."

Elijah didn't answer that. He'd broken his own mother's heart. He was the kind of man Sadie would want to keep her boy away from—the bad influence, the danger to his innocence. There had been a woman who left home and went Mennonite back when they were all kids. She came back after her Englisher husband left her, and while she was rebaptized into the church again, she was never trusted, and the children were told to stay clear of her.

Elijah was in her shoes now, and he knew it.

"Sammie won't," Elijah said with more certainty than he felt.

"I have to make Samuel my priority," she said. "I'm a mamm, Elijah. That responsibility is deeper than any other."

"So you'll marry some man you hardly know?" Elijah asked, hearing the edge in his own voice.

"Maybe," she said.

"Don't." He sighed. "You're better than that. You always were. Wait for the right man, the one who will love you properly."

Tears rose in her eyes and she looked away. Her words were so quiet that he had to step closer still to catch them. "He wanted his food cooked like she used to cook it. . . . He wanted his shirts folded the way she used to fold them." She wiped at her eyes. "I didn't like coming second. Is that sinful of me?"

So he'd been right—Mervin wasn't the saintly older man after all. He'd sensed it, somehow. Elijah stepped closer still and slid a hand around her waist. What had she been through? Had she really been stationed under a dead woman's shadow in her own home with her husband? What would that have done to her?

"You deserved better than him," Elijah murmured.

"I was vain and stupid." Her voice trembled. "I thought because I was young and . . . relatively attractive . . . that he would love me. I thought that I could be enough."

"You are enough," he retorted. "Sadie—"

She raised her gaze tentatively, and he dipped his head down, catching her lips with his. Her eyes fluttered shut, and he pulled her against him in a slow kiss. After a moment, she pulled back, pulling out of his arms abruptly.

"Don't do that . . ." she whispered.

"I'm sorry."

"No, you aren't." Anger flashed in her eyes and she crossed her arms over her stomach. "This is what you always did—took advantage of any moment of weakness I might have . . ."

Took advantage. That stung. He'd never preyed on her like a prowling animal.

"And you don't do *that*." He closed the distance between them again, but didn't touch her. "Don't rewrite our history to make it into something sordid. We cared for each other, and maybe we didn't have much of a future, and maybe we were too young to think it all through properly, but don't lower what it was. The memory of *you* got me through literally years of loneliness out there with the Englishers."

She opened her mouth as if to reply, then shut it again, emotion sparkling in her eyes. Elijah stepped away from her. She'd been right of course—he had no right in kissing her, not now when they both knew better.

"You should have come home, then," she whispered.

"For what?" he asked bitterly. "To watch you marry another guy? To try to fit into my father's vision of my future around here?"

"This is where you belong, Elijah." She shook her head. "You were born to this life. What are you looking for out there?"

"A little less judgment," he replied. "Out there, we're considered really good guys. Here—your brother and I were rebels."

Sadie rubbed her hands over her arms again. The night was chilling, and he could smell September in the air. She took a step back toward the house.

"It doesn't matter where you go, Elijah, you'll be judged by someone." She sighed. "Duties and expectations are a part of community life. Without them, you are free as a bird and very much alone."

Sadie tucked a stray tendril of hair under her kapp, then turned back toward the house. Gone were the days of her brilliant laughter. What was pressing her down like that? The expectations were heavy on her shoulders, too, it seemed. Of all the people in her life wanting things from her, he wanted to be someone who offered something instead. Or maybe he just wanted to keep her with him for a moment or two longer. Was he no better than the others, tugging at her attention?

"Sadie, I could bring you to see your brother." The words were out before he could think better of them. It was the one thing he could do that no other man could offer her.

"What?" Sadie stopped in her tracks and turned around.

"If you wanted to see him again, I could bring you there."

Elijah knew that here in Morinville there would be potential husbands brought around, and while the women could only choose from suitors who had chosen her first, the men wouldn't be fool enough to pass up on Sadie. She was mature, beautiful, talented. She'd successfully had a child, so she was fertile. Amish men considered those things, even if Elijah didn't, and her father's respected position would be like honey to men like that, men whose own families hadn't been tilled under by the bishop's righteous fervor. Who wouldn't want to take her as a wife? He could almost smell the wedding soup in the air along with September's chill.

Absolom had asked Elijah to look out for his sister, and he felt like he wasn't going to be able to do too much to aid her. He had no influence anywhere. But he could offer this—a chance to speak with her brother herself, to see why he did what he did. To get some answers.

"My father wouldn't allow it," she said, but she'd stopped moving away from him.

"Maybe not," Elijah agreed. "But I'm leaving the offer there. If you want to see him, I'll take you."

"We aren't supposed to be friends, you and I," she countered.

"Unless I do what's expected of me and come back properly," he replied with a bitter smile. "I know. You aren't the only one."

"Meaning?" she asked.

"Meaning, my own daet wouldn't talk to me unless I came back and did as I was told. You're in good company, Sadie."

"I'm not—" She sighed. Yet they both knew it. It was what they'd been taught since childhood.

"But I'm a little more stubborn than you are," he said. "I don't like being pushed into corners. Besides," he added, "I'm perfectly safe. I'm obviously not courting you."

She slowly shook her head. "You are more of a danger than you think, Elijah Fisher."

And maybe he was. He'd just offered to bring her to the Englisher world and to open her mind in a way that would make all of her comforting platitudes fall flat. There was little more dangerous than that. But he wouldn't apologize for it.

Sadie turned toward the house again.

"Good night," he whispered after her, and she turned once to look at him with an unreadable expression before she walked resolutely back toward the house, up the steps, and in the front door.

Elijah sighed. Sometimes a mind filled with experiences that no one else could understand was the heaviest burden. He'd thought he wanted to offer Sadie something, but did he? Maybe he only wanted to have another person he could talk to, to drag her out into this no man's land that he inhab-ited. What was that she'd said—duties and expectations were a part of community life? Without them, he'd be free as a bird, but very much alone. And he was. This weight of loneliness could smother a man.

If he cared at all for her, he'd let her marry some stern farmer who would never love her well enough, and let her stay in the world she knew.

Chapter Seven

That night, Sadie lay in bed, unable to sleep. Her window was open, the curtain pulled back to let a cool breeze into the room, and with it the soft night sounds of crickets. Samuel was sound asleep in his little bed, his blankets flung aside. The excitement of his grandparents' visit had worn him out.

But as she lay in her bed, she was equally exhausted but unable to sleep. Elijah's kiss was replaying itself in her head. The softness of his lips, the way he'd pulled her close, not once asking for permission. Her heart pounded at the memory. That was how Elijah was different from Mervin. Elijah had always been able to awaken a spark in her, and Mervin had been, for the most part, properly distant. Mervin had never pulled her in for a forbidden kiss in the heat of an emotional moment. His fingers had never splayed over the small of her back like that, his lips hovering over hers before he sank down into the heat of her lips . . .

She should have walked away then—not stayed for more conversation. Because his offer to take her to see her brother was more tempting than she was comfortable with. She had been right to walk away. Elijah was the reason that

Absolom had left to begin with, and she'd be stupid to follow the same man out into the Englisher world. He could be so tempting . . . she knew that well enough. He could look into her eyes and give her one of those half-cocked smiles, and she longed to follow. He was most definitely dangerous.

But she couldn't quite put his offer out of her mind, either. Just one visit. She could see where her brother lived, meet this ominous Sharon. Maybe she could understand the draw, because part of the heartbreak was her complete inability to comprehend *why* her brother would do such a thing. How could an Englisher life be better than a solid, respectable life within the Amish community?

She rolled over, her legs getting tangled in her sheet, and she irritably kicked them free. Could she simply turn away from a chance to see her brother *just once*? It might be her last time seeing him—she could accept that. It would be painful, but at least it would be a proper good-bye. When the Amish left home, it was always in the dead of night because they knew if they had to look their parents in the face, they'd never be able to do it. Absolom had been no different.

Besides, she had a few regrets of her own when it came to her brother. The last time she saw Absolom, she'd argued with him about tramping his muddy boots into the kitchen, making messes for his sisters to clean.

He'd called her bossy, she'd called him spoiled, and he'd stomped off to bed, leaving her to clean it up alone. She'd left the kitchen as it was—to let Mamm see it so she could give Absolom what for. But there'd been no time for that. By the next morning, Absolom had vanished, and he'd wiped up the mud before he left. That was the last she'd seen of her brother.

Elijah was offering her a chance to change that—to wrap her arms around her brother's neck and tell him how she missed him. She'd be able to say all the things she'd rehearsed year after year. She'd be able to plead with him to come back, because if she was part of the problem—her bossiness, her short temper—maybe she could fix her part of it to bring him home.

She lay on her side, her mind spinning and her heart swelling with hope. What if she *could* see Absolom again?

And mingled with the thoughts of her brother were thoughts of Elijah, too. He made it all seem innocent enough—just a visit. Was that what he'd done with Absolom? Because Elijah had a lonely sort of air about him and he reached out to her with memories of their adolescent romance, but she wasn't made of stone. He'd been an older boy who listened when she talked. He'd shoot that sparkling grin of his in her direction, and while she'd huff and put up an act of being indifferent, she was privately happy that she could awaken those feelings in him. She'd taken it for granted in many ways, too, but now she knew that captivating a man wasn't quite so easy as she'd assumed.

She and Elijah hadn't been alone often, but when they were, he'd reach for her hand and twine his fingers through hers. He'd give her that slow, warm smile of his, and she would melt in reply. It was scandalous and wrong, but she hadn't stopped him. She hadn't pulled her hand back, told him to behave. If she had, she'd never have indulged in those heart-pounding entanglements by the creek—and she wouldn't have longed for more of it.

Maybe it was best that he'd left Morinville after all, or she might have let things go too far and ended up pregnant. These things happened, even in Amish communities. When Elijah left with Absolom, she'd been heartbroken to lose them both, but more than that . . . she'd been wounded that Elijah hadn't breathed a word of it to *her*. After those secret moments shared together, she'd been left out. He didn't even give her a chance to talk him out of it.

And that was the most dangerous part of his influence—he was so likeable that she might have followed after him, too, given half a chance nine years ago. If she couldn't have convinced him to stay, she'd have packed a bag, too. She'd have crept out of the house with Absolom and walked with him to whatever meeting place he and Elijah had decided upon. And she'd have told herself it was only to make sure that they both came back.

Sadie finally did fall asleep, and her dreams were plagued by dirty floors, her mother-in-law's appalled expression as she surveyed the mess, and the dreadful certainty that while she stood there trying to explain herself to the old woman, her brother was slipping further and further away from them all . . . but she couldn't stop explaining, and every time she tried to turn toward the door, there was more mud.

Sadie, what have you done?

She awoke to someone shaking her shoulder, and Sadie sputtered awake, sitting bolt upright.

"Shh . . . I'm sorry, Sadie." It was Mamm. "I didn't mean to scare you."

"Mamm?" Sadie rubbed a hand over her face. "What's the matter? What time is it?"

"It's four-ten. You haven't overslept. Daet pushed it too hard yesterday, and I don't want him to go out for chores this morning. He needs rest."

"Oh . . ." Sadie let out a breath, trying to shake the dream from her mind as she fully woke up. Samuel was next to her—he'd climbed up into her bed at some point during the night, and she smoothed a hand over his rumpled curls.

Mamm's voice held apology. "I know it's early, but if we can get things done quickly, maybe no one will notice."

Sadie understood all too well. They didn't want to spread the rumors that Daet was ailing. He might get better yet, but if the council of elders decided that the bishop couldn't do his job anymore, they'd have a new lottery for another bishop . . . Daet would be crushed. He was already losing his ability to run his own farm. To take away his spiritual responsibilities would be cruelty.

"You'll have to do the chores, Sadie," Mamm urged her. "Let's hope that Elizabeth and Amos sleep long this morning. I'll keep things as quiet as possible downstairs."

Sadie settled the sheet around Samuel's sleeping form and swung her legs over the edge of the bed. She'd been waiting for a chance to speak to Mamm alone ever since her in-laws had arrived, but that hadn't been so easy.

"Mamm, there's something I need to give you," Sadie whispered after her mother. Sadie's apron hung over the back of a chair, and she reached for it, fumbling in the pocket for the now familiar square of folded paper.

"This." Sadie held out the letter. "I was waiting to catch you alone. It's from Absolom."

"Oh?!" Mamm snatched up the letter. "He wrote to you?"

"No." Sadie shook her head. "He wrote to Elijah. Elijah gave it to me yesterday."

Mamm nodded, her enthusiasm dampening. She swallowed a couple of times. She knew her mother was feeling the stab of that detail. She'd felt it, too.

"I'll read it downstairs when I light the lamp. Now you hurry and get out there. Elijah arrives in an hour and a half, and if you can get a start before he gets here, maybe you can both be back inside before Elizabeth and Amos come down."

Proprieties would have to wait for another time, it seemed, even with the Hochstetlers here to see.

"Mamm," she whispered. "He named his daughter after you."

Her mother put a hand across her mouth and shut her eyes for a moment as if holding back tears. Then she nodded slowly. "A girl . . ." She opened her eyes, and her tone firmed. "Well, he shouldn't have bothered if I'll never meet her."

"Still . . ." Sadie said.

Mamm met her gaze for an agonizing moment and then slipped out into the hallway, closing the bedroom door softly behind her. Sadie stood in the darkness, her heart feeling heavy and sodden. It was impossible, wasn't it? She wanted to see her brother so badly, but for what? He'd never come back, and she'd never go to the Englishers. They'd never speak again . . .

Sadie felt around for her clothes, pinning her dress into place by touch. She combed her hair quickly, then twisted it up into a bun at the back of her head to be concealed by a fresh white kapp that she pulled from her drawer. When she looked back to her sleeping son, he hadn't moved an inch, and his breath came in a slow, even rhythm. May her in-laws be blessed with the blissful slumber of a tired toddler.

By the time Sadie got downstairs, the lamp was lit, and the downstairs was uncomfortably warm as it always was this time of year. Mamm stood by the lamp with the open letter pressed against her chest. Tears sparkled in her eyes.

"Mamm . . ." Sadie moved toward her mother, but Mamm folded the page quickly and slipped it into her pocket.

"I will show this to your father, and he and I will discuss it."

"Absolom is a daet now," Sadie said quietly.

"And still not married." Mamm shook her head. "Again, I'm not sure if I should be glad for that, or not."

"He's thinking of you, though," Sadie said. "He wouldn't have named his baby for you if he weren't."

"And yet he did not write to me." Her mother pressed her trembling lips together. "I'm his *mamm*."

Sadie couldn't comfort her mother there. She had

nothing to offer. That offense was a private one between mother and son. Her son had left her, and he refused to come home. He'd left not only her, but his faith and the way of life she'd taught him so lovingly as he grew. Only a mother could feel the pain of that rejection.

"I don't know what it's worth," Sadie said quietly. "But Elijah offered to take me to see Absolom. I could see his baby, talk to him. Maybe there's hope he'll change his mind if we go to him. I don't think he'll come to us."

Mamm turned toward the stove and bent to light the burner. "Maybe." Her voice was soft. "I'll talk to your father. But I'm not sure it would be a good example to the rest of the community. We have a responsibility to them, too."

"Okay." They'd talk. That's all she could ask. "I'll go start the chores now."

Sadie went into the mudroom and pulled on her rubber boots. There was work to be done, and as always, there was a strange comfort in that fact. Work gave them purpose, and kept them putting one foot in front of the other when they'd rather indulge their emotions.

Mamm would cook up a big breakfast, and Sadie would tend to the cattle. And when she got back, she would smile brightly, and they'd all pretend that nothing whatsoever was wrong. They were a good family, they were respected members of the community, and appearances must reflect that fact. People were watching, and people would talk. Their grief would have to remain private.

Elijah arrived at the Graber farm a few minutes later than usual, and he was deeply regretting having kissed Sadie the night before. It had been spontaneous and stupid, sparked by that dewy look in her eyes—her belief that she'd some-how not been enough for a man who was too blind to see the beautiful creature he'd married. And he wanted to erase that for her—as if a kiss could even do that.

Stupid. That's what it had been, and she'd been right to tell him off.

His own morning chores at home had taken longer, and Elijah hadn't wanted to leave everything to his mother to finish on her own. They were all tired. Elijah's father had been working extralong hours trying to make up for his slower production on the bishop's large order, and the bishop's ever-growing demands on Elijah's time took away from any physical help he could offer to his parents now that he was back. Still, his mother remained steadfastly grateful for that paycheck, and Elijah couldn't tell her what time on this farm was doing to him . . . the idiotic things he was coming to because he couldn't quite tear his heart free from the one woman he'd never had a right to.

The sky was still dark as he unhitched his horses and brought them into the stable for some hay and oats, next to the Grabers' draft horses. Then he headed for the cow barn where his morning chores would begin. The nights were getting chillier on this end of August, and Elijah picked up his pace to warm up. His boots crunched against gravel as he walked down the road. It was strange to be back on the Graber property this way. He'd spent years on this farm with his best friend, helping out with the haying, the calving, or just spending a Sunday evening with the family. And now he was here as an employee . . . still overstepping bounds with the same woman. He had to stop this. Coming back had been to help out his parents, not to get himself entangled in old mistakes.

The only sound was the far-off lowing of cattle and the chirp of insects. Back in the city, the constant hum of traffic and voices had been distracting until he'd learned how to tune it all out, but, by deafening himself to one thing, he found himself deafened to others, as well. He could not block out the sounds of the city without also cutting himself away from the whisper of his own mind. So many times, he'd lain in bed wishing for silence, remembering how it felt to walk outside in the predawn gray when he could actually hear himself think.

When Elijah pushed open the side door to the barn, he could see the soft glow of a lamp already hanging from a hook, and the sound of metal against concrete met his ears. But instead of the bishop, he saw the soft gray of a woman's dress contrasting with a white kapp.

"Sadie?"

She turned and wiped her forehead with her wrist as she met his gaze. "Good morning."

Her complexion was pale, and faint rings showed in that fragile flesh under her eyes. She heaved the last shovelful of soiled hay into the wheelbarrow and put the shovel down with a heavy clank.

"So you managed to beat your daet out here, did you?" he asked.

She kept a hand on the cow's rump as she moved around it toward the fresh hay. "Mamm woke me up. We're hoping to be back inside before Mamm and Daet Hochstetler realize how much I'm doing for my father."

"They don't know about his illness?" he asked.

Sadie shook her head. "They know that he's seen a doctor and has some medication, but we're trying to hide how bad it really is. If the elders decided to replace Daet, he'd have nothing left."

"He'd have a fully paid farm," Elijah said.

She paused, met his gaze earnestly. "What is that compared to the purpose he gets from his position with the church? Money . . . there is a reason we aren't supposed to be focused on all that."

She was no longer the vulnerable woman from last night, and he felt his ire rise. If money weren't a consideration, he wouldn't even be here.

"The work—I know." Elijah pulled a knife from his pocket and cut through the twine that held together a bail of hay. The twine broke with a *ping*, and the hay sprung free. He picked up a pitchfork and began transferring clean hay to the cow's stall. Sadie moved toward the wheelbarrow.

"I'll get that," he said. "It's heavy."

And dirty, and smelly. Sadie didn't belong out here in the barn, working her hands to blisters in men's work. But there weren't enough men to carry the weight around here on a regular basis. The Grabers hired seasonal workers normally, and as far as Elijah knew, he was the first full-time regular employee.

"Thanks." She reached for the milking stool and a clean metal bucket instead.

"You know, the Englisher women get offended if you tell them they belong in the kitchen," Elijah said.

Sadie set the stool on the ground and settled herself onto it. "A woman belongs where she's needed."

Elijah couldn't help but smile. She was more like them than she thought—that urge to prove herself capable. He'd struggled with how to talk to Englisher women. They were so direct, and he didn't understand the difference between a woman who was flirting with him and a woman who felt sorry for him. It had been awkward all around.

"I once told a woman that she should focus more on taking care of her home," Elijah admitted.

"Insulting her housekeeping?" Sadie asked incredulously. "That's a stupid move."

"No, I meant that she shouldn't be working in manual labor with us men. She didn't take kindly to it, let me tell you. She reported me to our boss, and I almost got fired. The Englishers have rules against that sort of thing."

"What sort of thing?" She frowned.

"Suggesting that a woman doesn't belong doing men's work."

The sound of milk hissing into the bucket filled the air, and Elijah added another forkful of hay into the trough for the cow.

"If you're saying I shouldn't be out here—" she began.

"No, I—" Elijah sighed. He hadn't meant the story to be a judgment on her. He was just talking—sharing a little bit of his life from Chicago with the only person he could speak to about it. He was still sorting out the Englisher irregularities, trying to piece it all together and make sense of it. "I was just remembering. Sorry. That wasn't aimed at you."

"I have little choice, Elijah." She sounded offended. "Daet is ill. My brothers have land of their own, and if word gets out—"

"Sadie!" His voice reverberated through the barn, and she fell silent. "I didn't mean that. I was just talking."

The milk drummed into the bucket in a steady rhythm, and Elijah took the wheelbarrow outside to empty it. Sadie seemed to be expecting judgment from every corner. Maybe because she'd been experiencing it, he realized. He'd felt like a failure in that construction job. He'd been the least-skilled worker there; even the women knew more than he did. He'd bumbled through everything from the job to the social interactions. He didn't know how to banter with the men, and the women who seemed friendlier toward him hadn't stayed that way. He'd kept putting his foot in his mouth.

When Elijah came back inside, Sadie had moved on to the next cow, her fingers working in a steady rhythm as the milk sprayed into the bucket.

"Why do you tell those stories?" Sadie asked, and he paused at the stall where she milked. "They're all like that—strange and uncomfortable."

"I guess I have all these memories I can't do anything with. They don't belong anywhere, but I can't just shove them into a drawer, either. Nine years is a long time. I need to—" He shook his head, looking for the words. "Sometimes a man just needs to be heard. I do the same thing with the Englishers—tell them stories that make no sense to them."

"You could just admit that you made a nine-year mistake," she replied. "That would make it easier to sort out."

Sadie rose from the stool and she reached for the milk pail, her arm trembling under the weight of it. He caught the pail in his own grip as she exited the stall, and her fingers lingered next to his as he caught her gaze.

"So what am I supposed to do?" he asked, his voice low.

"You ask me?" She met his gaze uncertainly.

"Who else do I ask?" He felt a rush of frustration. He'd honestly wanted an answer—some piece of Amish wisdom that had eluded him, that filled in the gaps. She'd lived some hard years, too—whether she admitted to it or not. She wasn't the same teenage girl who'd caught his eye all those years ago. She was a woman, warm and fragrant right in front of him, her chin raised so she could look him in the face—always so fearless when it came to him.

"You should just come home," she said softly. "Permanently, and then put it all in the past. That's my advice."

She didn't get it. A man could want to erase a part of himself so much, and it could still be impossible.

"Back in the city, I used to lie in bed at night listening to the traffic. It was frustrating—so noisy and bright. The lights would move along my wall, shining through the curtains. But I'd lie there trying to sleep, and I'd think of the things I loved about Morinville. Like the creek, or

walking down that dusty road with you and Absolom when
we'd talk about the future and what we wanted out of life.
Absolom and I had craved freedom—and we have it. But
what we scramble for isn't always what makes us happy."

She let out a pent-up breath, but her fingers remained on
the pail handle next to his. She smelled of soap and something like vanilla. Her complexion was pale and spattered
with the faintest of freckles, and he found his gaze moving
down to her lips in spite of himself.

"I *would have been* happy," she said. "If my husband
had lived long enough for us to figure each other out."

Elijah released the pail, and she moved away from him
a few steps.

"I'm sorry it was so difficult," he said.

"Don't be," she replied softly. "Like anything, happiness
requires some work first."

She had a point, he realized. Life didn't just fall together.
People worked for it—in the fields, in the home. . . . Even
Englishers scrambled after happiness as they milled through
shopping malls.

"So what are your plans now?" she asked.

Elijah shrugged. "To help my daet get his finances settled, and then go back, I suppose."

"Still?" She shook her head. "Why not work your daet's
business?"

It would certainly be the Amish way, but his daet's
business had been driven into the ground, thanks to her
overzealous father. He shook his head. "There's no future
with it."

"The future is in the family," she countered. "In building
something over generations and—"

"My father's business is nearly bankrupt." The words
tasted bitter in his mouth. "Your father insisted that he take
out an electric tool, and his competitors overran him."

She fell silent for a moment, then licked her lips. "But

those are the sacrifices we make, aren't they? The Amish life is one of simplicity and there is a cost to that, but the benefits outweigh what we might give up."

She was one to talk!

"Sadie, I'm sorry to be the one to tell you, but you've never experienced a day of financial hardship in your life. You have no idea what a family faces when their livelihood is at stake. The ideals get tilled under with the money."

"Then we work harder—"

"We?" he asked bitterly. "Your father could have made an exception as he did for other businesses. Our home has stayed staunchly Amish. A family can't live by the Ordnung if it can't make enough to survive, and poverty is shameful."

"My father is fair," she retorted. "A line has to be drawn somewhere, Elijah. You know that."

There were other businesses that were treated more leniently, but she wasn't going to see that right now.

"Your father is capable of great flexibility," Elijah said bitterly. "Where it comes to Absolom, he'll bend so far that he'll brush the ground—wait and see."

"My father has shown no partiality—" she began angrily.

"Oh, he will."

Sadie glared at him, her blue eyes icy in the glow of the gas lantern. "Absolom is *his son*. I dearly hope he bends for him and brings him home where he belongs!"

"I know." Elijah gave her a tight smile. Was she going to finally understand this? "And that will make all the difference. For you. Your family will flourish, Sadie. But no, I won't follow my father's business down into the dust. I want a whole lot more than that."

Elijah pushed open the side door and chill, morning air rushed around him, bracing him against whatever it was he kept feeling for this woman. She was blind to her father's faults, and perhaps that was even understandable. But it didn't help him. Whenever he was around Sadie, he found himself opening up to her, longing to be understood by someone in this blasted community. And was it so stupid of him to want that from her? Except he wasn't planning on staying, so what was he trying to do here?

Sadie came outside behind him, the door banging shut. Elijah turned, and she rubbed her hands over her arms, but her eyes still flashed fire.

"So tell me this, Elijah. If you resent my father so much, why did you take this job?"

"Why do you think?" Had she forgotten so much about him already?

"The money?" She sounded embarrassed to even say it.

He laughed bitterly. "It factors in, believe me. But as I told you before, I promised your brother I'd make sure you were okay."

"And I am." She straightened her spine as she said the words.

"Are you?"

He raised an eyebrow, waiting for a response. Color infused her cheeks and she dropped her gaze. She wasn't okay. She was scared—and while she'd always been cautious in the past, she'd never been afraid.

"The only difference between you and I, Sadie, is that I'm willing to do something if I'm not happy. That's it. No husband is going to solve your problems. If you don't take charge of your own life, someone else will do it for you."

She was no better than he was, no purer or more righteous. She was just more afraid.

Chapter Eight

The next afternoon, Elizabeth and Amos Hochstetler caught a van carrying various Amish travelers back to Pennsylvania. Sadie stood outside as they loaded their one small suitcase into the back of the van. Samuel stood next to her, his little hands clutched in front of him. But Sadie's mind was still fixed on Elijah's words: If she didn't take charge of her own life, somebody else would do it for her—the right husband wasn't going to solve her problems.

And while she agreed with the sentiment, the wrong husband would only add to her problems, and she couldn't make that mistake, either. But she couldn't just shake off what he'd said. Elijah had been willing to do something to rectify his situation, and she might disagree with his choices, but at least he'd done something. Was she stagnating here?

"Dawdy has to go?" Samuel asked plaintively.

"Yes, Sammie."

The boy had bonded with his grandfather over the last couple of days, and as much as Sadie wanted to be enough for her son, she was struck with how important men were in her little boy's life. Mammi was all fine and good— Samuel had sopped up all that extra attention like biscuits and gravy—but his dawdy had filled Samuel's little heart to overflowing. Dawdy had given him wooden horses.

"Come give Mammi a hug," Elizabeth said, turning back toward them. Samuel permitted himself to be squeezed once more, and then Elizabeth turned her attention to Sadie.

"You'll find a good Amish husband, won't you?" she asked softly. "A man who will raise that little boy right."

"The Lord will lead," Sadie said, and Elizabeth pursed her lips, then gave a curt nod. What Amish woman could argue with divine leadership? It was a righteous conversation ender.

Even the most honorable and noble of Amish husbands could be obstinate, illogical, and moody. And, just because those sacred vows had been said before God and everyone they knew, it didn't mean that behind closed doors he would open his heart. It didn't mean that he could fill hers, either. Good Amish husbands were men—nothing more and nothing less.

"Travel safely," Sadie said. "We were so glad to have you with us these last two days."

"You'll come to see us, too," Elizabeth replied with a warm squeeze of her hand. "And I will introduce you to some nice young men."

Sadie had no doubt—she'd been put on matchmaking notice. But she was in no hurry to visit her in-laws, either. While she needed her family and her community, she was tired of being pushed around by them—always doing what would make her appear to be a "good woman." Even the best of women could end up with a miserable marriage, and then she'd be alone enduring it.

The van pulled away, and Sadie stood somberly watching as it turned onto the main road and disappeared behind some trees. She looked down at Samuel then, and gave him a relieved smile. The pressure was off for the moment, and it was just her family again.

"Dawdy gave me horses," Samuel said sadly.

Sadie reached down for her son's pudgy hand. "Let's go inside and start supper."

The next day was a service Sunday, so the morning was busy with getting ready to leave the house all together. Chores were completed as efficiently as possible, breakfast was eaten, and then Sadie dressed her son in his crisp Sunday best.

Sadie and Rosmanda got into the back of the buggy, with Daet and Mamm in the front. Sadie wore her sky-blue wedding dress—as did all the married women, and it was nearly as bright and new as the day she'd married Mervin, except for the waistline that she'd had to let out since Samuel's birth.

Samuel settled on his mother's lap as they jiggled their way down the road toward the Yoder farm where service would be held this week. Usually, service Sundays brought Mervin to mind more sharply than other days, considering her attire, but today, her mind kept moving back to Elijah. He was determined to go back to Chicago, and she shouldn't care so deeply what he chose to do. But she did. And then there was his certainty that her father would bend. It irritated her. The Amish life was one of discipline, but it wasn't the dictatorship that Elijah made it out to be. Leadership was necessary for any community, and Elijah had never tolerated authority very well.

Sadie sighed, looking out the small square window as a car crept past them, the Englisher occupants straining to get a look at her. She pulled back, out of their view.

Samuel was more cuddly than usual, and when she placed a hand across his forehead, he felt a little warm. Not dangerously warm, but it was noticeable.

"How are you feeling, Sammie?" she asked.

"Good."

Fair enough. Maybe it was nothing. It was summer after all, and maybe his church clothes were overheating him a little. She blew across his head, trying to cool him a bit. It would be a long day—it always was when trying to keep a small child quiet during service.

When they arrived at the Yoder farm, they parked their buggy with the others, and the horses were unhitched and taken out to the pasture to graze. The Yoders had a meeting barn that stood empty most of the year, except for just after harvest when they used half of it for hay bales. The congregation mutually owned some benches that were carried by cart from farm to farm on meeting Sundays. The cart was left at the farm where the service had just been held, and it was that family's responsibility to hitch up the cart and bring it to the next farm the following service day. It was an old, reliable system.

Sadie talked with a few friends, a sister-in-law, and a cousin, outside, before the service was set to begin. Samuel, who usually liked to run with the bigger boys, stayed close to her side, her apron clutched in his grasp.

"You'd better play now," she told him. "You won't be able to later."

Sammie ignored the warning and popped a thumb into his mouth.

When it was time to go into the barn, Sadie settled herself on the women's side, on one of the community benches next to Mamm. Mamm was looking down at her hands, likely in silent prayer. Samuel didn't want to sit beside Sadie, so she pulled the boy onto her lap. Sadie's friend Hadassah sat on her other side, drawing Samuel's attention with her smiles and by holding his hand. Sammie loved attention, especially from women. Rosmanda sat a row back with some of her friends.

The men's side was directly opposite them, and Sadie

scanned the familiar faces as she always did, spotting her uncles, some younger cousins, her oldest brother, Amos, who still lived within the church district, and her father, seated far to the right on the front bench. And just behind her father sat Elijah.

She wasn't the only one noticing Elijah, either. Elijah Fisher was a curiosity. He was no Rumspringa youth back home after a few weeks of learning the hard way that the Amish life was preferable. He was a grown man who'd been gone for enough years that most people had written him off as already halfway to hell. He'd lost that gangly quality he used to sport, and now he sat with broad shoulders and a cleanly shaven face to show his single status amid all the bearded, married men. He sat with his knees wide apart, resolutely still, his black service hat slightly crooked and his expression brooding and introverted.

"Elijah Fisher is still here," Hadassah said quietly, nudging Sadie's arm.

"Yah." What more was there to say?

"If he came back, he'll stay," her friend went on.

"He isn't baptized," Sadie whispered back. "So don't go getting ideas—"

"With the right incentive, he will be." Hadassah hadn't always been this forward, but the years had plodded on without any proposals, and even the most demure Amish girl could be pushed to the limit at the prospect of Old Maid status. "He works on your farm, doesn't he?"

When Sadie looked over at her friend, she saw that Hadassah's gaze was fixed on Elijah, and a small smile curved her lips. Hadassah wasn't an overly attractive girl. She was thin and pale with prominent teeth. But that look in her eye left no question about her intentions.

"He does," Sadie said, eyeing her friend, and then glancing to see if Elijah had noticed the attention. He licked his lips, then pursed them slightly, deep in thought by all appearances, and Sadie could see why he drew her friend's eye. He had always been cute in that way that relied more on personality and self-confidence than it did on the bare building blocks, but he'd matured into something more rugged over the last nine years. He was a mixture of strength, muscle, and vulnerability, and watching him from across the barn in service was different from working with him side by side. In service, he wasn't only hers to dismiss.

"Is he going to the hymn sing tonight?" Hadassah asked.

"I wouldn't know." The words were more curt than she'd intended, and Hadassah startled, then looked at Sadie.

"What?" Hadassah whispered. "I know he was out in the world, Sadie. I'm not stupid. But he's also single and gorgeous, too. Not all of us got scooped up so quickly as you did."

A single man wasn't to be sneezed at in this community, and Sadie understood her friend's perspective. Hadassah was twenty-three and single. Most of the single men were younger than her. It was time to take anyone who would have her—even a risk like Elijah.

"I'm not the only one," Hadassah murmured, keeping her voice low. And Sadie followed her friend's gaze to see two other young women staring at Elijah with bold curiosity. Sadie dragged her eyes away from them as Samuel whimpered and rubbed at his eyes with his fists.

"He's a danger," Sadie murmured. "He's not so settled in our ways as he looks."

Hadassah deserved a warning at least. The younger woman might not see it, but a bad husband was worse than no husband—and this man had no intention of even staying in Morinville.

Sadie put a hand over her son's head once more. Samuel's forehead was still overly warm, and his cheeks were flushed. He wasn't feeling well.

"I'd settle him into our ways myself," Hadassah said with

an impish smile. "Shoofly pie and a girlfriend? He'd come home to me, I can assure you. I'd be ever so agreeable."

Elijah was going to have no trouble getting female attention, appropriate or not—pious or not—and that realization piqued her more than she liked to admit. After all Elijah had done, a few grudges were in order, but he was male and single. That's all some girls needed.

An elder with a hymnal in hand rose to his feet and made his way to the center of the stage. It was time to begin the song service, and as everyone stopped their whispering, Elijah's gaze suddenly snapped up, and Sadie found his dark eyes drilling straight in to hers. He hadn't searched the faces to find her—he'd simply looked up into her eyes and held her there as if nailing her to the spot. Her heart did a little jump.

Samuel started to cry plaintively, and Sadie rose to her feet. She'd have to bring Samuel out of the service and find some shade and water. He hadn't been sick in a couple of years. He was a hearty little boy, and this sudden fever worried her.

"Sadie!" Hadassah tugged at her apron.

"I'll be fine. You stay in service," Sadie whispered, assuming her friend meant to lend a hand with Sammie.

"Tell Elijah to come to the hymn sing," Hadassah whispered back, then her attention moved back to the men's side of the barn.

Sadie didn't answer, and she edged past the knees of the women, Samuel clinging to her neck with clammy hands. She patted his back soothingly, and as she escaped the benches, she glanced back to see the two other girls who had been staring at Elijah now watching her with a mixture of curiosity and something slightly sharper in their clear gazes. They'd noticed Elijah's intense stare, and she was no longer just a young widow in the congregation. She'd just become competition.

There was a small part of her heart—a petty little part—that sparked. She wasn't to be disregarded yet. Widowed, perhaps, but still in the ring.

"Mamm . . ." Samuel whimpered, and she turned her attention to her son.

She shushed him softly, her lips pressed against his head, and headed out of the barn to allow the other worshipers to continue without disruption.

Elijah wasn't listening to the hum of voices around him. Men were murmuring to each other—greetings, a few conversations kept quiet out of respect for the day. Across the center of the "stage" where the preachers would speak, the women sat in rows of muted-color dresses. Purple, blue, and some pink for the younger women who weren't yet married. He could still remember how scandalized he'd felt when he'd walked into a Mennonite church for the first time and found himself seated shoulder to shoulder between two women.

Elijah sucked in a breath, straightening his back. This would be a long service—three sermons, normally, plus the singing and some lengthy prayers. But he wasn't thinking about worship—his thoughts were fixed on the argument he'd had with his father the night before. Elijah told his daet that he'd been thinking of going back to visit Absolom for a day—just to check in on him. He hadn't mentioned his offer to bring Sadie with him. His father had been upset.

"Daet, you know I'm not staying."

"You could stay, son. You could. The Lord brought you back—"

"YOU brought me back! I came to help out, Daet, but this isn't my home anymore!"

Elijah was doing his best by everyone, but he couldn't just slip back into Amish life. It wasn't so easy as that. His father—and the bishop, too, for that matter—saw it as a choice between right and wrong, but it was a lot more complicated than that. Elijah wasn't afraid of eternal damnation for staying away, but he was afraid of crushing himself down for so long that he turned into an angry, hard, bitter man. He had one life to live, and he believed that he'd be held accountable for it. He also thought he was capable of a whole lot more than the Amish life would allow.

His father had suggested that he might find a nice girl to get to know . . . but the sharp looks he received from the other men, including Mr. Yoder, Hadassah's father, were dissuading enough. He was a threat—and he understood why they felt that way. He glanced toward the women's seats once more, and he noticed both Hadassah's doe-eyed stare and Sadie carrying Samuel toward the door.

Elijah tugged at his collar, the air hot and thick. An elder cleared his throat several times, then began singing the first few words of a familiar hymn, and the congregation quickly joined in. Hadassah's lingering looks were making him more and more uncomfortable—and the singing didn't seem to distract her any.

Elijah rose from his seat and edged around the outside of the bench area. The men's voices rose together in song, and Elijah felt his breath coming more easily as he left the crowded seats behind him, heading for the door. He wasn't following Sadie, exactly, just escaping. As he stepped outside, the warm, fragrant breeze swept around him in a welcome embrace. He just needed to breathe.

Sadie walked across the grass ahead of him, Sammie propped on her hip. She reached the pump and heaved the handle to get a few splashes of fresh water in the tin bucket. Then she dipped the corner of her apron into the water and put the boy on the ground. She knelt down to wipe his face. Sammie kept trying to climb back into her lap, his cry surfing the warm wind. Sadie gathered the boy up into her arms again and dipped her hand into the bucket instead, stroking water through his hair.

She looked alone. That was the best way to describe her. Many a woman took a child outside for similar reasons, but never had a woman looked so utterly bereft as Sadie did, balancing her child on her knees and using her own apron to wipe him. He sighed, then headed in her direction.

"Is Sammie okay?" Elijah asked as he approached.

"He's not feeling well." She dipped her hand into the bucket again. "I noticed he was warm just as we were leaving. I should have stayed home with him. I just—" She sighed, not finishing her thought.

She'd been lonely for her community, no doubt. She'd wanted to see her friends. He understood that well enough. The Amish only met to worship together once every two weeks, so this was a time that people looked forward to.

Sadie used the corner of her apron to wipe Sammie's head again. Elijah pulled a clean handkerchief from his pocket. He gave the pump a good heave, and put the cloth underneath the icy gush. He wrung it out, then laid it over Samuel's forehead. The boy stopped crying as the cold cloth touched his skin.

"Thank you." Sadie sank down to the wooden platform and leaned her back against the pump. She raised her gaze to meet his. "Why are you out here?"

"I needed air."

She smiled wryly. "You should need worship more."

"Maybe." But that was the problem, wasn't it? He wasn't an Amish ideal of anything—including what should comfort him. Right now, the very community he'd longed for when he was in Chicago made him feel suffocated.

Sadie dipped the handkerchief into the bucket and Elijah wrung it out for her again before she placed it back over Samuel's head.

"I'm not used to it anymore," he confessed. "The long services, I mean."

"You went to church, though—with them."

"Yah. It's shorter, though. And the men and women sit together. In families. All in a row."

She nodded slowly. "I heard that."

The Englishers had their own way of doing things. There were youth group activities which he'd been invited to join in on, but no formal dating. Not like the Amish had. How did a man even ask a girl out, if there were no ground rules already set out? He'd been informed that a man asked a girl to "a coffee," and they would sit in a little shop and drink a hot beverage together with only a cup to fiddle with instead of the reins of his horses.

"You should go to the hymn sing tonight," Sadie said quietly.

"Why?" It was like she'd read his mind, and he swallowed, looking away.

"It's what single men do. They go to the hymn sing and they talk to the girls. Then they offer one a ride home." She shot him a wry look, as if he needed schooling in the art of courting a girl. And perhaps he did, because now that he was back, he found himself wondering if "a coffee" weren't just a little less intimidating than full-out courting. It was just a conversation.

Elijah barked out a low laugh. "I'm not baptized. The girls are safe from my courting."

"You might change your mind if you talked to a few of them."

"Is that what you want?" he asked pointedly. "For me to stay and find some other girl?"

"What do *you* want?" she hedged. "It's not about me, is it?"

He sighed. "I can't do the drama, Sadie."

She smoothed down Samuel's wet hair. "It isn't drama. It's life."

It was the cost of living in a close-knit community, and Elijah recognized that. A man could live lonely and free, or he could bind himself to people and live with some drama. Those were the choices—and he'd opted for freedom.

Samuel started to cry again, and Sadie looked toward the shade, then back at the pump.

"I should take him home," she said. "I'll get my sister to drive me back."

"I can take you," he said.

"No—" She shook her head, then struggled to get to her feet under the weight of her son. Elijah grabbed her hand and helped her up.

"Why not?" he asked. "You need to go home, and I need to get away."

"You should try a little harder to fit in, Elijah," she said. "Have some fun."

"Sage advice," he retorted. "When is the last time you had fun?"

"I'm a mother." She met his gaze evenly. "I'm past that."

"And I'm just an unmarried boy, beneath you." He couldn't help the irritation in his tone.

"Maybe you are!" She shook her head. "I've already been married. I can't go to the hymn sings anymore. I have a child to worry about. It isn't the same for me—so yes, you should go have some fun while you can."

He hadn't expected her to admit it, but it sparked a challenge inside of him. She'd always been the "little sister" to him, and now she was treating him like the little brother. Well, he wasn't keen on that role—especially not with her. He was most certainly a man—something that the Englishers didn't quibble about once someone passed the age of twenty-one, but the Amish required a little more proof. And he wanted to provide that for her—in some form, at least.

"Let me drive you back," he said, his voice low.

She met his gaze, then licked her lips and looked away. "I'm not sure I should."

"Would being seen with me be so very scandalous?" he asked with a slow smile.

Sadie ran her hand over Samuel's head once more and the boy began to whimper.

"Okay," she said with a sigh. "But I'll have to leave a message with someone so my family knows where I went."

Elijah nodded toward an older woman, Miriam Graber, who came out of the barn, heading in the direction of the outhouse. She paused, looking in their direction and no doubt jumping to a few conclusions.

"Your aunt," he said.

Sadie hoisted her son out of her arms and into Elijah's.

"Hold him, would you?" she breathed, and then hurried across the grass toward her aunt.

Elijah looked down into Sammie's flushed face and glassy eyes. He wasn't very big, and he felt as light as a piglet in Elijah's arms. Samuel whimpered again, tipped his head against Elijah's shoulder and let out a shuddering sigh.

"Hey, buddy," Elijah said quietly. "Feeling sick?"

Samuel nodded against his shoulder. "I want my mamm."

"She'll be right back," he said. "You know if I'm holding you that she won't be long."

Samuel lifted his head and regarded Elijah solemnly. He seemed to accept that as truth, because he stopped whimpering.

Elijah watched her as she talked with her aunt, then both women turned and looked toward him. There was a pause, a little more discussion, then Sadie squeezed her aunt's hand and headed back across the grass.

When Sadie reached his side, slightly out of breath, she held her arms out for her son. Samuel reached back, sliding into his mother's embrace. Elijah had to admit that having a child had matured Sadie in ways he hadn't experienced yet. She was a mother—the soft bosom and the final answer for her little boy—but the fact that he hadn't married yet didn't make him any less of a man.

One of these days she would look up at him and recognize that fact.

Chapter Nine

Elijah guided the horses into the Grabers' drive, flicking the reins to keep them moving at a trot. Sadie put a hand on her son's forehead, then pressed a kiss against his flushed skin. He should drop her off, turn around, and head back to the Yoders' farm. That would be the wise course of action right now, but he realized he didn't want to.

It was stupid. He knew why he was back in Morinville, and it wasn't to get himself emotionally entangled with Sadie again. But he was finding himself more and more drawn to her, despite his better instincts, and he felt a strange surge of protectiveness toward Samuel, too.

This was what it would be like to have a family, he realized, to have a wife and a child under his care. Absolom had a little family of his own . . . was it terrible to want this for himself, too?

"Do you want a hand in there for a few minutes?" Elijah asked.

"Actually, I wouldn't mind." She shot him a grateful smile.

And that was that. He'd offered now. They were alone—the whole family was at the Sunday service. There was no one to walk in and interrupt in silent disapproval. It was both freeing and unnerving.

Sadie gathered Samuel into her arms, and Elijah helped her down from the buggy. She cast him a smile as she eased past him, and he caught the scent of honey in her wake. His heart sped up, and he forced himself to take a step back. She still awoke the man in him—that much hadn't changed.

Elijah brought the horses into the buggy barn and set them up with some oats, then as he angled his steps toward the house, he found his stomach flipping in anticipation. It was an old feeling that he wished was connected to his adolescence, but it wasn't the case. She still made him feel like this at the prospect of being alone with her. Except he wasn't seventeen anymore, and it couldn't be about sneaking a kiss or holding her hand. He'd have to cut that out.

Elijah tapped on the side door before he let himself in, and when he came through the mudroom into the kitchen, he saw Sadie clutching a whimpering Samuel on her hip as she attempted to work one-handed at getting another wet cloth.

"Let me help," Elijah said.

Sadie looked between the cloth and her son, and then eased the boy into Elijah's arms. It was strangely gratifying that she trusted her little boy to him, even for a little while. He looked down at his flushed cheeks and teary eyes.

"Hey, buddy," he murmured.

"You can just sit and hold him," she said. "I know where everything is. Just take his shirt off, would you? He's so hot."

Elijah sank into a kitchen chair, balancing the boy in his arms somewhat awkwardly. He unbuttoned the little shirt and took it off, then took the wet cloth she held out to him and wiped down Samuel's face and arms. The Amish Budget lay on the table, and Elijah used it to fan Sammie as the boy leaned back against Elijah's broad chest.

"Here, Sammie." Sadie crouched down next to him and held a glass of water to his lips. "Have a drink."

Samuel drank half the glass, then held out his arms for his mother, and she picked him up again. "Let's move to the sitting room. It's cooler in there."

Sadie was definitely deeper, stronger, more intriguing now, which only made his feelings for her more complicated. He was supposed to be finding a way to purge himself of her, not getting more attached, but Elijah followed her through to the sitting room. She sank down onto the sofa, and he was struck with a memory of her from years ago when he'd be visiting Absolom, sitting in that exact spot, and how he'd felt looking at her—like his heart would burst out of his chest.

"I should probably head out," Elijah said, jutting his chin toward the hallway. "Now that you're settled."

It was inappropriate for them to be alone together. People would talk.

"You don't have to." She smiled faintly. "I don't mind the company."

"You sure?"

She nodded toward the couch next to her. "It's a good breeze from here."

Either appearances mattered less to Sadie now, or Elijah wasn't much of a threat to her reputation. Elijah sank into the sofa next to her, and he looked over at Samuel, whose eyes were shut, his breath starting to slow. She was right about the breeze, and Elijah let out a long breath. It was strange to be sitting here with her like this, when both of them were supposed to be in church. Normally, a man and a woman did this on the day their wedding banns were read in the church—sitting in her parents' home together as a couple and unchaperoned for the first time. Except he and Sadie weren't a couple.

Still, she'd invited him to stay.

"There's something I've been wondering," Sadie said

quietly, keeping her voice low so as not to disturb her slumbering child.

"Yah?"

"What did my daet say to you, exactly? When you left, I mean. Back then?"

Elijah sucked in a breath, then let it out slowly. "First of all, I was seventeen," he said. "And that makes everything a little more dramatic, I suppose. But your father told me straight that I'd never be enough for you, or for the family. He said that you were above me, and from that moment on, I was no longer welcome on this farm. I was to stay away from you, or my father would pay."

"Pay how?" She frowned.

"I don't know. It was a broad threat, but I took him seriously."

"So that's what pushed you away?"

Elijah's mind went back to that fateful day when he'd stood there in front of the bishop, his palms sweaty and his heart pounding. He'd been scared, angry, resentful. And the bishop's tone had been dripping with disdain.

"He said I should know my place." Elijah shook his head slowly. "I know that sounds like nothing, but it pounded everything home for me. There was a place for me here in Morinville, but there was no flexibility, no choice on my part. I would work with my daet at a business I found deathly boring, and I would marry some girl I didn't love. I don't think your father understood how much I loved you. Watching you marry another man, being forced into finding some appropriate plain girl to drive home from singing. . . . It was too much . . ."

Sadie was silent.

"Does that make sense?" he asked, turning toward her.

"So leaving was your only option?" she said. "Going English."

"I saw a future with the Englishers, a chance at more.

I still do. Besides, you were right." Emotion hollowed out his voice. "Absolom wouldn't have left if it weren't for me."

"I thought you said he was angry with my father."

"He was. He was furious. But leaving? That was my idea, and he didn't want to go. I said I'd go without him, and I knew that would allow me to get my way. Absolom and I were best friends, and he figured he could talk me into coming back."

"So what changed?" Sadie shifted Samuel in her arms. He was sleeping now, his pale lips parted.

"It's different out there, Sadie . . ." How to explain this to a woman who knew nothing but the sheltered life in Morinville? "There's freedom like you've never experienced it. I was tired of being told who I was and where I fit. I wanted to define that for myself."

"But Absolom wanted to come home?"

"Until he didn't . . ." Elijah searched her face, looking for some understanding. "He had girlfriends, freedom. There comes a point when you know that the stain is too dark. If you go back, you'll always be the one who left. Besides, we'd both changed. Do you remember the place in the Bible that says it's better to cut off your hand than to go with both hands into hell?"

"Coming home wouldn't be like that—"

"It would be," he interjected. "You grow as the years pass, and in order to fit back in here in Morinville, you'd have to cut all that growth away."

She winced at the imagery, and he shook his head. "Sadie, I know what I did, and I know how much is my fault. I was an angry teenager who loved a girl he'd never have. I was stupid, stubborn, and if I'd just left by myself . . ."

He sighed. If he'd left by himself, maybe he could have made the adjustment to come home again. Maybe he could have cut off that pound of flesh. But this wasn't about him anymore . . . at least not him alone. He'd dragged his best friend with him. Elijah had been the one with no future. Absolom had been an angry teen, but he'd have been able to marry any girl he liked. He would have had a future.

"You feel obliged to stand by my brother," she concluded.

"Yah. Among other things. I owe him. He stood by me for all these years. We've helped each other get jobs, we've navigated the Englisher ways together. . . . We've been there for each other through all the hard stuff. I owe him more than walking out on him now."

"If you came back, he might, too," Sadie countered.

"If I came back without him, he'd probably never come back at all," Elijah replied. "Besides, our business needs both of us. He can't do it without me."

"It isn't like you have a wife and children out there—" Sadie shook her head.

Elijah reached out and caught her hand, annoyance simmering deep under the surface of his conflicted feelings.

"Are you going to call me a boy again?" His voice came out in a growl, and her eyes widened, but she didn't answer. "I may not have married yet, Sadie, but I'm no boy. I've taken care of myself since I was seventeen, and I've seen more in the last nine years than any of the men living here. I'm every inch a man."

Outside, the clop of horse hooves and the rattle of a buggy pulled both of their attention away, and they looked out the window to see the Graber buggy coming down the drive.

"You can't come back without him," Sadie said hollowly. "And you won't leave him alone out there, either."

"I won't. A man has responsibilities, debts, obligations. Englishers are no different in that respect."

Outside, Elijah heard the bishop's voice. "Whoa, now."

Their time alone was over. Elijah suspected the news that he'd brought Sadie home was more alarming than

Sadie intended. He was a bigger threat to their daughter's future than Elijah liked to think.

"So I'll have to say good-bye to you again," she said, looking away.

"We knew that," he countered.

"Did we?"

Maybe she'd expected something different, but he'd been up front from the start. He wasn't the kind of man who would mislead her . . . not again. There were footsteps on the stairs outside, and Elijah's heart jammed in his chest. There was so much more to say.

"Whatever we're feeling for each other," he said quietly, "we'll just have to keep it under control. We know how this ends."

"We aren't feeling anything," she snapped.

That was a lie. Their kisses, their moments alone . . . they were all charged with some undeniable energy. They weren't the same teenagers they'd been nine years ago, but whatever they'd started back then hadn't been snuffed out.

"I don't know what you want from me," Elijah murmured.

The door opened, and Rosmanda's voice filtered through the walls, her words muffled. Footsteps sounded from the mudroom, and then the kitchen.

"Nothing." Sadie smoothed a hand over her sleeping son's forehead, and her chin trembled ever so little. "I don't want anything from you, Elijah."

And even though he knew that he was in no position to offer her any of the things he longed to, that "nothing" gouged deeper than being called "boy."

"There you are." Sarah appeared in the doorway, and her sharp gaze moved between them, evaluating the situation silently. "Come, Sadie. Let me help you with Samuel. Elijah, my husband will need you for the chores. He says that you can finish early and then go home."

There was a slight emphasis on the words "go home," and he smiled wanly. Apparently, he was still very much a threat.

Sadie watched as Elijah tramped out the side door with her father.

"Your daet isn't feeling as bad as before," Mamm assured her. "And Elijah won't let him work too hard."

The door slammed, and Sadie cast her mother a thin smile. Her heart hammered in her chest, and she hoped it wasn't noticeable. Elijah had a way of filling up that space in a room, and squeezing out her peace of mind. That man shouldn't be preoccupying her thoughts when there were more serious things to worry about. And yet he did.

He was making her feel things she didn't want to feel— like the way her heart sped up when he stared down into her eyes like that. He was every inch a man, he'd said, and she was grudgingly forced to agree. He was, and the woman in her was responding to him as urgently as she had when they were much too young. She wanted to feel his arms around her, to lean into his kisses. And, wicked as it was, she yearned for even more. She might resent him for a good many things, but she hadn't expected to feel so betrayed at his plans to leave town again—his eagerness to build a decent Englisher life for himself—and she tried to push back the nagging emotions as she worked with Rosmanda and Mamm, putting together a meal of chicken, potatoes, and gravy.

Two hours later, the side door opened and the sound of men's boots tramped into the mudroom. Sadie's back was sticky with sweat, and she wiped her face with a hand-kerchief. Rosmanda's cheeks bloomed red from the heat of the stove, but Mamm managed to look as cool as a winter's morning. How she did it, Sadie would never know.

"I'm hungry, Mamm," Samuel said, standing next to his chair. He looked like he was feeling better, and she bent to touch his forehead. He still had a bit of a fever, but it wasn't as bad as before.

"Are you?" she asked with a smile. "Here."

She slipped him a roll to munch on while he waited for the meal. An appetite was a good sign. Sadie lifted him up onto his seat atop a wooden booster that had been used in this family for generations. She'd sat on that same booster as a little girl. It nudged her up high enough to let her eat from her plate at the table. The men came into the kitchen at that moment, hands and face wet from their wash-up at the pump.

"It smells delicious," Daet said, and Sadie was relieved to see that her father didn't look quite so tired as she'd expected. There was still some color in his face.

Elijah's nose looked sunburnt, and he held her gaze a beat longer than necessary—then he turned away. Just like the old days, she realized, when Elijah would stay for dinner and stand there all awkwardly—freckled feet and hands too big for the rest of him. He'd grown into his limbs, finally, and he still made her feel too many things at once.

"Sit down," Mamm said, and if she noticed any tension in the room, she ignored it. "The food is hot. Everyone's hungry."

The men slid into their places—Elijah opposite Sadie, and Daet at the head of the table. Sadie reached over to stop Samuel's hand from creeping toward the bowl of dinner rolls.

"Bow for prayer," Daet said, and they all did as he bade, bowing their heads in silence. A moment later, Daet said, "Amen," and they all raised their heads and reached for the food.

"Your mamm and I were discussing things," Daet said as he speared a baked potato and plunked it onto his plate. "And we've come to a decision."

Sadie glanced toward her mother, but Mamm's expression remained carefully neutral. Whatever it was, Mamm hadn't even hinted about it.

"About what, Daet?" Sadie asked.

"You'll be going to see Absolom's child." Daet's somber gaze met Sadie's, and she stared at him in shock.

"I'm going to visit Absolom? Really?"

"Yes. Really. Pass the chicken, please."

Sadie's hands shook as she picked up the platter of chicken with both hands and passed it over her son's plate to her father. Daet took a wing from the side of the platter and put it on Samuel's plate, then took a leg for himself.

Sadie looked over to Elijah. Had he known about this? But he looked as stunned as she was. At least she wasn't the last to know this time.

"Who's going?" Rosmanda asked excitedly. "Because I'd so love to see my brother . . ."

"Your sister," Daet replied. "And Elijah. He'll be able to escort her to and from most easily."

"Can't I go, too?" Rosmanda pressed. "I want to see him! And the baby—"

"No." Daet didn't raise his voice, but his tone was final.

Elijah was to bring her to her brother. . . . She looked over at Elijah again, and misgiving rose up inside of her. She'd see the world that Elijah had chosen over theirs, see the home that her brother had built for himself.

Daet passed the chicken along to Rosmanda, who sullenly took some meat onto her plate. She chewed the side of her cheek.

"I haven't seen my brother in so long," Rosmanda said quietly. "I want to see him."

"Sadie is going," Daet replied. "You are too young and

impressionable. Sadie is old enough to see the evils of the Englisher world for what they are. She won't be lured astray."

Elijah coughed, reaching for a cup of lemonade. Should Sadie tell her father about Elijah's confession that he was going back? But if she did, he was liable to change his mind and forbid any of them to see Absolom, and the very thought closed off Sadie's throat. A chance to see her brother was dangling in front of her . . .

"What about Mamm?" Rosmanda pressed. "She'll want to see Absolom, too!"

Mamm's chair scraped back, and she turned to the counter to fetch another bowl of buns. The extra bowl of buns wasn't needed. She was hiding her face.

"Never mind, Rosmanda," Mamm said as she turned back toward them, more composed. "There will be work enough to keep us busy with Sadie gone for the day. And you, my dear, are not ready to care for the house alone, even for a day."

Mamm wanted to see her son, too. Desperately. Sadie instinctively reached toward Samuel and placed a protective hand on his back. Sammie wasn't eating much more than the bun she'd already given him. She felt his head, and while he was still warm, he wasn't as feverish as earlier.

"Send me along!" Rosmanda pressed. "If I'm useless here—"

"Do not question your mamm," Daet barked. "As for being useless, don't take that as a compliment. You need to learn to care for a home if you intend to marry! Your mamm was married by sixteen."

Rosmanda clamped her mouth shut, her cheeks flaming, and her eyes filled with tears.

"And Samuel will stay here," Daet added. "I think Sadie will agree."

"Yes, I agree with that," Sadie said quickly. She didn't want her child exposed to any of it. She didn't want him to have some lurking memories from his toddler years, some image that would take root in his sensitive little mind.

"And the appearances, Benjamin . . ." Mamm prompted quietly.

"Yes, of course." Daet wiped his mouth. "We will not speak of this, if we can help it. We are an example to this community, and if we appear to weaken in our resolve, we will hurt more than just ourselves. We must keep this visit to the city private. No one is to mention it. If anyone asks where Sadie has gone, you will only say that she's gone on an errand."

"It will look like there is something between Sadie and Elijah," Rosmanda said. "If I was along, though—"

"More reason to keep your own counsel," Daet replied curtly. "We don't want to tarnish Sadie's reputation, either. But she has options in Pennsylvania with the Hochstetlers. She'll marry again. You, Rosmanda, are my bigger worry."

Silence descended around the table, and Sadie eyed her father cautiously. This would be a secret—something done for Absolom's sake alone. This wasn't for them, because if it were, Mamm would be the one going, and Sadie's reputation wouldn't be risked. If she wanted another good, Amish husband, she could back out of this fool's errand. She could protect her image and find another solid, pious man who would embrace Samuel as his own . . .

But she wouldn't do that, because she wanted to see her brother too badly. This was a priceless opportunity, one that wouldn't come again. If she let this chance pass her by, the only way to see her brother would be in defiance of her father.

"Absolom is most likely to listen to Sadie," Mamm added. "They were always close, and he seems to have a soft place in his heart for her still. But this is delicate. You all understand that, don't you?"

They were bending for Absolom's sake. According to the Ordnung, tough love was the way to deal with these things—silence and disapproval until Absolom returned to them and admitted his sin. And returning to the community was supposed to solidify a person back into their place. Except that wasn't working with Elijah, and Sadie was beginning to doubt it would work with her brother, either. But this wasn't the Ordnung's way, and Elijah's words sprang back to her mind: *Your father is capable of great flexibility. Where it comes to Absolom, he'll bend so far that he'll brush the ground—wait and see.*

She could feel Elijah's gaze burning into her, and she refused to meet it. Instead she filled her plate and forced herself to take a bite, her mouth dry. Daet was bending for Absolom, and she didn't blame him one bit. Elijah might judge her father for this, but she didn't. Absolom was Daet's child, and Elijah had no idea how viciously a parent could love.

If this were Samuel, she'd camp herself on his doorstep and sit there night and day until he came home again—anything but lose her son. She expected nothing less of her daet.

"When will we go?" Sadie asked.

"Soon. I'm aiming for Tuesday. I'll let you know when I have it arranged," Daet said.

Somewhere just outside of Chicago—a place that meant nothing to her in a concrete way—her brother would be sitting down to his own dinner with his own little family. In her mind's eye, he was still wearing his Amish suspenders and straw hat, even though she knew logically that he'd be dressed like any other Englisher. But he'd be there, eating a meal cooked by the woman he'd had a child with, but hadn't married.

Was that bond strong enough to hold them all together through the good and the bad? Did that woman fill his heart? She'd always thought that marriage would miraculously instill a blessed sort of love between the partners, and she'd been proven very wrong. And yet her brother had a woman he wasn't married to . . . a woman who had given him a daughter, and who had a son from another relationship. And yet, she seemed to be enough for him. Absolom had found something that Sadie missed out on, despite doing everything the Amish way.

On the coming Tuesday—the weekday that the Amish held their weddings, ironically enough—she would meet that scandalous woman, and see the Englisher life that Elijah had left behind . . . the life he intended to go back to. Everything she'd believed to be so obviously true seemed to be slanting now, tipping off balance.

But someone had to go after Absolom, and, as Mamm had said, Sadie might be the only one he would listen to.

Chapter Ten

Elijah swallowed a mouthful of food. Sadie's gaze flickered up toward him, and she gave him a faint smile. She had her precious permission—she'd see Absolom again. She claimed not to want anything from him, but she did want *this*.

He was going to be responsible for her, too—to both her father and her brother, whose hopes for her future were vastly different. The blind enthusiasm from that night when he'd offered this had evaporated. It wasn't just about giving her something no one else could, or getting some time alone with her. Going to the city changed people—Elijah had seen that firsthand.

He'd wanted Absolom to go with him the first time he left home because he was afraid of going alone. Elijah knew the risks of companionship now, like the apple from the tree of knowledge. There was no unseeing what she'd see out there, and she'd be changed by the experience, whether she wanted to be or not. Sometimes ignorance really was preferable, especially if she wanted a peaceful Amish life.

"Are you sure this is a good idea?" Elijah asked, and all eyes whipped toward him.

"It was *your* idea, wasn't it?" the bishop asked, eyebrows raised.

"It might have been impetuous," Elijah replied. An offer sparked by a moment in the dark with Sadie—less logical than it was competitive with the other men he imagined courting her in the near future.

"It seems appropriate to me," Sarah Graber said quietly. "You brought my son to the city with you nine years ago, and you can bring him home again. You can make up for the impetuosity of youth. But I do appreciate your caution now, Elijah. I do."

Elijah looked back down to his plate. He was no longer hungry, and he could feel the weight of that responsibility—because their expectations weren't realistic. He wouldn't be able to deliver what they wanted with Absolom or Sadie. He couldn't turn back time.

Little Sammie was munching on a dinner roll, but the rest of his food sat untouched on his plate. Sadie pushed back her chair and her son crawled into her lap, leaning his cheek against her shoulder. Sadie smoothed his flaxen curls away from his face.

"Will you take Sadie to see her brother?" the bishop asked.

Elijah could refuse, but nothing would change. Not for him. He'd be even more alone, having alienated the only family who remotely understood where he'd been. Or he could do as they asked, and bring Sadie to the city.

"If you insist," he said at last. "But you can't hold me responsible for anything more than delivering her back home again."

The bishop met his gaze and held it for a beat, then nodded in agreement. It was something.

The meal ended soon after, and Elijah thanked Sarah for

the meal, then headed to the mudroom for his boots. He needed to get away—to go home—and think this all through. The bishop followed him to the door.

"Thank you," Elijah said with a deferential nod. "I'll see you in the morning."

Elijah had his own thoughts to wade through tonight. He wasn't doing anything behind the bishop's back, but he was still wary. He'd caused enough hardship for this family.

"I would like to speak with you." The older man's voice held the gravelly weight of a church leader.

Bishop Graber led the way outside, and Elijah followed, their boots clomping down the wooden steps. Once they were a few yards from the house, the bishop stopped.

"Is there a problem?" the bishop asked quietly. "From what I understand, you offered to take my daughter to see her brother. Or were you hoping to bring her to the Englishers without my blessing?"

"Not the case." Elijah eyed the bishop for a moment. "And if you distrust me so much, why did you hire me on?"

"For such a time as this," the older man replied curtly.

There it was—the reason for all of this. The bishop had plans of his own. Whatever the older man hoped to accomplish, Elijah felt wary.

"I'm still not completely comfortable with bringing Sadie to the city," Elijah said. "It changes people . . ."

"Sadie is our chance, Elijah," the bishop said tightly. "Don't you see that?"

That stab of jealousy was back again, because, whether Absolom knew it or not, his father was willing to trample any boundary to bring him home. Elijah's daet hadn't dared. Moreover, he'd been held back by the bishop's orders.

"I see it," Elijah admitted. "But seeing her brother will have a profound effect on her. I can't stop that."

"You don't know my daughter like I do." The bishop

scrubbed a hand over his beard. "What is our faith if it can't stand a test? She wants her brother back home as badly as we do. I'm asking you to bring her back. And, if at all possible, bring her brother, too."

No small request there. He crossed his arms over his chest, his mind spinning. But what about Elijah? If he hadn't come back to help his father, would the bishop have allowed all of this for *him*? Not a chance.

"I met a man in a Mennonite church who left the Amish life about twenty years ago," Elijah said slowly. "He was only a teenager at the time. His father followed him and would sit on the steps in front of his hotel room every single night for several weeks straight. He'd just sit there. All night long, because he couldn't bring himself to be away from his boy. And he wanted to protect him—if he could." The bishop was silent, and Elijah eyed the older man skeptically. "What does the Ordnung say about that?"

"The community must come first, of course," the bishop replied. "Every man has a choice, and that man's son made his."

That Mennonite man had told the story with tears sparkling in his eyes when he remembered his daet. Choices, even the hard ones a young man had made for his own future, didn't erase the heartbreak.

"Would you have allowed my father to go to such lengths?" Elijah asked.

"He didn't need to." Bishop Graber sucked in a slow breath.

"Because I'm back," Elijah confirmed. Because the bishop had so ruined his father's ability to run a successful business that his father had been forced to swallow any pride he might have and ask his only son for financial help.

And yet, Elijah's father *hadn't* come to the city. He hadn't sent anyone after him. It might have been different if his father had—he might have come back to Morinville for the sake of his parents, before it was too late, before he'd seen too much and changed too much to fit back in. At the very least, this visit back would have been different. It would have been good to know that he was worth a risk to his own father.

"Yes. You're back." The bishop shook his head, not seeming to understand where Elijah was coming from. "The letters worked."

"It wasn't the letters on church teachings," Elijah said with a bitter laugh. "It was the one letter he likely never showed you."

"What letter?" the bishop asked with a frown.

"That's between me and my daet. I'm not telling you."

"Whatever you think of me," the older man said quietly, "I have no wish to intrude upon your relationship with your parents. You're back—that was all any of us wanted."

It was ironic that the same constricting rules that had chased him off and been the source of his father's business failure had brought him back, no matter how temporary it might be. This was success in the bishop's eyes?

"What about you, then?" Elijah shot back. "Is this secrecy abiding by the Ordnung?"

The older man's face colored, but he crossed his arms over his chest and met Elijah's gaze regardless.

"He's my *son*." This wasn't the church leader talking. This was the father.

Elijah shouldn't be doing this—meddling in the Graber family's business. He shouldn't care. He'd come back in spite of the bishop, not because of him. And even his memories of Sadie had paled in the face of his new reality. There was no peace to be found here in the bosom of the Grabers' problems.

"All I ask is that you keep this plan a secret until we have

Absolom home," Bishop Graber said earnestly. "Including from your parents."

"You don't think *my father* can be trusted?" Elijah barked out a bitter laugh. "He followed your instructions with me, didn't he? With *his* son."

The bishop considered for a moment. "Your father is a good man. But this is a private matter, and all it takes is for one person to breathe a worry to another. . . . I expect you to protect my daughter while she's in the city, and discretion is in *her* best interest," the bishop said, his voice hardening.

Elijah put his hat back onto his head. He wanted to set everything right again—more than Bishop Graber might realize. But what was right at this point in time? Was Absolom better off working his father's farm, abandoning his family in the city?

"I'll bring her back." It was all he could promise.

"And the discretion?" the bishop pressed.

"You'll just have to trust my judgment on that."

They regarded each other, but this time there was more equality between them. The Amish believed that no man was above another, but ideals didn't always match reality. Was this what it took to bring the old bishop down to Elijah's level, the unforgiving grind of the mill?

"One more thing," the bishop said quietly. "I want you to drive your own car."

"It would go against the Ordnung." And if the bishop was asking Elijah to do that—was his return really so important? Not compared to Absolom's.

"It will help keep things discreet," the bishop went on when Elijah hadn't responded. "No one need know. Leave early while it's still dark, and come back after sunset. Turn off the lights when you turn into the drive."

The older man had put some thought into this. Elijah stared

at him, mute. The thought of driving again was appealing—he couldn't deny it. It was one of the Englisher pleasures he missed most, but the bishop was putting the Ordnung aside completely for his son, it seemed. And Elijah's spiritual integrity, as well.

And what was Elijah fighting this for? He had no intention of staying in Morinville, whatever the bishop believed. The Grabers wanted Sadie to see their son—who was Elijah to stand in the way? The fallout would be theirs to bear.

"All right," Elijah agreed. "I'll drive."

He felt a simmer of anger at the prospect, though. The bishop was willing to sacrifice anyone at all to bring his son back, it seemed. Like wheat kernels on a flour mill, ground up for the sake of community.

The bishop stood there on the grass as Elijah walked toward the buggy barn to hitch up and go home. Elijah looked back once, and the bishop was still there, his spine straight and his thumbs tucked into the front of his pants.

Elijah would take Sadie to the city, but he couldn't guarantee what it would do to her. Not everyone wanted to be ground up into the community flour. Some Amish fell off the millstone and lay panting on the ground, grateful to be in one piece. Sadie's freedom might mean more to her than even her father suspected.

What then?

That evening, Sadie and Rosmanda stood in front of the kitchen sink washing the dishes. Such an ordinary chore to do, with her visit to the city looming in a matter of days. She'd imagined seeing her brother again a thousand times over the years, but in her imagination, he'd come to them. Going to see him—her heart sped up at the thought. What would she say? Would her brother even expect them? What if he didn't want to see *her*?

Except that Elijah had said that her brother did miss her. . . . That was something. But he'd never written to her. And she'd never written to him. That was for Mamm and Daet, and after she was married, Mervin had forbidden it. The constraints still chafed. And yet, even given all the freedom in the world, what would she do?

Sadie's hands were deep in the hot water, and her sister stood next to her, a dishtowel in one hand and a scowl on her face.

"What's the matter?" Sadie asked.

"Hmm?" Rosmanda immediately adjusted her expression. "Nothing."

"That's not true." Sadie pulled a plate out of the sudsy water and ran it under the tap to rinse it off. "Are you still upset about not being allowed to see Absolom?"

"No." Rosmanda sighed. "Maybe. I don't know."

Sadie eyed her sister a little more closely. "You're going to the sing-along tonight, aren't you? You should still go."

"Yes, I'm going." Rosmanda picked up the next dish. "But I wish Daet would let me be baptized. Mamm was married at my age."

"You're too young," Sadie said with a small smile. How many times would they go over this?

"Oh, stop that! What else am I to do? I have no more school. I do chores and see my friends sometimes. . . . I'm bored! I want a home of my own."

"You hardly clean the one you live in," Sadie said with a short laugh, but her sister didn't take the bait. She took the next dish, her jaw set. There was more to this. Rosmanda could be stubborn, but she wasn't stupid. This didn't make sense, unless—

"Is there someone you're thinking of?" Sadie asked.

"What if there were?" Rosmanda raised her chin slightly.

Sadie ran through the available young men in her mind. None of them seemed appropriate for her sister. "Who is it?"

"I didn't say—"

"Don't lie to me, Rosmanda." Sadie wasn't in the mood for this. Her sister had been getting more and more defiant as the year wore on.

"It doesn't matter. He's courting someone else," her sister replied tightly.

"Jonathan Yoder?" Sadie turned to her sister, the certainty of it slapping into her like a wet towel.

Rosmanda's cheeks pinked, but she didn't answer.

"But he's courting Mary Beiler. You know that! What would you do, break them up?"

"He would be with me if I were available. But I'm not baptized yet."

"What makes you so sure about that?" Sadie shook her head.

"He said so."

That changed things. Sadie shot her sister a cautious look. "When?"

"At service. He told me that he feels the same way I do, but I'm too young, and he can't wait anymore."

Sadie shook the suds from her hands and dried them on her apron. "You realize he's doing this behind Mary's back."

"He doesn't feel about her the way he feels about me." Rosmanda looked away. "He feels about Mary the way you felt for Mervin."

Sadie's heart skipped a beat. "What do you mean?"

"She's . . ." Rosmanda turned back, her cheeks still flushed. "She's boring."

"What do you know about that?" Sadie shook her head and turned back to the sink. "Marriage needs some consistency, and I'm glad that Jonathan Yoder can see that much. Mary is a good choice."

"Marriage needs love, too."

"Love?" Sadie pulled another plate from the sink and rinsed it. "Rosmanda, you are young. And a boy who would talk like that to you behind his girlfriend's back isn't much of a catch."

"Unless I'm the one who fills his heart," Rosmanda replied with a small smile. "And then it isn't about him being unfaithful so much as him having to choose."

"He can't court you yet." Sadie shook her head.

"He could if I were baptized." Rosmanda's eyes glowed. "He does love me, Sadie. He's told me so. He says that he thinks of me day and night, and he—"

"You haven't let him touch you, have you?" Sadie interrupted.

"Yes, he's kissed me." Rosmanda's chin rose again. "And he's held me close, and I fit right under his chin in the most perfect way. He says that no girl has ever made him feel the way I make him feel, and—"

All words Sadie had heard before at about the same age, too. What was it about boys that made them so eloquent right when a girl was the most vulnerable?

"They say that," Sadie said with a sigh. "But he's still courting another girl. And your reputation is at risk letting him kiss you. You know where babies come from, don't you?"

"Not kissing." Rosmanda rolled her eyes.

"Fine. But that's where it starts. He has no right kissing you if he isn't courting you." Advice she should have taken herself with Elijah back then. A mangled heart could ache for years.

"He has to marry." Rosmanda's eyes welled with tears.

"So what happens when he does?" Sadie demanded. "What then? Will you keep seeing him?"

Rosmanda looked startled, but didn't answer that. She turned away, picking up another dish to dry. Was that a yes?

How had this happened? When had Rosmanda had the time to take up with an older boy, and no one noticed? Sadie had been busy with her son, and with Daet's sickness, they'd all been distracted.

Then there was Mary—Sadie's friend, and she deserved better treatment than this. To think that Jonathan would go behind her back like that and spout off all sorts of romantic garbage to a girl young enough to believe it!

"Rosmanda, boys will say things because they want to take advantage—"

"That isn't it," Rosmanda snapped.

"You're young—"

"I've *watched*!" Rosmanda turned on Sadie, her eyes snapping fire. "I've watched my older sister get married to a very nice man the whole family liked. And I saw what it did to you. You started out happy and excited, and then you just . . . you went flat. You turned pale. You stopped laughing."

So her marriage to Mervin had impacted Rosmanda, too, had it? It wasn't her fault. If she'd had a little more privacy, some space from her family, she might have been able to hide it.

"And what did that tell you?" Sadie asked, her throat tight with emotion.

"That it's possible to marry someone perfectly respectable and still be miserably unhappy."

"And you think you won't be miserable in the end, playing this game?" Sadie asked quietly.

"I'm not going to marry some boring old man," Rosmanda retorted. "I'm going to marry the man who makes my heart race. I'm going to take a chance on love."

"He isn't taking a chance on you, Rosmanda. He's courting another girl!"

"But he *loves* me!"

"Love is an action. Not a feeling. Love is cooking for your family, ironing your husband's shirts, raising children together."

"Is it pretending you're his dead wife?" Rosmanda snapped, and Sadie's breath knocked out of her chest.

"What?"

"Isn't that what your mother-in-law said?" Rosmanda retorted. "He made you do everything like his dead wife used to do it. He most certainly loved *her*."

Sadie's eyes filled with tears, and she had to hold herself back from slapping her sister straight across the face. How *dare* she? What did she know about life or men? She wasn't even old enough for a Rumspringa!

"Love isn't some soggy feeling, you little idiot," Sadie hissed. "And if you were a little older you'd know that!"

"Then you've never felt it." Rosmanda's tone was quiet and confident. "Because if you ever had, you'd know what I'm feeling now."

Sadie swallowed a retort. She'd never loved? That wasn't fair at all. She loved her son with all her heart. She loved her brother so much that she was willing to risk her own reputation to bring him home. She'd learned to love her husband, even though marriage had been difficult and jarring. . . . And a long time ago, when she was about Rosmanda's age, she'd thought she loved a boy, too—but then he ran off with her brother and left her behind.

"Things feel different at your age," Sadie said at last.

"Meaning what?" Rosmanda demanded.

"Meaning, I had someone I thought I loved, too, and I can assure you that some kisses and honeyed words don't make them stick around."

"Who?" Rosmanda breathed.

"It doesn't matter."

"Elijah Fisher?"

Was Sadie so transparent? She licked her lips. "You should listen to someone who has some experience, Rosmanda. That boy, Jonathan, isn't going to leave Mary for you. He's using you for some cuddles. That's it."

"Are you going to tell Mamm about this?" Rosmanda asked.

"Of course!" Sadie shook her head. "You're playing with fire, Rosmanda!"

"If you tell her"—her sister's voice shook—"I'll never tell you anything again. Anything. It won't stop Jonathan from loving me, or me from loving Jonathan. I just won't tell you anything again. Ever."

Nine years ago, Sadie had come downstairs to start the fire in the stove, and she'd found a letter on the table from her brother. Elijah and Absolom hadn't told her, either, and that feeling of being the one left behind came flooding back over her so forcefully that tears pricked her eyes.

"Rosie, I only want to protect you!" Sadie put her hands on her sister's shoulders and turned her to face her. "If you were caught kissing Jonathan Yoder, you'd ruin any chance you have of getting married. At least in this county. And if you were to get pregnant—"

"I'm going to *marry* Jonathan Yoder," Rosmanda said. "You'll see. Are you going to tell Mamm?"

Sadie stood in silence for a moment. What if Jonathan tried to run off with Rosmanda? What if she awoke to another letter on the kitchen table? Elijah had told her that he and Absolom hadn't let her in on their plans because they were sure she'd tell Daet. She hadn't even had the chance to make them see reason, and she wouldn't give up that chance with Rosie.

"I won't tell her, on one condition."

"What's that?" Rosmanda eyed her distrustfully.

"That you won't see Jonathan Yoder again without telling me first."

"Why?"

"To give me the chance to talk you into some sense," Sadie said with a shrug. "That should be obvious enough."

Rosmanda picked up another plate from the sink. "All right."

"You promise me?" Sadie asked.

"Yes."

It would have to do. She'd had one sibling run off and ruin his life, and she couldn't take a chance on Rosmanda doing the same. Sadie might not have loved her husband with the same kind of youthful abandon she'd felt back when Elijah had tugged her around by her heartstrings, but that was a good thing. Life was long and hard, and trials would come. Commitment and steadfastness counted for more—they lasted. Those fluttering, intoxicating feelings of whatever it was she'd felt for Elijah had only melted into heartbreak.

Chapter Eleven

Early Tuesday morning, Elijah stood with his parents in the gas-lamp-lit kitchen, weighing his car keys in his hand, which even after only a few weeks back in Morinville felt foreign. The jingling in his palm was like an echo from somewhere far, far away. Funny how the memories of Chicago clung so close, but when faced with driving his own vehicle, those same memories felt so distant.

The car had been put under a tarp in the buggy barn when he returned. And while his decision to come back hadn't had anything to do with the Ordnung, he felt the discrepancy of this request that he drive Sadie into the city. He hadn't come home to corrupt anyone, and he was afraid of doing just that.

"The bishop gave his permission?" his mother asked in disbelief. She was still in her nightgown, a shawl thrown over her shoulders and her hair hanging loose down her back. At first, he thought he'd just slip out, but he'd changed his mind outside on the dew-laden grass. His parents would only worry. If they heard the engine and then saw the car missing, they'd think he'd abandoned them when they needed him most, and he'd break his mother's heart all over again. As it was, she stood in the center of the kitchen in bare feet, her expression filled with misgiving.

"He gave more than permission. He gave an order," Elijah replied.

It was early, and the sky was still fully dark. He and Sadie would need to be out of town by sunrise, and by the time they were drawing stares as an Amish couple in a hatchback car, they should be far away from anyone they knew. It was the only way to get to Absolom's home without a vanload of Amish people seeing them do it.

"It's wrong!" Mamm shook her head, tears springing to her eyes. "We Amish walk the narrow way, and we don't deviate from the path—not even for our *children*!" At least, his parents hadn't deviated from the Amish way—even an inch.

"I thought you supported the bishop's leadership," he replied bitterly.

"Now is not the time, Elijah," his father said, his voice low.

"Abram?" His mother whirled around to face his daet, who stood by the door, his lips pursed and his expression grim. She seemed to be expecting some solidarity from him.

"And you weren't to tell us anything," his father confirmed.

Elijah chewed on the side of his cheek. "He didn't want to risk gossip."

"Gossip!" Mamm shook her head in exasperation. "Gossip is unfounded lies. *This* would be truth!"

"Nettie . . ." Daet's tone held quiet warning. "We are not going to discuss this with anyone."

"Don't go." Mamm turned toward Elijah pleadingly. "Don't do this, son. You've only just come back."

"Mamm, you know I'm not here to join the community

again," Elijah said quietly. He knew she hoped for more—
the same as Sadie seemed to.

"But you might yet," she pressed. "You don't know.
What if you want to stay? And if you go now, it will be too
much of a temptation to stay away. Once you start one part
of your old life, you'll slip into the rest, and—"

"Nettie." Daet's voice was firm. "He came home to help
us, and we agreed not to pressure him."

"No!" She sucked in an audible breath. "Stop trying to
shush me, Abram! I followed the bishop's leadership. When
my son left, I did as he told us. I begged to be allowed to go
visit him, but the bishop forbade us. I *obeyed*! And now he
sends my son back into the lion's den, in a car, no less? For
his boy?"

Daet was immobile, his expression staying granite.

"Absolom is my friend, Mamm." Elijah looked down at
the keys again. "He's more alone than anyone realizes. If
you'd come to see me—"

"We were *forbidden*!" Tears sparkled in his mother's
weathered face.

"I know, Mamm. I'm doing it for Absolom."

And possibly for Sadie. He wasn't sure if this would be
good for her or not, but if seeing her brother could bring
her peace after all the misery he'd caused, then he'd do this
for her, too.

"And you think this will bring him home?" Daet asked.

"I don't know." Elijah shrugged helplessly. "Probably
not. But coming home isn't everything. Maybe it will give
him some strength to face his new life."

"Coming home *is* everything!" Mamm rubbed her
hands over her face. "I know why the Grabers want him
back so badly. I do! But I'm not willing to sacrifice my boy
for theirs!"

"We aren't sacrificing him," Daet said with a sigh. "He

told us about it, didn't he? He hasn't snuck off in the night. He's told us straight. He's promised to come back."

Mamm stood there looking small and betrayed. She tugged her shawl tighter around her body, and Elijah's heart nearly cracked at the sight of her. She was reliving the last time he left home—he knew it. Elijah crossed the room and wrapped his arms around his mother. She reached up and pulled him down the way she used to when he was a teen, towering over her, and she rocked him back and forth.

"Mamm, I'm not a boy anymore," he said quietly. "I can take care of myself."

She released him, then put her hands on the sides of his face, looking up into his eyes imploringly. "No one is quite so self-sufficient as they think, son. You still need us."

And he did—he always would. They were his parents . . . but he understood his mother's panic.

"What is the plan, then?" Daet asked.

"We leave town before sunrise, and we return after dark. Nobody sees us, and the bishop hopes I'll return with his son."

"All right then," Daet replied. "Your mamm and I will wait up for you. We trust that we'll see you tonight, son."

Elijah nodded. "I'll be back, Daet."

He turned toward the door. There wasn't time to waste if he and Sadie were to be far away from anyone they knew by sunrise. He tucked the keys into his pocket and had his hand on the doorknob when his mother's voice stopped him.

"Elijah?"

He turned back. "Yes, Mamm?"

"If you don't return, I'm going to hire a van and I'll go find you. This time, nothing will stop me, and if you choose that Englisher life, then you'll be responsible for my damnation as well as your own. We'll be shunned. That will be on you." Her voice trembled and she met his gaze with glittering determination.

Elijah nodded slowly. Somehow, he didn't doubt her. She'd been forbidden from going to her son once, but the bishop had lost his credibility in this house. Elijah never thought he'd see that day, and now that his parents were seeing things the way he did, he wasn't sure if it was a good thing or not. Their blind faith had been comforting, in a way. He could rail against it, but it had been a central pillar in his life that he kept coming back to. Would they all be adrift now?

He'd come back irreparably changed. Now that Englisher life was rubbing off on the people closest to him, changing them, too. There was a bitter wisdom in the Ordnung's inflexible orders. The seal around the community had been compromised, and change was seeping in like a water leak.

"Mamm, I'm bringing Sadie to see her brother, and I've promised the bishop that I'll bring her home. My word has to count for something."

It would have to be enough, because it was all he could offer.

Elijah and his father clomped outside together. They pulled the tarp off the car, and they pushed the car up the drive to the road. No one was around to see them, and when they got to the end of the drive, his father put a hand on his shoulder.

"Be safe, son."

Elijah nodded, then eased into the driver's seat and put the key into the ignition. The engine rumbled to life, and he slammed the door and stepped on the gas, easing onto the road.

It had only been a few weeks since he had last driven this car, and it felt good to be back in the driver's seat again.

It gave the illusion of having more control over his life than he really did. The Englishers had songs about this feeling of control as a man drove down the highway . . . but he knew better. The Englisher life wasn't quite so free as everyone believed. There were fences for everyone, gullies and mountains. Everything might be permissible, but not everything was possible.

The bishop was hoping for something that Elijah couldn't deliver. If Absolom came back home again, it wouldn't be because of Elijah. And right now, he didn't even think that it would be because of a miracle, either. If Absolom came home, it would be out of heartbreak, and he couldn't wish that on his friend.

As Elijah drove down the road toward the Graber home, the horizon in the east was turning from black to gray. Morning was coming.

Sadie stood at the end of the drive. The morning was chilly, goose bumps standing up on her skin. She clasped a small, paper-wrapped parcel in front of her—a little baby quilt made by Mamm. Mamm had a store of baby items for when women welcomed their newborns, baby clothes and tiny quilts made by hand in the quiet of a winter evening. Mamm had chosen a soft, square quilt made with mauve and pink—girl's colors. In a pinch, it would have to do.

A few minutes ago when Sadie was still inside the house, her mother had tied the strings around that package, and Daet had informed her of her travel arrangements. Elijah's words still echoed through her mind.

He'll bend. You'll see.

She'd defiantly defended her father because they all wanted Absolom back, but what about Elijah? Her father was not only sending Elijah back to the city, but he was ordering him to drive his car into the city . . . a distinct difference there. Elijah had been right.

Sadie had ridden in several cars over the years. Sometimes an Englisher neighbor would give them a ride to a doctor's appointment, or there would be a van hired for a trip somewhere. She and Mervin had visited his parents once by van. So riding in a vehicle wasn't shocking for her—the shocking bit was that the car would be driven by Elijah.

A pair of headlights bounced up the road, then the car slowed and the headlights flicked off. That would be Elijah, and she glanced back toward the house, where she could just make out the white of her mamm's apron on the front porch where her parents stood, watching to make sure she left safely.

The car slowed to a stop, and she bent down to see Elijah peering at her through the window. He leaned over and pushed the passenger side door open. She looked back at her parents one last time, then eased into the seat and reached for the seat belt. Elijah stepped on the gas and the car started forward again while she was still buckling up.

"Hi," he said, and his voice was warm and comforting in the chilly morning.

"Hi." She looked out the window, back toward her house that was already disappearing behind them.

"Are you okay?" he asked.

"Of course." She sighed. She was missing her son. She'd left when he was still asleep and wouldn't see him until late tonight when he'd be asleep again; she missed him already.

"I called Absolom last night from the pay phone outside the post office," Elijah said. "He said he'd be there today, even if he has to call in sick."

"You mean he'll lie?"

"Afraid so."

Sadie stole a glance at Elijah. "And that doesn't bother you?"

He compressed his lips into a flat line. "Yah, it does still. I'm not that different. But at least he'll be there to see you."

Elijah's left hand was draped over the steering wheel, his right tapping on his leg in a rhythm she didn't recognize. He was more confident than she'd ever seen him before—she could tell by the way he leaned his head back and the relaxed look on his face. His gaze flickered toward her, and he gave her a half smile.

"When did you learn how to drive?" she asked.

"I had to get ID first," he replied. "That took a few months to gather it all. And then I had to buy the car."

"This one?"

He glanced over at her, and a smile tickled at the corners of his lips. "This one."

He seemed attached to this piece of machinery, the way a man might be attached to the first horse he purchased with his own earnings. But this was no horse. She looked back out the window.

"You like this too much," she said. But that wasn't her only issue. He looked more self-assured like this—more so than he did on the farm—and that sent a warning prickle over her arms. What was her father thinking asking Elijah to drive again?

"Yah, I like it." Elijah shrugged. "That doesn't mean I wanted to take my car today, though. I was against it."

"So you'll just drive us straight to Absolom's home, then?" she asked.

"That's the plan." He was silent for a few beats. "Sadie, you don't need to worry. I fully intend to bring you home again, even if I have to throw you over my shoulder to do it."

An image of him doing just that popped into her mind, and she felt a rush of heat hit her cheeks.

"I'm not the one who's the risk," she retorted.

Elijah took off his straw hat and tossed it into the back seat. With his Englisher hairstyle, and his hand draped over the steering wheel, he looked even more foreign than he had before.

"Why did you do that?" she asked.

"I can't see the road as well with my eyes shaded like that," he said. "Safety first, Sadie."

His smile was teasing—a throwback from their teen years, but the rest of him was every inch the rugged rebel. He was attractive in a way that made her breath catch, and she realized in a rush that she was about to see more than her brother—she was going to see the Elijah from Chicago. He'd be different from the man she knew now, and that realization made her stomach churn. She'd rather block his past out, but she wasn't going to be able to do that.

Elijah glanced over at her a couple of times, his eyes flicking back to the road. "What's the matter?"

"You seem different," she replied hollowly.

"I'm not."

"You're driving a car without your hat," she said. "That's different."

"It's just a hat," he said quietly, then glanced toward her again. "And your father ordered me to drive the car."

But he *could* drive. That was the thing . . . she was seeing his capabilities from his Englisher life. And worst of all, she found herself even more attracted to him this way.

"You're relaxing into the role," she said. "Whatever you are in Chicago, you're becoming that man again."

"Yah. I'm . . . free." He adjusted his position in the seat.

So this was the liberated version of Elijah. Perhaps he didn't realize how competent he looked, how in control of it all. If only he appeared more uncomfortable—mirroring her own uncertainty—she might feel more connected to him.

"You didn't want to bring me," she said. "Isn't that what you said over dinner?"

"Because I don't want to be the one they blame if you change." He shot her a direct look. "The city changes people, Sadie."

And looking at him, she couldn't argue with that.

"My faith is stronger than that," she replied quietly.

"You think I have no faith?"

She swallowed. "Well, you left . . ."

"Not because I lost my faith in God, Sadie. I still had that. I lost my faith in the church. Those are two different things."

"Oh." She'd offended him. She could hear it in his voice.

"Even in service, though, you seemed—out of place." An image of him sitting with his legs spread, his elbows resting on his knees and his brooding expression was stamped on her mind. That wasn't the image of a man at peace.

"Again—church and God. Not the same thing, Sadie."

Weren't they? Sadie had never seen them as separate before. She went to church to feel connected to God. The church was the body of Christ. They connected to God by connecting with each other. . . . Salvation was through community. And yet, he looked very sure of himself.

"Is that what you learned with the Englishers?" she asked.

He chuckled softly. "You think it's heresy, but yah. You learn things when you have to face life on your own. What is our faith if it's never tested?"

He was quoting her father there, and she could grudgingly see his point. What was their faith if they couldn't cling to it when they had nothing else? And yet she still couldn't imagine a life outside of their Amish community. Life was sweeter together . . . except not everyone seemed to think so.

"What did Absolom say when you talked to him?" she asked.

"Uh . . ." Elijah shrugged. "It was a short conversation. The baby started to cry, so he had to go."

"The baby was at a telephone?" She shook her head as she realized her mistake. "Sorry, he has a phone inside his home, doesn't he?"

"Yah. Of course."

Of course. "But what did he say?"

"He asked if your daet and mamm were coming along, and I said no. He asked if you were looking forward to it or dreading it, and I said you wanted to see him."

"And does he . . . want to see me?" she asked.

"He's excited to see you. He asked about Sammie, and I said that he'd stay home. He told Sharon that we were coming, and then the baby started to cry, and I guess he must have been holding the baby, because he said he had to go, and that he'd be sure to be home. That's about it."

Her brother holding his baby daughter and talking on a telephone inside his own home. She couldn't even imagine it. How could the family get any quiet with a telephone right there to interrupt them constantly with other people's greetings and questions? It sounded overwhelming, and frustrating.

The sun peeked over the horizon, spilling rosy light over the fields. They were passing an Amish farm, and she spotted a man with two boys tramping toward a barn. She didn't know this family. They were already outside of their local church boundaries. A car made distances evaporate so quickly.

"Are *you* excited to see him?" she asked.

"Yah." His tone was grave, and she looked over to see his jaw clenched and his eyes fixed on the road. "It'll be good to see him."

"But it's not the same for you, is it?" she said. "You're

going back one of these days. You weren't saying good-bye forever, like you did with me."

"I didn't think it would be forever when I left Morin-ville." He glanced toward her, and his dark eyes drilled into hers. "Not with you."

"And how could it not be?" she demanded. There was no connection between the Englisher and the Amish besides some sales and a few tourists, most of whom they avoided.

"I thought I'd find some deep Amish truth to bring me back," he said. "And I didn't leave you easily. I almost came back for you. That first night, we slept in a barn. And I lay awake all night thinking of you, and what you'd think when you found out that we'd left. We were young and stupid, and we liked the idea of causing a bit of pain when it came to our parents, but you . . ." He swallowed. "I almost came back for you."

"What stopped you?" she breathed.

Elijah shrugged. "Like I said, I couldn't take care of you out there. I wasn't man enough, Sadie. That's what it all came down to."

Like she'd told her sister, some stolen kisses and hand holding didn't add up to enough to make a lifetime to-gether. She hadn't been enough to keep Elijah at home. He'd had grudges bigger than his love for her.

She let her gaze follow the loops of telephone wire that dipped along the side of the road, and her heart seemed to rise and fall with the wire.

She'd loved Elijah back then . . . loved him so deeply that she thought it would never end. There was no way an-other girl could draw his attention away from her. But in the end, it hadn't been the siren call of another woman that pulled him away. And Sadie hadn't wanted him to take her along—she'd wanted him to choose her and stay. Mervin *had* chosen her. There was something deeply satisfying in a man saying, "I want her. For better or for worse." That was the part that Elijah hadn't been capable of.

The sun rose steadily into the sky, and the car warmed up with the golden rays that flooded inside. Sadie settled back into her seat and closed her eyes. It would be a long drive to Chicago.

Chapter Twelve

It was nine o'clock in the morning when they entered Chicago's suburbs, and Elijah felt that familiar tug of coming home. Strange how much more familiar this city felt after having been away for a few weeks. When he lived here, it still felt foreign, but now that he was coming back, he felt an unexpected relief. Elijah pulled to a stop at a red light.

"We paved this," Elijah said.

"You . . . what?" Sadie looked over at him blearily. She was only just waking up from another cat nap. She looked slightly rumpled, and she rubbed her hand over her eyes, then adjusted her kapp.

"You were sleeping," he said. "I said that we paved this intersection. Put down the asphalt."

"Oh." She looked out the window. "So that was your job?"

"Yah. That was my job."

He worked a lot of overtime for this project. Not all of the guys wanted to work more, but he'd been lonely, and he'd been grateful for a chance to keep busy. When his body was aching from hard work, he slept more easily and could escape the drifting thoughts of Sadie, his parents, the life he used to have.

Traffic started moving again, and he eased forward, following the familiar streets that he knew so well.

"Over there—" He pointed out her window toward a fast food chicken joint. "That restaurant. Absolom and I liked going there. Really cheap food, but tasty."

"Did you cook for yourself?" she asked, squinting at him.

"I cook rather well." He shot her a grin. "The Englishers expect men to be able to cook. In fact, men will brag about their cooking to the women folk—it's sort of . . . the women like the idea."

Sadie flattened her lips—disapproval. He couldn't help but chuckle. "It's different with them. But, yes, I learned to cook for myself. Not as well as you can, I'm sure, but—I ate."

"And my brother?" she asked.

"He cooks better than I do." Elijah nodded toward a grassy area as they drove past. "And I used to go sit there. That's a park. It's just some greenery for folk. I used to go there early in the morning so I could smell the dew and feel the morning air."

It was barely an acre of grass, a few trees, a path that meandered through. And it was surrounded by roads and apartment buildings—constant noise. There was no silence to be had in the city.

"It looks . . ." She paused.

"Pathetic." Elijah finished it for her. "I know. It's nothing compared to a farm, is it? I used to think it was like a prison window with a small square of blue sky. I used it like a prisoner would that window—a place to focus my hopes."

"Hopes for what?" she asked.

Elijah signaled to change lanes and pulled out in front of a dump truck lumbering up behind. "I don't even know. It changed from day to day."

Some days he hoped for some little bit of belonging. Other days he hoped for a woman in his life to make him feel loved. And then there were the days that all he wanted was to be Englisher to the core and to forget his Amish roots that were holding him back.

Absolom's apartment building was ahead, and Elijah slowed as he approached.

"Are we there?" Sadie asked.

"This is it."

Sadie leaned forward so she could see better, her gaze moving up the building. Twenty floors of apartments and rusted balcony railings—it was a far cry from the white-washed farmhouses, chicken coops, and rolling fields of Morinville. For a lot of people, *home* was as simple as a TV and a hot plate.

Elijah turned into the parking area and found a spot in visitor parking. Sadie was silent, and she clutched that small package in her lap, knuckles white. When he turned off the engine, he turned toward her.

"Are you ready?" he asked.

"No." She licked her lips. "I'm not."

Maybe all of this was more of a shock than he'd antici-pated. He reached over and put a hand over hers.

"It's not so bad. You get used to it."

She nodded slowly, then pulled her hand out from under his. She leaned forward again, attempting to look up at the building, but she wouldn't be able to see much. Through her eyes, it was probably ugly and horrible. But there were worse places to live in the city—which he and Absolom had discovered early on. This was safe, relatively clean, and wasn't infested by bugs. The thing was, there were some beautiful neighborhoods with houses and yards, trees that offered languid shade. There were places in this city that would have made life here much more comfortable.

He'd prayed for a home like that. It was a possibility, if he and Absolom could build a successful business.

"All right," she said, smoothing her hand over the paper-covered package. "I'm ready now."

They got out of the car, and Elijah waited for her to join him on his side before they walked together past the parked cars. Sadie held that package against her stomach, and Elijah put an arm around her to nudge her away from a dead bird that lay splayed on the asphalt. She followed his nudge, moving closer against him, and he felt a flip in his stomach.

In his memories, in his fantasies, on her father's farm, or even here in Chicago, this woman in his arms made him feel the same way—facing her was supposed to make it easier. So far, it had only made it worse.

He opened the front door, letting her go inside ahead of him, then he punched the buzzer number on the keypad. There was a crackly ringing tone. Sadie didn't ask any questions, but her gaze followed his every move.

"Yeah?" a tired female voice said.

"Sharon? It's Eli."

"Oh, hey!" Sharon sounded more cheerful. "Come on up."

There was a buzz, and he reached for the second door and pulled it open while it was momentarily unlocked. Sadie didn't move until he gestured for her to go inside ahead of him.

"Eli," she murmured. "That's what they call you here?"

"Yah. Just a . . . nickname, I guess."

He wasn't the same old Elijah in the city, and he could sense that she was starting to see that. A man had to adjust to his surroundings, and he'd done that as best he could. There was no other way to make it. He led the way to the elevator and pushed the call button.

"Just a couple of things," Elijah said. "Sharon's not like you Amish women. She's not a particular housekeeper like Amish women are, and she's going to be dressed a lot differently than you're used to. Less modestly, I guess. You get used to it, but it might be a surprise at first."

Sadie remained silent, and when the door slid open, they stepped inside. He punched the sixteenth floor and the doors slid shut again. Sadie felt her hair, then glanced toward Elijah.

"Do I look okay?" she asked uncertainly, and Elijah shot her a grin. She stood there in her long, Amish cut, mauve dress, and a white apron and kapp. Very proper and neat, her hair smoothed back under the crisp, white cloth of her kapp. Her lips were pale, though—nerves, probably. And she held that package in front of her like a shield.

"Yah. You look very nice," he said. Not that Absolom and Sharon would be judging. Still, she comforted Elijah, somehow. And it wasn't just the familiar Amish dress, either. Having her here in the city, in this building . . . too many nights he'd lain awake and tried to imagine what this would be like.

The elevator door pinged then slid open, and he led her into a hallway that smelled of fried foods, curry, and some other spices he didn't recognize. Sadie looked around, then followed him toward the end. Elijah knew the door, and he paused in front of it.

"This is it," he said quietly.

Sadie nodded quickly, then reached out and rapped sharply on the door. From inside, Elijah could hear the sound of the TV murmuring away, and there was the soft cry of a baby that grew louder with the shuffle of slippers. Then the lock scraped back, and the door opened.

Sharon stood there in a pair of yoga pants and a tank top, the baby on her shoulder. Her hair was pulled up into a ponytail on the top of her head, and she shot Elijah a relieved grin.

"Hey, you, get in here," she said, stepping back. "Long

time no see. Oh, my God, you look like—" Sharon stopped, turning her attention to Sadie. "Hi."

"Hello." Sadie's voice sounded slightly strangled. "I'm Sadie. Absolom's sister."

"Yeah, Eli said you were coming. Hi. Nice to meet you. Come on in. It's a mess in here, so watch where you step." Sharon wandered back into the apartment. "Chase, Uncle Eli's here."

Elijah gestured Sadie inside. He shut the door behind him, locking it, and he caught sight of little Chase peeking around the corner. He'd always been small for his age, but he made up for it with energy.

"Hey, buddy," Elijah said with a grin. "Come say hi."

The little boy scampered up, holding an action figure out in front of him. "Look what I got!"

"Pretty great." Elijah reached out and ruffled the boy's hair, then raised his voice so Sharon could hear him. "Is Absolom home?"

"Not yet. He worked last night," Sharon replied. "And believe me, I can't wait for him to get here. I'm wiped."

Elijah peeked into the living room, past the heaps of clothes piled on the couch and the piles of fast food wrappers on the coffee table.

"Yeah, I know," Sharon muttered. "Absolom doesn't help out with 'women's work'"—she made air quotes—"and I'm not the only one who lives here."

"No, no, it's fine," Elijah said quickly.

Sadie stood statue stiff, and Elijah nudged her side with his elbow. She looked more horrified than anything, and by the look on Sharon's face, she was starting to notice.

"Congratulations on the baby," Elijah said. "Absolom said you named her Sarah."

"Yeah." Sharon eyed Sadie again, then sighed. She turned to Elijah. "Would you hold the baby? I desperately need a shower. I won't even tell you how long it's been. . . . Absolom should be here any time now."

Elijah awkwardly accepted the infant and pulled her into his chest. She was tiny and smelled like a dirty diaper. He shot Sadie a panicked look. What was he supposed to do with this baby? Sharon didn't seem worried, though. She plucked at the front of her shirt, fanning it out to cool off.

"Chase, turn down the TV," Sharon said. "I'm going for a shower."

Chase ignored his mother and put up the volume instead, where a movie was playing that looked way too mature for a boy his age to be watching. She headed down the hallway to the bathroom. The door shut, and a moment later the water came on.

Elijah met Sadie's wide-eyed gaze with a tentative smile of his own. He felt like he was presenting more than her brother . . . this was his life, too.

"So, this is your niece," Elijah said, looking down at the infant in his arms.

"Yah . . ." Sadie breathed, and little Sarah's face crumpled into a wail.

Sadie looked around at her brother's home. Amish homes were neat and relatively bare. This place was cluttered and smelled of old food and baby diapers. The boy sat in front of the TV, staring as fixedly as if he were watching an anthill. Her fingers itched to do something about the mess. If this were an Amish family member's home, she'd roll up her sleeves and get to work.

"Rock her," Sadie said, and Elijah did as she told him and moved from side to side. The baby settled, her cries turning into hiccoughs.

"Should I clean?" she asked softly, her gaze moving over

to the pile of wrappers on the coffee table. She could only imagine the state of the kitchen.

"No!" Elijah's eyes widened in alarm. "No, Sadie. It's not like that here. You don't come over and meddle in people's stuff."

"She's just had a baby, though," Sadie said. "It's not easy."

"Just . . . don't." Elijah looked down at the baby uneasily.

"Here." Sadie put the package down on the arm of the couch and reached for the infant. Elijah gratefully handed her over. "Find me a diaper. I can do this, at least."

It had been a while since Sammie was this small, but she'd helped with numerous babies since his birth. There was always a new baby arriving in their community, and when that happened, the women pulled together and helped each other out.

Elijah poked around the living room, looking for diapers.

"Chase," Elijah said. "Where does your mom keep the diapers?"

"In the bag." Chase pointed to a cloth bag hanging over the back of a kitchen chair, and Elijah headed over toward it. He peered inside, and then returned with the entire bag.

Sadie was used to working with cloth diapers, but she understood the general idea of the disposable kind. She laid little Sarah on the couch and leaned over her so that the baby could focus on her face.

"Hi there, sweetie," she crooned. "I'm going to clean you right up and it's going to feel so nice to have a fresh diaper . . . yes, it is . . ."

Chase turned away from the TV and crept closer to watch her work.

"That's my sister," the boy announced.

"And she's very cute," Sadie said with a smile. "I heard that you're four."

"Yup. Four." Chase poked at his sister. "She's zero."

Sadie reached for a wipe and set to work on the little

bottom. It didn't take her long to get the baby cleaned up. When Sarah was smelling fresh once more, Sadie leaned back against the couch and looked down into the tiny face. This was her niece. It was hard to tell at this age—babies all looked alike. But maybe she could see some Graber in that little nose.

"Her name's Sarah," Chase babbled on. "And she's named after Uncle Abe's mom. She's named Sarah, too."

"That's right." Sadie reached out and ruffled his hair. "I'm"—she hesitated over the boy's name for her brother— "Uncle Abe's sister. So Sarah is my mom, too."

The boy froze, his eyes widening. "You don't love Uncle Abe no more."

"What?" Sadie felt the words hit her in the chest.

"Uncle Abe's mom and dad and all them, they don't love him no more."

Was that what he told people? Is that what everyone thought—that the family that had born him, raised him, loved him, had suddenly turned into monsters who turned off their feelings? Who had told them that?

"That's not true, Chase. We love Absolom very much. Very, very much. No one has stopped loving him," she said. "Elijah, is that what you told them?"

But Chase had turned away. He knew the version that he'd been told, apparently, and she and her parents were villains in that story—the ones who rejected Absolom. But there was always another side to a tale like that—more rejection, more heartbreak.

Before Elijah could reply, there was the sound of a key in the lock of the front door, and it opened. Sadie's breath caught in her throat and she carefully rose to her feet, the baby clutched close in her arms.

He was the same old Absolom—except he wasn't smooth-shaven anymore. He looked scruffy, and his hair was cut in an Englisher style. He wore a pair of dirty jeans

and a dusty white T-shirt. When he saw Sadie, the color
drained from his face and tears sprung to his eyes.

"Hey—" he said gruffly. "Wow. Hey . . ."

He didn't know what to say any more than she did. He
came over and gave her an awkward hug, the baby between them. It wasn't the satisfactory sort of greeting she'd
imagined.

"How are Mamm and Daet?" Absolom asked, taking the
baby from Sadie's arms.

"Good . . ." She nodded. "They miss you. So much.
Mamm was really touched to know that you named the
baby after her."

"Yah. Good." Absolom looked down at his daughter in
his arms. "It seemed to fit her. And Daet?"

"He sent me, didn't he?" Sadie shrugged faintly, and
their eyes met—siblings with that mutual understanding of
their parents' quirks, even after all these years. In some
ways, it was like no time had passed at all.

"Taking care of Elijah?" Absolom asked with a low
laugh. "Good to see you, buddy."

"Yah." Elijah reached out and they shook hands. "Didn't
think it would be so soon."

"Hey, I was hoping. The sooner we start collecting
clients the better." Absolom nodded a few more times, then
licked his lips and looked down. "How is everyone else?"

For the next few minutes, Sadie filled her brother in on
their other siblings—marriages, children—and on their
great-uncle who had died, along with a distant cousin who'd
been in an accident, between his buggy and a truck that had
been speeding along the back roads.

"And Rosie is boy crazy now," Sadie finished with a
short laugh.

"Yah?" Absolom shook his head. "In my mind, she's just
a little girl . . ."

"It's been nine years," Sadie said. "She's almost a

woman now." There were a couple of beats of silence. "But what about you, Absolom?"

"Well, there's my daughter." He looked lovingly down at the baby. "And you've met Chase, I see. And Sharon . . ."

Just then, Sharon came out from the hallway, wearing the same clothes as earlier, but her hair was wet. She eyed Sadie uncomfortably, then gave Absolom a tired smile.

"I'm going out," she said curtly. "I just need some space. I'm going crazy."

Absolom rose to give her a peck on her cheek, and they murmured together at the door for a moment or two, Absolom's words too quiet to hear, Sharon's harsher and more frustrated. When she'd left, Absolom came back, the baby still snuggled in his arms. He smiled faintly.

"She just gets tired. Being with the kids all day," Absolom said.

Sadie looked down. This wasn't the happy home she'd imagined her brother to have. Something was wrong here, but who was she to talk? There had been plenty wrong in her home, as well. Marriage, family—none of it came easily. What had her mother-in-law said? It took a few years to settle in properly? Maybe it was the same for Absolom.

Chase lost interest in the TV and crawled up onto the couch next to Absolom. Absolom put an arm around the boy, and Elijah reached for a little black box, pushed a button, and the TV fell silent.

"No!" Chase said, jumping up with fury in his young eyes. "No, Uncle Eli!"

"What did your mom say?" Absolom asked tiredly. "Are you allowed to watch that?"

"Yeah! Put it back on!"

Sadie had never seen a more defiant, bossy child before in her life. The boy jumped up and swung a small fist at Elijah, who put out a hand to catch it as gently as possible, then Chase went to the TV, and the screen burst back to life. She looked over at her brother, and he just shrugged.

"If his mamm lets him . . ." he said.

If Sammie tried acting like that, he'd find his bottom paddled right quick—by pretty much any adult within reach. Amish children didn't try defiance more than once, but this child was growing up with an exhausted mother and a stepfather who wasn't in the role of father . . . the confusing Englisher way of doing things. As she watched the little boy sink down in front of the TV again, his slender shoulders slumping, she had the urge to hug him. And maybe give him a job to do. Work started young for a reason.

She wouldn't meddle, though. This wasn't her son, and it wasn't her place. Sadie looked over at Elijah, but he looked mildly embarrassed and was looking down at the crumb-laden carpet between his feet. This was why young parents needed a community—none of this was easy.

"Sadie, how are you doing?" Absolom asked after a moment of silence.

"Fine." What could she say?

"Your little boy—Samuel," Absolom said. "He's doing well?"

"He's doing very well." She couldn't help the smile that came to her lips. "He's three now, and talks a whole lot. He sweeps the kitchen and follows Mamm out to the garden. His favorite job is holding the clothespins for me while I hang up the laundry."

Absolom smiled, too. "Who does he look like? Our side or Mervin's?"

"Ours." She was proud to say it. He was *her* child, and he looked like her, too, people said.

"I was sorry to hear about Mervin's passing," Absolom added.

Was he really? Elijah had already told her their opinion of her late husband. "You didn't write," she said instead.

"I—" He nodded. "I know. You know how it is. If I had, it would have been pored over by the whole family, and . . . I don't know."

There was a gulf between them—the life Absolom had refused, and the world that the rest of the family avoided with as much fervor as they avoided hellfire itself.

"Mervin's parents visited," she said suddenly. "They want me to marry again."

"Who?" Absolom's expression turned protective, and she felt a wave of gratitude for that. Her big brother had been her biggest ally over the years, and it felt good to have that back, if only for a few minutes.

"No one in particular," she said. "But Sammie needs a father, and I must provide one."

Absolom shook his head. "That doesn't always work, Sadie."

Her brother glanced toward Chase in front of the TV, and she could guess at what he was thinking. He must have tried to be more to that boy at some point.

"I'm a burden on Daet," she said. "With his illness . . . he can't keep working the farm much longer, and I'm just another mouth to feed."

"You're their daughter." Absolom's eyes snapped fire. "You aren't a burden to feed, Sadie."

But she was a grown woman, and back in the family home. She had to find a husband sooner or later. If not for her parents, then for her son.

"You know how it is, Absolom," she said quietly, and her brother heaved a sigh. That seemed to be how they resolved everything—the mutual acceptance of how things were.

"Don't be pushed into anything, Sadie," Absolom said earnestly. "You know how they are. They want every string tied up, and you're a loose string right now. There are worse things than being single."

"Absolom, I'm not an Englisher," she replied pointedly.

"Maybe not, but you don't have to obey them, either. Take a stand."

"And who will back me up?" she retorted. "You? Because you aren't back home where you belong, are you?"

Silence stretched between them, and Absolom sighed. "I'm sorry. I don't want to fight and waste the time we've got."

The time they had . . . everything was slipping away. They had one day to make up for nine years of silence, and after she went back home again, Elijah would eventually leave, too. This felt like the good-bye they'd skipped nine years ago.

Chapter Thirteen

The day passed by more quickly than Sadie expected it to. While her brother looked like any other Englisher with his close-cropped hair, jeans, and a T-shirt, he was still the same old Absolom who told irreverent jokes and reminisced about their childhood in Morinville. He was just the same, but perhaps freer than he'd ever been before. This was the Absolom who used to lie down in the grass by the creek, no one looking over his shoulder. He could come back, couldn't he? If he hadn't changed so very much. . . . It was the hope they had all cherished for so long—that Absolom could simply decide to return one day, and everything could go back to the way it was, as if he'd never left. But even now, she knew it could never be so easy.

They talked for hours, and Absolom told stories about how they had first arrived in the city with no job and no money. They'd stayed in a homeless shelter and gotten some assistance from a Mennonite church that helped them to acquire their first jobs and get some Englisher clothes. They stayed in a house owned by a woman who'd left her Amish community decades earlier—a woman who never went back to her family and her home, who married an Englisher man, had several children, and still decorated her home in the plain, Amish fashion, but *didn't go back*. People like her had made it easier for Absolom to stay away. They'd soothed the culture shock for Absolom and Elijah—a little cocoon in the middle of Englisher chaos.

There seemed to be a whole clutch of these ex-Amish Mennonites who reached out to the runaways, and hearing about them made her angry. Her father had told her that there were people whose sole aim was to undo the work of shunning. That was a few years ago, and she hadn't believed him. Her father could be a little zealous sometimes. But perhaps Daet had been wiser than she thought, because she could plainly see that the lessons the Amish community was trying to give were unraveled by these do-gooder Mennonites.

Chase sat in front of the TV, munching on a packaged crunchy snack that she'd never seen before, the crumbs falling into the carpet. They'd tried turning off the TV a couple more times, but the boy would shout and stamp his feet, and every time, Absolom would flick it back on.

"Sharon lets him" was all Absolom could say. "Besides, if he kicks up too much of a fuss, the neighbors complain. The last thing we need is a visit from social services."

Sadie tried to look away from the screen. Chase needed the outdoors—some bugs to chase, some snakes to catch, and some chores that would tire him out so efficiently that he wouldn't have the energy for tantrums. Maybe even a spanking on occasion. . . . But again, this wasn't her home, and Chase wasn't an Amish boy.

The day passed easily enough. Sadie told her brother about Sammie—his antics and the funny things he said—and the more she talked about her son, the more she missed him. It was better that he was safely at home with Mamm, Daet, and his auntie Rosie—away from this. And now, after a few hours in her brother's home, Sadie had grown more comfortable, and that in itself unnerved her.

Sadie cooked up some lunch to feed them all—after Elijah showed her how the electric stove worked—and a few hours later, she headed back to the kitchen to start supper. Sharon didn't come back, and the more time slid by, the more antsy Absolom got. He called Sharon's cell phone a few times, and texted her several more.

"She goes out," Absolom said hollowly.

"To do what?" Sadie asked. Besides helping out a neighbor, Amish women stayed home and took care of their homes. She couldn't imagine what could keep a woman away for this length of time—away from both her children.

"I don't know. She hangs out with friends. She just needs to get away sometimes. The kids are too much for her."

Sadie's gaze slid over to the newborn sleeping in a little crib at the side of the couch. "When will she come back?"

Her brother didn't answer that, and the question hung in the air. She could feel the tension radiating off of him, though—anger, uncertainty, anxiety. He loved Sharon, she could tell, but their situation wasn't an easy one.

"Mommy comes back," Chase said without turning from the TV, and he sounded much older than his four years—the kind of maturity that came from necessity.

"Oh, good," Sadie said faintly, trying with all her might not to judge this woman who had walked away from her children, from her man, and left them worrying.

Sadie found a plastic grocery bag and proceeded to swipe the fast food wrappers into it. She couldn't look at the mess anymore.

"You don't have to do that," Elijah said after a moment, dark eyes meeting hers.

She looked back to the job in front of her. "I know. You already told me."

She didn't want to offend her brother's girlfriend, but it was better than the jangle of the television and her brother's veiled unhappiness.

Absolom put a hand on her wrist, stopping her. "Elijah's right. You don't have to do that, Sadie. Here, the women don't have to be the only ones who cook and clean. You're not the maid."

"Keeping house isn't shameful," she said with a shake of her head. "If the Englishers do things differently, Absolom, then maybe you should clean up. Because someone has to."

Her brother's cheeks tinged pink, and she immediately regretted her words. She wasn't here to fight with him, and it wasn't as if she resented women's work. She took pride in her contributions to a peaceful, well-run home. But something had gone wrong here, and she couldn't be the only one who saw it.

Outside the window, the sun slipped behind the buildings, and Absolom rose to his feet and flicked on some lights. He turned away from them and dialed a number into his cell phone. Sharon. Sadie could see his worry in the way he held his shoulders. No one seemed to answer, and he dropped his phone into his pocket.

"*Will* she come back?" Sadie asked in German to protect the boy from this conversation.

"Yes. She always does." Absolom sighed. "She does this a lot lately. It's gotten worse. She struggles with depression and anxiety, and the kids . . ." He sighed, not finishing. He didn't have to. Children were work—there was no way around it. Absolom looked very much alone in this apartment. Her brother, the angry little four-year-old, and this helpless infant . . . the children *needed* Absolom. He was all they had when their mother disappeared.

"Are you happy, Absolom?" she asked.

Her brother looked away for a moment, his eyes brimming with tears. "I don't know. I'm doing what I have to do. We'll sort it out, Sharon and I. Sometimes it just takes some time."

It was the same thing Elizabeth had said—if Sadie had had a little more time with her husband, maybe it would have gotten better. Perhaps it was the same for her brother's relationship, too. Sadie could offer to bring him back with them, but she knew it would be wrong to even speak it out loud. What was he supposed to do, walk away with the children? There were Englisher laws against that. He'd made his bed, all right.

"We have a long drive back," Elijah said, his voice rising above the sound of the television. "I told your father I'd have Sadie back tonight."

Absolom's gaze flicked toward his sister. "You could stay a few days—"

She longed to say yes—to help him, somehow. Her brother had come out to the Englisher freedom, and she could see how empty he was. He was lonesome, and lost. . . . But that was how it started, and even though she could see how much her brother needed her right now—a woman's presence in this home to pull things back together—she knew better than that. She was not a Mennonite do-gooder, and Samuel swam in her thoughts. She missed him desperately.

"I have a son at home," she said with a shake of her head. "And he needs his mamm."

"Yah." Absolom sucked in a deep breath, then rose to his feet. "He needs his mamm."

She had no way of knowing what her brother was thinking, but she wished they had just a little more time together. Absolom needed his mamm, too, from what she could see, and he needed his community, his daet, his siblings. He needed more than a job, more than a struggling relationship with the mother of his daughter. There was solace in work, but what could it comfort a man without a loving home waiting for him at the end of a long day?

"What should I tell Mamm?" Sadie asked.

Absolom shoved his hands into his pockets. "That I love her."

"And Daet?"

"Tell him that I'm working hard. I've got kids to feed now, and I can appreciate all that Daet did in the feeding of us. I know he doesn't approve of any of this, but maybe he'll understand my responsibility."

Chase turned away from the TV, at last, and his big brown eyes moved between them.

"We have to go home now, Chase," Sadie said softly, bending down to his level. "I'm very glad to have met you."

The boy regarded her seriously. "Can you come back?"

Sadie's heart thudded hollowly in her own ears, and she suddenly realized that she'd like nothing more. This visit with her brother hadn't been enough, and these children needed more nurturing than they'd been getting.

"I wish I could, Chase," she said, her throat tight. "But I can't come back."

"Why?" Chase whispered.

"My father would never allow it." She reached out and ruffled his hair. "Tell your mamm that I said good-bye."

"My mommy," he corrected her.

"Yes." She forced a smile. She'd used the German instead of English. "And you take very good care of your baby sister, okay?"

Chase nodded, but he didn't come any closer to her. Instead, he sidled up to Absolom and leaned into her brother's leg.

"Sadie, *try* to come back," Absolom said quietly. "Or write me letters, at least."

"I will if Daet allows it," she said, and her brother deflated.

"Then I won't hear from you," he said.

"You don't know that, Absolom." But she suspected the same. Her father might be willing to bend in order to bring

Absolom back, but he wouldn't condone an easy and open relationship with him if he stayed with the Englishers.

"Thank you for today," Absolom said gruffly, and he wrapped his arms around her, giving her a quick squeeze.

"Absolom, if you can"—her chin trembled—"I know it looks impossible, but if you ever find a way, *come home*."

Her brother nodded, dashing a tear from his cheek with the back of one hand. "Yah."

And they both knew that wouldn't happen, either. Sadie bent over the bassinette to press a kiss against Sarah's downy head. She wouldn't see this child again, and she looked silently over the little girl with a heavy heart. Her brother's choices had come with weighty consequences.

Elijah and Absolom hugged roughly, then her brother pulled open the front door.

"You're coming back, aren't you?" Absolom asked Elijah.

"Yah. Of course. I'll need another couple of weeks, at least."

"The customers won't wait forever, Eli. I'm lining them up for leaf and snow removal, and that's around the corner."

"I know. But you can count on me. You know that."

The men shook hands, and as Sadie stepped out of her brother's home, she felt a rush of regret. One day—that's all they'd had—and she'd found no solutions.

Sadie followed Elijah to the elevator. They were both silent, but Elijah reached over and took her hand in his broad, calloused palm. This was no longer the tentative touch of a teen doing the forbidden in holding a girl's hand, but the strong grip of a man who knew her pain. She leaned into his muscular arm and let her head rest against his shoulder. Her heart felt sodden with unshed tears.

"You okay?" he murmured as they stepped into the elevator and the door slid shut. His solid presence beside her was comforting—at least she wasn't alone. But her brother was.

"No," she whispered. "I'm not."

She'd seen Absolom—she'd held her niece. And she could see exactly why her brother could never come home again. Her brother's choices had nailed him firmly into the Englisher world.

A few weeks ago, Elijah had driven this route back to Morinville. He'd been packed full of conflicted feelings. The first letter his daet sent that was different from the ordinary explanation of church teachings was the one where he confessed that he'd lost a great deal of money investing in a piece of machinery he wouldn't be permitted to use. The next letter after that had been the one where his father had asked for help.

I can't make my bills, son. I can't compete. I hate to humble myself like this, but I need your help. I don't think I'll be able to stay afloat unless you come back to help us. This isn't a ploy, son. Your mamm and I won't pressure you to stay, but we don't know what else to do.

He hadn't had any Amish clothes to change into, and he'd known that he'd have to drive to his parents' house like a common Englisher, drawing curious stares the entire way. A few weeks ago, he wondered what his parents would say—if his daet would be happy to see him, or furious at how long he'd been away. He had sisters and their husbands who would be angry, too. He'd abandoned the family, after all, and the faith—selfishness. It was never just one relationship—there was a web of extended family, all feeling personally betrayed.

Now he was driving this same road again, and as he followed the traffic out of the city, he had a lump in his throat. This time there was no uncertainty, but the memories from his first drive back flooded through him like a recent trauma.

Traffic was light at this time of the evening, and once they reached open highway, he could lean back and rest his hand at the top of the steering wheel and let his mind wander. How long until he came back to Chicago for good? And would he be able to finally put his feelings for Sadie to rest, or was he stuck with these rogue emotions that refused to be ruled by logic?

He glanced over at Sadie. She had a hand clamped over her mouth, her eyes brimming with unshed tears. His heart stuttered, and he reached over and grabbed her hand.

"Hey . . ." He didn't know what to say, because words couldn't make this better, and even if they could, he'd never been a man who knew what to say. He could joke and laugh, but the heavier, more painful subjects left him muzzled.

"I'm fine." She sniffled and pulled her hand out of his grip. He wished she hadn't. Because he didn't have anything else to offer her, and that felt achingly wrong.

"Sharon isn't as bad as she seems, you know," Elijah said after a few beats of silence.

"No Amish woman would do that," she replied, ice in her tone.

"Maybe not. They'd be pushed out of the community first. We only keep the ones who can play the part."

Sadie shot him a sharp look. "That's not true."

"Isn't it?" He shook his head. "She struggles with depression, and it can get really bad. Having a few women come and pitch in for housework now and again wouldn't be enough. Doctors have given her medication for it, but that isn't a cure. The more pressure on her, the worse it gets, and sometimes she just has to get away."

Sadie was silent.

"We don't talk about mental illness in Morinville. We talk about faith, and God, and prayer. And when people can't handle the pressure, we call them sinful and shun them. Sharon isn't a bad person. She's just . . . struggling."

"She doesn't seem to love my brother much," Sadie said.

"Well . . . I guess they're struggling, too. They weren't always like that. She used to be the one who understood him best out of the Englishers. She could just let him be different."

"Do you feel like we're abandoning him?" Sadie asked.

Elijah sucked in a deep breath. "Yah."

"Me, too."

"But I can only do one thing at a time, and right now, I'm honor bound to get you home."

She smiled wanly. "You had any doubt?"

"Only a small one," he said. "More of fear."

Or perhaps a hope? Absolom had Sharon, and Elijah had gone all these years with a few casual girlfriends who'd never really understood him. And cherished in his heart was the memory of the one girl he'd adored—the one who'd always been out of reach for the long term.

"I don't know why you feel drawn to that life . . ." She sighed, and he wondered exactly what she was picturing from their visit.

"That life?" Elijah laughed softly. "That isn't the life I want. I want a better life than that. I want a house—a nice one, with a two-car garage and a decent yard." The image rose up in his mind—the green of the grass, the flower beds vibrant with color. "There would be a job of some sort, where I would be respected and well paid. And I want a beautiful wife to live in that house with me, and four or five kinner of my own."

"So you endure all that for a hope of something more?" Sadie's eyes glittered in the low light.

"It's possible," he said. "With enough work. I've met a few ex-Amish men who've built careers in the Englisher world and have very comfortable lives. We can hold out a long time in the hope of something better."

The headlights from oncoming traffic zipped by, and Elijah leaned his head back against the headrest.

"I held out, too," she murmured.

"What?"

"I held out for something better . . . with Mervin. They say if you wait, it gets better. There are bumps in the beginning that can be smoothed over . . ." Her voice trailed away.

"What bumps?" he asked quietly.

"He didn't love me." Her voice was choked, and Elijah reached for her hand again. This time she didn't pull away. He twined his fingers through hers. Elijah might dislike the very idea of Mervin Hochstetler, but the thought of a man getting to pull this woman into his arms at night—to have her in his bed, in his home, and to still not love her—that wasn't in the realm of possibility.

"He might have been bad at loving you, but—"

"No, it's true. He loved his first wife, and he thought he could love me, but after a year together, he still didn't. A woman knows—she can feel it. I wasn't enough."

"You're enough," he said gruffly.

"I cooked. I cleaned. I folded everything the way he told me to." Silence stretched for a moment. "I was holding out for some improvement, too. And my mother-in-law says that it gets easier as the years go by. But I'm not sure it would have with Mervin."

"Was he angry? Mean?" Elijah needed something to latch onto here, something he could nail down.

"No. He was perfectly kind and sensible. He never even raised his voice."

And yet he'd made it abundantly clear that she wasn't loved. To think that she'd faced day after day like that. . . .

The Englishers were right when they said that a woman's place wasn't in the kitchen, after all. Her place was in her husband's arms, and Mervin had denied her that right.

"I think my brother is in the same position," Sadie said after a moment.

"He's nothing like Mervin," Elijah countered.

"No, he's more like me," she said. "Sharon doesn't love him."

"She used to."

"Then she's stopped."

Was it possible for love to just stop like that? The sky was dark, the moon hanging full and silvery over the fields that rolled out on either side of the highway. The miles melted beneath them as the car hummed along the road.

Sadie had been holding out for something more—something she'd never get from that man. And maybe Elijah wasn't so different. He'd held out with the Englishers, waiting for something he'd never achieve, even with his new high school diploma. And perhaps Absolom was doing the same with Sharon. Were any of them so very different?

Sadie turned toward the window, her shoulders hunched up. He couldn't see her face, but the depth of her sadness filled the vehicle like rising water.

"Sadie," he murmured.

"I want to sleep, Elijah," she said, her voice thick with emotion.

She wasn't fooling him. It was obvious that she wasn't going to sleep, and he could make out the soft, choked sound of repressed tears.

She'd lost her husband, and all hope of being loved. She'd lost her favorite brother and everything he'd been to her. . . . And now she was knowingly turning her back on her newborn niece. Sadie had always had a ferocious heart, but even the most valiant of warriors had a limit to what they could endure.

Elijah signaled, then slowed the car, easing to the side of the road. Sadie wiped her face and looked over at him in alarm.

"It's okay," he said, and he put on the hazard lights.

"Where, what—"

But Elijah was out of the car before she could finish, and he slammed his door shut. A car whipped past, the sound of the engine raising goose bumps. Then he headed around the car to the passenger side and pulled open the door.

"Elijah?" Sadie squinted up at him, her eyes puffy from her hidden crying.

"Come here." He held out his hand, and she tentatively took it. Then he tugged her out of the car. As she stood up straight, he slid his arms around her waist and pulled her close.

"Elijah—" she gasped, but he didn't let go. She needed this, whether she knew it or not, and there was no way he could drive on with this woman sobbing silently next to him. He had nothing to offer—no words would fix the pain inside of her—but he did have a big, strong body that could shoulder the weight of her.

"Shh . . ." he murmured against her hair, and he shut his eyes, breathing in the scent of her—soft soap and just a hint of vanilla.

She pulled back enough to look toward the road. "People will see—" she whispered.

"What people? We're alone out here, Sadie. No one will see anything. Your reputation is safe." She slowly sank against him, her resistance leaking away until she started to shake with silent sobs once more. Her hot tears soaked into his shirt. He tightened his embrace, pulling her against his chest as if by holding her close enough, he could absorb some of her pain along with the tears.

"You were always enough, Sadie," he murmured against her kapp. "Always."

If he could have protected her from all of this, he would have. If he could have brought Absolom home, if he could have stopped her from marrying the respectable church elder . . .

Sometimes life just hurt.

Moonlight bathed the field in liquid silver, and beside them, another vehicle zipped past, the engine fading away as quickly as it had approached. He wanted to give her so much more than he could. He was jealous of the next husband who would get to do this—hold her close, dry her tears. Even though he knew he wasn't the man for her.

She was the bishop's daughter, and she was meant for another elder, a respectable man in the church. Elijah was dangerous—a walking risk, now that he'd abandoned the community for as long as he had. Whatever they'd shared was in the past, and he knew better than to hope for more, but holding her in his arms like this, he couldn't help but think of the kisses they'd shared since he'd been back. All logic aside, he wanted more with her, too.

Sadie pulled back and wiped her eyes.

"I'm sorry," she said, wiping a tear from her cheek with the palm of her hand. He let his arms drop, and those few inches between them felt like yards. There were so many excellent reasons why they could never be more than friends, but he ached for her as if she were a part of him.

Except his feelings for her were that part of himself that he'd had to carve from his own body. She'd never be his.

"If I'd stayed in Morinville," he said. "Would you have still married him?"

He didn't know why he was punishing himself this way. Sadie looked up, ocean-blue eyes meeting his for only a fraction of a second before she dropped her gaze again.

"Yes," she said quietly. "I'd still have married him. I knew what I wanted."

Not Elijah. That was the implication, wasn't it? She'd known what she wanted, and he'd never measured up—not in that way. He'd been a friend of the family, and she wanted a man with something more to offer her than a strong chest and arms that ached to hold her. And why shouldn't she? Mervin might have been a bad choice, but that didn't change what she wanted.

"Yah," he said, forcing some joviality into his voice that he didn't really feel. "That's what I thought. Just makes me feel better knowing I couldn't have set you straight, anyway."

A lie to save face. She looked up at him again, and her quizzical look made him wonder if she saw through it. Her tears had stopped, though, and she licked her lips, then gave him a wobbly smile.

"As much as I'd love to blame you for absolutely everything, I don't think I can," she said. "I made my own choices."

Sadie slid back into her seat. Elijah slammed the door shut, and stood there in the cool night breeze as another car sped past them on the highway. He knew why Absolom wouldn't leave Sharon. Sometimes, a man just couldn't let go of the possibility of something better. But it wasn't the house or the cars, or the respect. It was that hope that the naïve happiness of the past would resurface.

It never did, though. Time tramped on, and there was only forward. Elijah, of all people, should know that.

Chapter Fourteen

I'm no boy, Sadie. Isn't that what he'd said? And Sadie realized with a rush that he was right about that. He was most definitely a man—of the most dangerous kind. He was alluring, and he woke her up in ways that only a husband should do. Her body responded to him; her heartbeat seemed to slow as she rested against his broad chest. He'd smelled slightly musky—warm and spicy, and she'd longed to simply raise her lips and let him kiss her . . . to just let herself slip into another mistake would be ever so easy . . .

But she knew better than to let her body rule her choices, because Elijah had one foot in Chicago already. There was no future between them, so why was she allowing herself to rest in his arms like that? She'd only end up heartbroken in the end.

If there was one thing that had been pounded home in her visit with her brother, it was that the children were the most vulnerable, and the influences around them made a traumatic difference. It would be the same for little Sarah, too, which was equally heartbreaking. But Sammie could still be spared. *Her* son could grow up safe and secure in an Amish community that would hold him safely to the narrow path. So why couldn't she dampen whatever it was she was feeling for this man?

The last few miles went by too quickly, but when Elijah pulled into her family's drive with the headlights flicked off to draw less attention, her heart gave a grateful squeeze. This adventure was over—she was back where she belonged.

Elijah turned off the engine, and Sadie reached for the door handle.

"Thank you," she said, turning back. "For . . . all of it."

For bringing her to her brother, for sitting by her side, and for holding her close beside the highway while she cried it all out.

"Yah," he said gruffly. "It was nothing."

"I talked a lot—too much, probably." Now that she was back on home soil, she was regretting opening up as she had. She felt exposed, vulnerable. She'd lost a piece of her armor by talking as heedlessly as she had.

"No, you didn't," he said quietly.

"Still—" Her heart sped up, and she licked her lips nervously. "I hadn't told anybody those things—about Mervin. I'd meant to keep the secret."

"You can trust me," he said. "Your secrets are safe with me."

Were they? Nothing else was safe with him. She looked toward the house as a lamp's light flickered behind a curtain and the side door opened. Her parents had stayed up for her, as she knew they would. They were anxious to hear the news about Absolom.

"I have to go," she said.

"I'll see you tomorrow morning." Those dark eyes met hers, and there was something in his gaze that tugged at her in a way she didn't want to feel. He'd trampled boundaries between them today that went beyond a kiss, and had sunk right into her heart. She couldn't let that happen again.

Sadie got out of the car without another word and shut

the door as quietly as she could behind her. Then she headed for the house, only glancing back when she heard the engine start again.

"Sadie!" Daet stood at the door. "It's later than we thought you'd be."

"I know, Daet." She looked back again, and Elijah's car was reversing into the darkness, headlights still out. She stepped inside. "We stayed until sunset, almost. It was hard to say good-bye."

Mamm and Daet were both still dressed, and there was a pot of tea on the stove, whistling comfortingly.

"Come inside and sit down," Mamm said, and she looked sadly toward the door as Sadie shut it behind her.

Sadie came inside and looked up toward the staircase. Her own son would be asleep in his little bed, and she longed to wake him up and snuggle him. She wouldn't, of course.

"Sammie didn't like going to bed without you, but he finally fell asleep. He'll be a handful tomorrow, though," Mamm said, turning toward the kettle.

"Is he in his bed, or mine?" she asked.

Her mother's face colored. "Yours. I did my best, but he wouldn't have it."

Sadie smiled. Her son had been without her for a day, and Mamm was right—Sammie would make her pay for it tomorrow by not letting her out of his sight. But what could Chase do when his mother returned? Nothing. He was already fighting the world with everything in his little arsenal.

Sadie accepted a mug of tea from her mother, and Daet sat down at his usual place at the head of the table. Her parents watched her in agonized silence.

"I saw him," Sadie said. "And he's . . . he's not doing well."

There was no use in sugarcoating the truth.

"Is he sick?" Mamm asked, leaning forward.

"No, no, he's healthy," Sadie replied. "And he has a job, which is important, of course. But he isn't happy."

"That's excellent news." Daet smiled. "As well, he shouldn't be. He's been raised on the narrow path, and he's finding out just how miserable the devil's way makes a man."

The devil's way. Yesterday, she wouldn't even have noticed the phrasing. Today, though, it irked, just a little.

"His girlfriend, Sharon, is struggling with depression," Sadie went on. "She has another child from a previous relationship—Chase. He's a handful, that boy. He's allowed to do pretty much anything he wants. He's the one who suffers the most, I think."

"And the baby?" her mother pressed.

"Sarah is healthy, too. The mother left while we were there, so we held her a lot. Absolom is a very doting father."

"So he's close to coming back." A smile toyed at Mamm's lips. "Isn't he?"

"No." Sadie could feel her parents' disappointment as the hopeful smiles slipped from their faces. "Sharon is having a hard time caring for those children, and Absolom was right about her not fitting in here in Morinville. She seems to have no love for us."

"Us?" Daet frowned. "Why?"

"I don't know. Whatever Absolom has told her, I imagine. She stomped off, left the children with Absolom, and hadn't returned yet by the time we left. But for all of that, Absolom loves her. And they are . . . a family."

"A family?" Daet shook his head. "They are *not* a family!"

"He has children who depend on him for food as well as love," Sadie replied quietly. "He has a woman he keeps house with. And he's standing by them, Daet. He said that he has responsibilities, and he hopes you'd understand that."

Daet's eyes filled with tears, and he turned away. He'd

been hoping, Sadie knew, that this would be the end of it all, that Absolom would come back.

"Does he miss us?" Mamm asked, a tremor in her voice.

"Desperately." Sadie swallowed a mist of tears. "He says to tell you that he loves you, Mamm."

"If he loved me, he wouldn't have done this!" Mamm pushed her chair back and rose to her feet. "Love is an action, not a feeling! Not a regret! If he loved his mother, he would come back!"

"He *can't* come back, Mamm!" Sadie's voice rose to meet her mother's. They wouldn't understand—they hadn't seen him, seen his life there. She wished that his choices made less sense—it would hurt less if there was some hope, or at least some indignant anger at his outrageous behavior. But she had neither.

Daet sat in somber silence, and when Sadie looked toward him, she read the grief in his face. He rubbed his hand over his gray hair.

"If this were another family," he said slowly, "I would advise shunning."

Sadie's mouth went dry. "Daet, please don't. He asked me to write to him. There might still be hope!"

"You are already defending his worldly ways." Daet shook his head. "I have to consider the community—the weaker members of the church who might stumble because of my own weakness."

"It isn't weakness to love your son!" Sadie was too tired to dampen her words. "I have a son of my own, and, Daet, I'd swim oceans for him." Tears prickled at her eyes.

"I have more children than just one," Daet said, his voice low and thick with emotion. "I have an entire congregation, as well. The Good Shepherd might have gone after his missing lamb, but he didn't do so at the risk of the rest of the flock."

Sadie looked toward her mother, but Mamm stood immobile, her face ashen.

"Daet—" Sadie rubbed her hands over her face. "Please, Daet."

"It is better for us to face facts than to have the elders come and inform us that we're straying from the Ordnung. I won't risk your reputation any further. We will never speak of this visit to your brother, and I will tell the elders of my decision for a vote."

Shunned. The word was ugly and sharp in her heart. It wouldn't be so very different from the way Absolom lived now, but it would solidify his position of outsider. And his letters would go unopened instead of just unanswered. No one would be permitted to speak to him, to look at him, to have anything to do with him until he came back, humble and penitent.

Small feet sounded on the stairs, and Sadie turned to see her bleary-eyed son coming down.

"Mamm?" he whimpered.

"Mamm is back," Sadie said with a misty smile. "Come here, sugar."

Samuel descended the last of the stairs, and she picked him up in her arms, cuddling him close. He smelled of the soap his grandmother had washed him with before bed, and Sadie closed her eyes, breathing him in. Her little boy.

"Sadie," Mamm said, and Sadie opened her eyes to see her mother's agonized face. "Your brother isn't a little boy any longer."

And she knew that—but she didn't care how big Sammie got; he'd never stop being hers.

"If you saw how sad he was . . ." Sadie said.

"Does he care about my broken heart?" Mamm asked, her lips quivering with repressed tears. "Does he care about your daet's heart?"

Sadie looked around, as if she could find some answer

hidden in the walls or the windows. She'd gone to see her brother in hopes of giving him a bridge back home, but she'd discovered that it wasn't the bridge that was holding him back.

"He cares! He's just . . . trapped."

Samuel squirmed in her arms and he caught one of her kapp strings, tugging it loose. Sadie reached back to pluck her kapp free, along with the bobby pin that held it in place. She'd bring him back to bed and tuck him in properly.

"Don't think I love him any less than you love Samuel," Mamm said, pressing her lips together to hold back the tears. "The Lord disciplines those He loves."

Sadie turned toward the stairs and started up them. Samuel was heavy now, and he felt like he'd grown over the last day—fitting into her arms just a little differently than he had last night. She climbed the stairs carefully, feeling her way since she couldn't see her feet past Sammie. As she made it to the top stair, she heard her mother's sobs burst out through the kitchen.

"My son . . ." Mamm wept. "Oh, Absolom, my son, my son . . ."

And her father's deep voice, hoarse with grief, murmured back to her.

Sadie looked down at her kapp in her hand. It represented submission before God and before the men God put over her. She'd always accepted that submission as a fact of life, but now she realized just how dangerous a potential husband could be. She'd be under his authority—as would her son—just like they were under Daet's authority here at home.

Sadie held Samuel a little closer as she carried him into her darkened bedroom. She knew the way by feel, and she brought him to his little bed.

"No, Mamm," Sammie pleaded. "Sleep with you . . ."

"No, you'll sleep in your own bed, son," she said, kissing

his forehead. "And I'll be in mine. But it's very late, and we both need to sleep, all right?"

Samuel's pale face crumpled into tears, and he reached for her. He'd missed her—he'd gone a whole day away from her—and she didn't have the heart to push him away. Sadie sank into the rocking chair in the corner instead, snuggling her son into her lap.

One day she would be forced to marry, and that thought was even more frightening than it had been before, because Samuel wouldn't be the natural child of whatever man chose her. And that was even more of a danger than she'd realized, because Samuel didn't have a living father to match her ardent love for him. No one on God's green earth loved this child just as deeply as she did.

No one.

But marry she must.

The next morning, Elijah arrived early at the Graber farm and unhitched his buggy in the barn. The morning quiet was punctuated by the first twitter of birds as the sun eased up over the horizon, spilling rosy light over the cattle-dotted fields. Elijah kicked the door to the buggy barn shut behind him and was about to head toward the cow barn when he saw the bishop standing on the porch.

Elijah hesitated—did the old man want something from him, or was he simply standing in the cool morning air?

"Elijah." The bishop's voice wasn't loud, but it carried, and Elijah suppressed a sigh. He suspected that the bishop would want to ask about his son, but Elijah had nothing to tell him that Sadie couldn't.

Elijah headed in the older man's direction, and the bishop came down the steps, meeting him down on the grass.

"Good morning, sir," Elijah said.

"Thank you for bringing my daughter home safely," the

bishop said quietly. "I appreciate your willingness to help us in this matter."

Elijah nodded in acknowledgment.

"I'm sure we can count on your discretion still . . ."

"Of course." He wouldn't be discussing this outside of his own home, and neither would his parents.

"Good." The older man paused. "Sadie told us about Absolom's situation. I understand why you weren't able to bring him back home with you."

"Thank you." It wasn't exactly the response he'd expected. Elijah tucked a thumb into the front of his pants.

Elijah was less worried about Absolom right now than he was about Sadie. She'd try to be strong for her parents, but she'd been shaken by the view into her brother's world . . . and maybe he should have expected that, but he thought that she'd use judgment and religious certainty as a shield. He'd even considered the possibility that she might offer a little discipline of her own to Sharon's wild and unruly son—but her heavy heartbreak had been worse. Elijah could still remember that distinctive scent of Sadie's hair as he wrapped his arms around her, trying for just one moment to be enough.

The bishop started to walk slowly toward the cow barn, and Elijah matched his pace. The older man wanted to say something—Elijah could feel the unspoken words humming in the air around him. Would this be the end of his employment? He couldn't imagine that the bishop was keeping him around for more reason than Elijah's connection to his son. Elijah would almost be relieved if the bishop replaced him, let him lick his wounds and get over whatever new, unsettling feelings he seemed to be developing for the bishop's daughter all over again.

"You said before that I am more flexible for my own

family than I am for anyone else," Bishop Graber said, coming to a stop.

They reached the gravel road that led up to the cattle barn, and Elijah let his gaze travel up the curving road.

"I'm sorry if I offended you," Elijah said at last.

"You were right. I was willing to give Absolom more grace than I'd have given anyone else's son."

"Including me?" Elijah asked bitterly.

The bishop's face clouded, but he nodded. "You were the reason my son left, Elijah. And while I do my best to be unbiased, I may have allowed my personal feelings to cloud my decisions."

"He would have left, with or without me," Elijah said, his voice low.

"No, there you are wrong."

"Am I?" Elijah asked, looking up to meet the bishop's gaze. "Can you be so sure?"

"Are you saying he lied to us when he said he would bring you back?" The older man laughed bitterly. "No, my son is many things, but not a liar."

"He was angry," Elijah said. "Yes, I pushed him to come with me, but I also asked him to come home with me several times over the years, and he turned me down. You expected perfection from him. Other boys could make a mistake, but if Absolom did, he was whipped."

"Spare the rod, spoil the child." The bishop's voice was less certain now.

"Spare the rod once in a while, and your son might not hate you so much that he leaves the community," Elijah snapped back.

"I quote the Bible. What's your foundation?" There was a low, dangerous simmer in the old man's eyes now.

"I'm simply looking at the fact that Absolom left and never looked back."

Bishop Graber looked ready to retort, but then he sighed. "Don't question a father's love, Elijah Fisher. I did all I could to bring him back into salvation. I did more than I'd have allowed anyone else to do. And in that, I was wrong." The older man nodded several times. "Very wrong."

Was he? Was compassion and an honest attempt to reach out to his son a mistake? The bishop should have bent more readily for other people's sons, other children who turned their backs on the community . . . but he hadn't done wrong by Absolom. Elijah might have said so, but the bishop raised a hand to silence him.

"It is time to stop bending with the wind and whim of a disobedient boy."

Elijah's breath froze in his throat. "What do you mean?"

"I have done more for my son than I allowed even your father to do for you. Now, I must do as I advise others. It is time to shun."

Shunning? Elijah swallowed. "Bishop . . . please . . ."

"No, there is no need for that," the bishop said with a tired sigh. "I have prayed and prayed over this matter, and I vowed to the Lord that if my son didn't return with you, that I'd follow the Lord's will through the Ordnung."

"He is already so far away," Elijah pressed. "Is it even necessary? If you shut him out this way—"

"You yourself told me that I am unfair in the public eye," the bishop interrupted. "If I don't take this step, the community will be weakened. I must not show favoritism. My son is in full defiance. The only answer is to shun him until he is willing to confess his sin and return home."

It was a cruel twist on Elijah's words. Now, not only was Elijah responsible for Absolom's defection, but he was responsible for his shunning, too. All because he'd pointed out the bishop's bias.

"Does Sadie know?" Elijah asked woodenly.

"Yes, she knows."

Did she blame him, too? That's what he wanted to know, but he couldn't ask that. If Elijah had taken his anger and left the community alone, it all might have been different . . .

"I will send for the elders today," the bishop went on, "and we will discuss the matter and take a vote."

"You don't have to do this."

If the bishop heard him, he showed no sign of it.

"Do not contact my son again," the bishop said, his words heavy and slow. "Do not answer his letters, or even open them. We are permitted to help him if he is going to suffer unduly, but we will not eat with him, talk with him, or even look at him until he has chosen the narrow path once more."

Elijah knew the rules for shunning. What Amish person didn't? It was a horrible consequence where the community had to cooperate in the punishment of the person in question. Everyone had a hand in it, and as long as Elijah was living with his parents, he would be forced to participate, too.

I shouldn't have taken her to see her brother. He'd known it was a mistake from the start. He'd known that Absolom couldn't come back as easily as all that, and now his father's hand had been forced. Absolom would be formally separated from everyone he'd ever known and loved in Morinville.

All because of a quiet moment in the dark with Sadie. . . . Who was he fooling? Elijah hadn't been trying to help her—he'd been offering her the only thing he could give that no other man could provide, and he'd proven himself to be even more damaging to her well-being than he'd imagined.

"Do you still want me to work for you?" Elijah asked.

"Yah. Of course. You've done well by us, Elijah Fisher." The bishop reached out and squeezed Elijah's shoulder.

So welcoming, so approving. Why? Was it because he knew their secrets?

"Then I should get to work." Without waiting to be dismissed, Elijah turned his steps toward the barn.

Shunning.

Elijah had only wanted to let Sadie connect with her brother, but it seemed like everything he touched was soiled somehow. He'd come back to Morinville to help his parents, but he wasn't improving Sadie's life by being here. If he really cared about her, he'd take a big step back and let her put together the traditional Amish life she craved.

Chapter Fifteen

Sadie bent down and kissed Sammie's damp forehead. It was naptime, and as predicted, Samuel had been following her around all day, wanting hugs and attention. He hadn't completely forgiven her for being gone the day before, and she knew he could sense the tension around the house, even though no one would speak about Absolom in front of the boy. Especially now. But the silent grief was still there—the disappointment that reaching out to Absolom hadn't changed a thing.

Sadie pushed the window open another few inches to let a tenuous breeze into the bedroom, and as she looked outside, she saw a buggy coming up the drive. Sadie waited until it came closer, and she recognized the girl holding the reins—her friend, Mary Beiler.

"Now you go to sleep, Sammie," she said. "You understand?"

Sammie rolled over onto his side, his eyes wide open. He'd fall asleep, but it was taking longer the last few weeks. So small still, but she could see the bigger boy inside of him starting to emerge. If he'd only hold off on that a little longer.

Sadie headed down the stairs. Mamm was seated at the

table shucking a bucket of peas from the garden. Her mother looked wan, faint circles under her eyes.

"Where are you going?" Mamm asked.

"Mary Beiler just drove up," Sadie said, and Mamm looked toward the side door instinctively, then to the sitting room where Daet was sleeping in the rocking chair again.

"Well, don't take too long," Mamm said, her voice low. "I've got your sister weeding the garden, and I'm going to need you to check on the goats."

They exchanged a somber look, and Sadie nodded. "I'll go check on them as soon as I see what Mary needs. Don't worry, Mamm. When Daet wakes up, you can tell him I've already done it."

Sadie headed out the side door, catching the screen door so that it wouldn't slam. It felt like a death in the family, except that their grief couldn't be shared. Sadie had been so hopeful that seeing her brother would make some kind of difference, but the letdown had been almost physically painful. And now, Daet was determined to have Absolom shunned.

It wouldn't bring him back, it would only allow the family to save face, as if that even mattered anymore.

Mary reined in her horses, and from here Sadie could see that her face was ashen, and her eyes were rimmed in red. Sadie picked up her pace and crossed the lawn.

"Mary?" Sadie stopped at the side of the buggy, looking up into her friend's face. "What's the matter?"

Mary's face crumpled into tears, and she covered her face in her hands. Sadie hoisted herself up into the buggy and settled onto the seat next to her friend. Something was terribly wrong, and her heart hammered just a little faster. Had someone died? Had there been an accident? Sadie grabbed Mary's hand in hers and gave it a squeeze.

"What's happened, Mary?"

"It's Jonathan—" Mary choked back a sob. "He just . . . he came by and he . . . we were supposed to get married, Sadie!"

"What do you mean, were?" Sadie asked, confused. "He didn't call it off, did he?"

Mary nodded, wiping her eyes. "An hour ago. He drove up in his buggy, told me we needed to talk, and said he couldn't do it."

"Just like that?" Sadie looked toward the garden where Rosmanda was pulling weeds, and her sister looked toward them, but didn't stop her work. Had her sister really managed to break them up? It hardly seemed possible. Rosie was young still—definitely naïve. Did Jonathan really think he felt that strongly for a sixteen-year-old girl?

"Oh, Mary, I'm so sorry . . ."

"I don't understand it," Mary went on, sniffling into a handkerchief. "One day he says he can't wait to make me his wife, and the next he's telling me he never loved me. How is that possible?"

"Is there another girl?" Sadie asked.

"Who?" Mary spread her hands. "I can't see who he'd be with!"

Sadie knew exactly who Jonathan Yoder had been fooling around with, but she was shocked that he'd actually called off his engagement. Rosmanda had insisted that they were in love—could there really be more between them than Sadie had imagined? She'd thought this was mostly one-sided, that Jonathan would tire of flirting with her sister soon enough, and Rosie would end up with a broken heart and a mite more wisdom . . . but a broken engagement changed things.

"What did he tell you?" Sadie pressed. "Exactly."

"He said that he'd made a mistake with me," Mary said, her lips trembling. "He said he loved me more like a sister, and he'd never really loved me like a wife, and that he now knew that. He wanted to save us both the misery of an unhappy marriage, and he said that he couldn't go through with it."

"Have you told your parents?" Sadie asked.

"No . . ." Mary shook her head and leaned back against the seat. "Not yet. I don't know . . . if he changes his mind back again, and he still wants to marry me, then I won't have to tell them, ever. Right?" She looked over at Sadie pleadingly. "Because they'd never forgive him for this."

"I'm not sure that I will, either," Sadie said grimly.

"Just help me figure this out!" Mary pleaded. "I know he loves me. I don't understand what happened, but he does love me. If you knew how he kissed me and held me . . ."

Rosmanda had a similar story to tell, but another realization put a rock into Sadie's gut. Rosmanda hadn't had her Rumspringa yet. She wasn't old enough to court, so if Jonathan had dumped Mary for Rosmanda, it certainly wasn't to do things the Amish way. Was he going to try to make Rosie run off with him?

"What do you want me to do?" Sadie asked.

"I don't even know." Mary sighed. "He'll have to come talk to your father, Sadie. Maybe you could speak with him. See what happened. Because I don't understand how he could change like this—it makes no sense."

"I'll keep an eye out for him," Sadie agreed. "Oh, Mary. I'm so sorry he did this to you. At least it was before the wedding. After would have been worse."

Mary's gaze shifted to the side, and she licked her lips. "Yes, much worse."

But something in her tone suggested that Mary didn't agree with that. And Sadie couldn't blame her. She'd gone from planning her wedding to sobbing her heart out. And she deserved much better treatment than this.

Mary could be sure that Sadie would be watching for

Jonathan Yoder's arrival, because he wouldn't be getting a moment alone with her sister if she could help it. If he was going to run away from his promises and responsibilities, he wouldn't be doing it with Rosie.

They talked together for a few more minutes, and then Mary wiped her eyes with her apron.

"Mamm needs me for the laundry. I have to go back . . ."

"Give it a day or so," Sadie said. "Maybe time will change his mind back again."

Mary nodded. "I don't have much choice, do I?"

When Mary left, Sadie headed for the garden, and Rosmanda pushed herself to her feet, brushing the dirt from her hands and tossing the last weed into the bucket at her feet. She looked anxiously toward Mary's receding buggy, then back to Sadie.

"What did Mary want?" Rosie asked hesitantly. She bent and brushed the dirt from her knees.

"You don't know?" Sadie demanded.

Rosmanda shook her head. "No. Of course not. What's happened?"

"Jonathan dumped her."

Pink shaded Rosmanda's cheeks, and she clasped her hands in front of her. "He's done it, then?"

"So you knew he was going to?" Sadie demanded. How long had this misery been plotted?

"No . . . maybe. He's been promising to do it for weeks now. I was starting to worry he wouldn't." Rosmanda licked her lips. "I told you he loved me, Sadie. I *told* you!"

Sadie rubbed her hands over her face, her stomach sinking. "Rosie, you know you can't marry *anyone* yet."

"I know." Rosie nodded.

"If Jonathan comes to talk to you, you'd better have someone with you, or it will look like you were—" Sadie shrugged weakly. "It will be obvious what you did."

"I didn't do anything wrong."

Sadie met her sister's gaze in silence, and the color in Rosmanda's cheeks deepened.

"I'm not ashamed," Rosmanda said archly.

"Maybe you should be."

Rosmanda didn't answer, and she walked away, then knelt back down to continue her weeding. Sadie watched her sister for a moment, her heart heavy. Rosie was old enough to know better than to cheat with a man who was officially dating another girl. She'd been raised better than her actions suggested, and now that Jonathan seemed to be making his choice, Sadie couldn't help but pity her sister.

One of two things would happen: Either Jonathan would get bored of waiting for Rosmanda and break her heart just as he had done to Mary, or he would be willing to wait and marry Rosmanda—and Rosie would have a husband capable of utterly deceiving a woman. As far as Sadie could see, no good could come out of this.

What was happening to this family? Heartbreak and poor choices seemed to follow at their heels lately. Even Sadie, who had done everything the Amish way, had ended up married to a man who hadn't been able to love her, try as he might. For all of her virtue, she might find herself in another marriage, equally disastrous.

The Grabers were supposed to be better than this, but more than that, the Amish principles were supposed to protect them better than this.

Where had they gone wrong?

Elijah put his pitchfork back into the corner where it was kept and wiped his forehead with the back of his hand. Dust motes danced in a square of sunlight that slanted in through the window, and he heaved a deep sigh.

He was done with his work for the time being. In a little while, he'd go check the feeders in the field, but right now, he'd earned himself a break that he wasn't even sure he wanted. Work helped him to focus his conflicting feelings so that he didn't have to think about them. Sweat was a great purifier.

He'd been trying not to think about Sadie all day today, but every time he stopped lifting or throwing or shoveling, she'd come creeping back into his mind.

At lunch time, Elijah had eaten quickly and excused himself to go back out to work before anyone else was done eating. A pall hung over the home, and Elijah knew he couldn't help them. Even shunning wouldn't fix this. Absolom was a grown man who'd made his choice—at this point, shunning was for the bishop, not for Absolom.

The very thought made his neck prickle, and he knew just how much this would hurt his friend . . . and Sadie. She was heartbroken, too, and that was part of the reason he couldn't banish her from his thoughts. He'd seen those tears—felt them soak into his shirt. If they'd stayed away from the city, maybe things could have continued as they were without any lines drawn by the bishop. But then, Sadie wouldn't have seen her brother, either, and while isolation might benefit the community, it didn't benefit *her*.

Except he wasn't supposed to be thinking about Sadie's internal workings—he was supposed to be focusing on his own future. If he could help his father get his business streamlined again, he'd be free.

And he had a few ideas to help his daet, but it would take his father changing his way of doing things . . . taking a few notes from the Englishers and moving away from the physical labor toward the planning end of the business— being a consultant of sorts. His daet wouldn't like that one bit, even if it would save the business.

Elijah pulled off his gloves and tossed them over a rail, then did the same with his hat. He used his handkerchief to wipe his face and neck, and just then the barn door handle jiggled, then the door creaked opened. Elijah turned to see a familiar shape backlit by the sunny outdoors. The very one he couldn't banish from his thoughts. It was just as well. Sadie stepped inside and pulled the door shut behind her, and he watched her blink a few times as her eyes adjusted.

"Hi," Elijah said.

Sadie startled and she squinted as she spotted him. "I didn't know you were here."

"I just finished up." He put his hat back on—it was only appropriate. "Is there a problem?"

"No." Sadie walked briskly into the barn, scanning the stalls. "Where are the goats?"

"In the back stall—over by the back door."

Sadie headed in that direction, and as she passed him, he saw tears glistening in her eyes. Before he could think better of it, he grabbed her arm and she skidded to a stop. He tugged her more gently toward him.

"Elijah—" She shook her head in annoyance. "Stop. Yesterday was strange and emotional, and . . . there's no point in any of this!"

"Any of what?" he demanded.

"Whatever we're doing!" She heaved a frustrated sigh. "You're not staying. Even if you were, I need a different kind of husband."

"Yah, I know."

"So we need to stop yielding to temptation," she said, pulling her arm from his grasp.

"Are you calling me tempting?" He shot her a teasing grin.

"I'm not here for you," she said curtly. "So if you have other work, I won't keep you. I'm busy."

She was trying to pry open that gap between them again, and he huffed out a sigh. There was no undoing any of it, and while he'd promised not to tell anyone else about that trip to the city, he wasn't going to live a lie with her.

"Aren't we all," he quipped. "What's the matter?"

"I'm checking on the goats. Daet was worried about the kid."

"They're fine. I've been watching them all day, and the kid is suckling well."

Sadie looked toward the back stall again, then sighed. "Good."

"Now, what's going on?"

"It's nothing I can talk about."

Of course. The Grabers had their secrets—some of which he was privy to, and others they would protect with rare ferocity. But he was tired of this—the secrets, the pressure, the demands.

"Your father told me about the shunning," he said. "If that helps."

Sadie sighed. "The elders should arrive this evening for a vote."

"Any chance they'll vote against your father's wishes?" Elijah asked.

Sadie's answer was in the sadness welling in her eyes. "We should never have gone to see him, Elijah."

"No!" Elijah shook his head. If she'd only folded herself into a small enough shape? If she'd only pushed her emotions down a little further? If he'd sealed his lips and never said a word to her about her brother, or their life in the city . . . "Sadie, listen to me. You wanted to see your brother because you missed him. You all miss him! He's more solidly in your thoughts now than he ever was when he was here! Your father doesn't have to do this."

"Yes, he does. He can't appear to be more lenient with his own son than he is with any other person in this community."

Elijah felt that old frustration rising. "He can choose mercy over punishment. He's the bishop—he has that power, you know!"

"My father is a good man," she snapped.

"Your father is an *ambitious* man."

Sadie spun around and stalked toward the back of the barn. Elijah watched her go, his frustration solidifying into anger.

"Where are you going?" he called after her.

"I'm checking the goats!" she snapped.

"I told you they're fine!"

"Take a hint, Elijah!" she said, casting him an angry look over her shoulder. "I'm doing my duty, and then I'm leaving. A whole lot like you."

Sadie stopped at the far stall and stood with her back to him. Her spine was ramrod straight, and he couldn't tell what she was feeling. But if she was mad, she had no right to aim that at him—not this time. But give him a few minutes, and maybe he'd give her reason. He was tired of playing a part around here.

"Your father's wrong," Elijah said, striding back to meet her.

Sadie turned, her eyes ablaze. "Is he? Because this community needs discipline as well as mercy. You can't just let people gallivant about doing whatever they please. Our community—our distinctiveness—would be gone in a generation!"

"People aren't so bad as you think," he shot back. "If they value the Amish life—"

"My sister has been fooling around with a boy who is publicly dating someone else!" Sadie burst out, her voice almost a shout. Tears welled up in her eyes. "My little sister! And while I blame her, she's only sixteen. She's not old enough for any of this, but the boy sure is, so I'm holding him just a little bit more accountable. He knows better! He's already promised to marry another girl!"

Elijah stared at her in silence, trying to absorb what she'd just said. Rosmanda had a boyfriend? His mind stuttered, trying to catch up.

"So what about that?" she snapped. "Do you think we should just be *merciful* and let them do whatever they please?"

"Who's the boy?" he asked at last.

She sighed. "It's Jonathan Yoder." He could hear the bitterness on her tongue. "Mary Beiler just came to see me, and Jonathan has dumped her. Their banns were to be published next week."

"And he wants to marry Rosmanda . . ." Elijah was still trying to make sense of this. What had just happened here?

"I have no idea! Rosmanda seems to think so, but I have two girls telling me that they know for a *fact* that Jonathan loves them because of the way he holds them close! What *is* that? It's nothing! A few kisses and snuggles don't create a future together—they don't prove a man's character!"

Elijah swallowed hard. Was she talking about her sister's situation alone? Because he and Sadie had shared some kisses, too.

"Love matters, Sadie," he said quietly.

"And what's love in this situation? We have a young man in our community who is playing with the hearts of two girls!"

Elijah shook his head. "Fine. There are times when a little harshness is necessary." What was Jonathan Yoder playing at? He found it distasteful, too. "But, Sadie—"

"As for Rosie," Sadie went on, not even slowing. "She's a little idiot! She knows he loves her by a *kiss*? I've been married—and I know for a fact that a kiss means *nothing*!"

"Sadie!" He raised his voice.

"What?" She wiped a tear from her cheek with an angry swipe.

"A kiss means *nothing*?" he demanded.

"And I stand by it," she retorted.

Elijah caught her by one wrist and pulled her into his arms. Her eyes widened in surprise, her anger slipping as he pulled her hard against him. Without pausing to breathe a word, he slid his hand behind her neck and lowered his lips onto hers. He didn't know why he was doing this—he'd likely regret it deeply within a matter of minutes—but right now, the only thing he wanted was to prove to her that a kiss could matter . . . because every single time he'd kissed her, it had meant something. It might not have had a future, but it *meant* something.

Sadie was stiff in his arms at first, and then she slowly relaxed, melting against him in soft heat, and he felt the soft pressure of her fingers on his biceps. Her lips were warm, and as his mouth moved over hers, he felt her sigh softly. He wanted more than this kiss—he wanted to be as close to her as a man could be, but that would never happen between them. Ever. He pulled back, breathing hard, then rested his forehead against hers.

"Oh . . ." she murmured, her chest rising and falling with her quickened breath.

"Is my point made?" he whispered huskily.

"I don't think—"

He lowered his lips onto hers again, this time tenderly, sweetly, and he wrapped his arms around her, nestling her into his body. She followed his nudges to pull her closer, and when she let out a little shuddering sigh, he felt the urge to do things that only a husband had a right to do. He was playing with fire, and he knew it. His body was responding to her more ardently than even in their youth. If he didn't stop now—

Elijah pulled back and said gruffly, "That's the kind of kiss that matters."

Sadie's eyes blinked open, and color crept into her cheeks.

"Elijah, we can't—" She pulled away, and he let her go. "Why did you do that?"

"You said a kiss means nothing," he said. "And that's not true."

She sucked in a breath and eyed him distrustfully. "She's too young—"

"I'm not talking about Jonathan Yoder," he said, rolling his eyes. Could she be more daft? He pinned her to the spot with one hot glance. "I'm talking about *you*. You said you'd been married, and so you know full well that a kiss like that means nothing. And I'm telling you that it does."

"And what does it mean?" she snapped. "Because you're not staying—"

"Shut up for a minute and listen to me," he barked back, cutting off her words. "The right kiss means that there is something between the two of you—chemistry, the Englishers call it. It means the man feels something for you on an emotional and a physical level. A man can love his sister, but a kiss like that"—he let a slow smile turn up one corner of his mouth—"a kiss like that shows that he doesn't see you as a sister at all. You're right—his ability to fire up your blood says nothing about his character, but if a man can't kiss you breathless, then you have no business marrying him to begin with. No matter how *good* he is."

Elijah's breath was still calming after that kiss, and he glared down at her, daring her to argue with him. He wanted an excuse to close that distance between them again, if she needed more proof of the point.

"You just kissed me. And we both know there's no future between us. So what did *that* mean?"

"Like I said," he said gruffly. "It doesn't mean I'm good for you. I think we both know I'm not. But I sure don't see you as a sister."

And he held her gaze, enjoying the blush that crept into her cheeks.

"I have to go," Sadie said, swallowing hard.

Elijah didn't move an inch as she slid past him and headed for the far door. And when she got there, she looked once over her shoulder.

"Sadie," he said, and she froze with her hand on the clasp. "I mean it. I know you'll have to get married sooner rather than later, but don't marry a man who can't kiss you like I just did."

"What do you care about how I'm kissed?" Her eyes sparkled with something close to anger.

"I just do."

Sadie pushed open the door and disappeared outside. The door swung shut with a clatter.

Kissing her was a mistake, and he was sure he'd feel that acutely later, but right now, he could feel her skin on his hands, her lips against his, her heart beating so close to his own . . .

Forget the break. He needed to keep working and try to purge her out of his system. Sadie had never been meant for him, but if she married another man who didn't love her well enough, he'd do something stupid that would get him shunned, too.

Sadie had said she wanted nothing from him. Well, he did want something from her—for her to see exactly how exquisite she really was.

Chapter Sixteen

Elijah didn't sleep well that night, his mind going back to that kiss in the barn. He knew better . . . and the regret he knew he'd experience came over him in a flood. Sadie was fragile right now, and she didn't need him jerking her around emotionally. He wasn't staying, and her life was entrenched in this Amish community. What did he hope to achieve by giving in to his feelings for her?

The next afternoon, the weather seemed to dog Elijah's mood, as did the bishop, who insisted on coming with him to check the herd when he brought hay out to the feeders in the field. Dark rain clouds loomed a few miles off, a brisk, chill wind driving the broiling storm ever closer. Cloud cover scudded in, blocking out the sun momentarily as the clouds sailed by. Hopefully they'd get back to the barn before the worst of the storm, but there was no way they'd outrun it.

Today, Sadie had been distant. She served him breakfast and said hardly a word to him besides what was absolutely necessary, which might explain her father's decision to go with him. Or maybe that was just Elijah's conscience bothering him, watching for someone to intervene again. He'd done this before when they were young—fallen headlong in love with her, even though he had no business doing so. And look what became of that!

If he were to face her in the barn again, though, he couldn't say that he'd do any differently. In some part of his heart, she was still his—as illogical and wrong as that was. He'd told himself that he wanted better for her than Mervin, but he'd realized something as he tossed and turned last night: he'd told her to find a man who could kiss her breathless, but what he really wanted was to be that man.

Except she wasn't his to kiss. He wasn't her husband, or even a man who could court her. He was officially an outsider, and playing with emotions this strong was foolhardy. Sadie might have kissed him back, but she'd made her feelings about him clear today. On this side of that kiss, he felt foolish. Her silence was rejection enough.

"We need that rain," the bishop said from his seat on the front bench of the hay wagon beside Elijah. "Just to cool it off a bit."

"Yah," Elijah agreed, and a damp breeze swept toward them, fraught with the scent of earth and lightning.

Elijah glanced toward the bishop. The lines around his mouth had deepened over the course of the day, and his face was now a grayish hue.

"I'm fine," the bishop said, as if reading his mind. "I'll get one of my sons to take over soon enough. But they each already have farms of their own, so taking over this one, too, wouldn't be easy."

The fact that his sons were hesitant to take over the family farm was suspicious in itself. Being busy wasn't reason enough, and Elijah suspected that the Graber family had more hard feelings swirling within its depths than he'd been able to see, even with his close connections. The Amish life was all about family, but as anyone knew, family wasn't only about togetherness and belonging. There were tensions, jealousies, rivalries, and bitter divides. Ideals didn't change reality, even in Morinville.

Overhead, thunder rumbled, and the last ray of sunlight was blocked out by the gathering clouds. A copse of trees whipped and bent under the rising wind. Elijah turned around, and he could see a veil of mist moving toward them across the hills, creeping up from behind.

"Sadie spoke to me about you this morning," the bishop added.

Elijah's heart skipped a beat. Had she told her father about what had happened in the barn? The bishop wouldn't look too kindly on a man—any man—taking liberties with his daughter. Although she *had* kissed him back—Elijah had that.

"What did she say?" he asked hesitantly.

"She has a friend who has expressed interest in you." The bishop rubbed at his chest again, then kneaded at his upper arm. "Hadassah Yoder."

"Hmm." He didn't want to give any response that would encourage this. He wasn't sticking around, and, even if he were, he wasn't interested in Hadassah Yoder. His heart was still in a snarl over Sadie.

"She's a fine girl, a good cook, and an excellent seamstress," the bishop went on. "She's also in danger of becoming an old maid."

That was the only kind of woman who'd risk her happiness on him right about now, he realized bitterly.

"And Sadie suggested I take Hadassah home from singing, I take it?" Elijah asked, trying to mask the resentment in his tone. It was her way of getting rid of him—turning him on to another woman. At least he wasn't toying with her emotions.

"If not Hadassah, it might be worth taking a look at the

single girls, Elijah. You could be baptized any time now, and start courting."

Sadie hadn't told her father Elijah's plans to leave, apparently.

"You should probably focus on your daughter's marriage options," Elijah grunted.

"Elijah, I have children older than you are, so I have seen more than you have," the bishop said quietly. "And the secret to creating a home begins and ends with a woman. It's a common experience for a young man to feel adrift— even if they've never left our people. But once they find a wife, it all settles down."

"Really." Elijah eyed the ever-darkening clouds. His disquiet wouldn't be fixed by Hadassah Yoder.

"I've seen it many times," he replied. "Every man thinks his experience is isolated, but it isn't. Many, many have walked this path before you. Trust me, Elijah. A wife is the key."

Ever matchmaking. Elijah wondered what the bishop would think if he knew that Elijah's feelings for his daughter hadn't changed. Very likely, this fatherly encouragement would disappear. The bishop leaned forward, kneading at his chest with the heel of one hand.

"Are you alright?" Elijah asked.

"It's just tight—" The older man grimaced. "It's time for my pill, but I left it in the house."

Chest pain was more than a missed pill, and Elijah's stomach dropped. He'd taken a first aid course with his job in the city, but he was drawing a blank on what he was supposed to do. Call 911—but the nearest phone was . . . was it in town?

"Hya! Keep on!" Elijah urged the horses, but they'd been pulling that wagon loaded down with bales of hay all afternoon, and they were hot and tired. Then, as if by providence, a crack of lightning lit up the sky, and the horses sped up to a trot of their own accord.

"It's not too bad. . . . Don't mention this to my daughter. Between Sadie and her mother, I can't take three steps without being coddled," the bishop said after a moment.

Coddled—he shouldn't have been out here! He was a sick man, and he belonged at home. Someone else should be running this farm—a son, a friend, a hired manager. But the bishop wouldn't let go of the reins on anything, least of all his land.

An image of Sadie rose in his mind—Sadie with her lips parted and her cheeks flushed as his mouth covered hers . . . an image he'd been trying to banish all day. The bishop would never let go of the reins when it came to his daughter, either. There was another flash of lightning, and the first fat drops of rain splattered to the ground.

A gust of wind blew rain into his face, and Elijah turned his head to the side, pulling his hat down. And it was then that he saw the bishop's face twisted in a grimace of pain.

"Bishop!" He put a hand on the older man's shoulder. "What's happening?"

"I—" the bishop gasped. "My chest . . ."

His breath came in ragged gasps, and he didn't even lift his hand to shield his face from the wind-driven rain.

"Hold on," Elijah said, snapping the reins again. "We're almost at the barn. Just hold on—"

The barn loomed ever closer, rain bouncing off the roof in a halo of mist. The sky suddenly opened up and rain poured down like a sheet. A wheel hit a bump and the bishop pitched to the side. Elijah barely managed to catch him by a handful of his shirt to keep him from toppling out of his seat and landing underneath a grinding wheel.

"Stay with me, sir," Elijah commanded. "We're almost there."

The bishop moaned in response, and, as the wagon

came up next to the barn, Elijah snapped the reins and shouted for the horses to keep moving. They were used to stopping here, especially if there was rain, and the horses balked at first, but Elijah shouted again. The horses plodded on through the downpour, clattering over a pothole that jarred the bishop so hard he almost went over the side again. They carried on around the side of the barn toward the gravel road that led down to the house.

As long as the bishop was still breathing and conscious, they had time.

"Mamm! Sadie!" Rosmanda shouted from the kitchen, and Sadie looked up from the folded laundry she was putting away in her bedroom. She darted a look over at Sammie, who stirred in his sleep but didn't wake. Rain pattered against the window pane in a soothing rhythm.

Sadie hurried out of the bedroom and ran down the stairs to see her sister holding open the side door, and Elijah half carrying her daet into the house. Her father's hat was gone, and his gray hair was plastered against his head. Both men were drenched, and their shirts clung to their bodies. Elijah's face was nearly as pale as her father's.

"What's happened?" Sadie gasped. "Daet, are you hurt?"

"He's been clutching his chest," Elijah said. "Lots of pain. He needs an ambulance."

"Benjamin!" Mamm cried, coming up behind Sadie, and then she straightened. "Get your father comfortable. I'm going to use the telephone at the neighbors'."

Mamm didn't even bother grabbing an umbrella; she just marched out into the deluge and headed straight for the wagon that Elijah had vacated. By the time she lifted her skirt and hoisted herself up onto the seat, her dress was soaked through and clung to her legs. She gave a shrill whistle and snapped the reins.

Sadie and Rosmanda brought their father into the living room where he lay down on the couch, and he rubbed at his chest, breathing shallowly.

"Daet?" Rosmanda wailed, her voice going higher. "Daet! What do we do?"

"Go get some towels," Sadie ordered, as much to get her sister out of the room as to get her father dry. Rosmanda's hands were shaking, but she left the room as ordered.

"You might want to get dry, too," Sadie said, glancing at Elijah, who stood there immobile, dripping onto the floor.

"I'm fine," he muttered. "If you need to lift him again, you're going to need me."

She had to agree—they would. Tears welled upside of her, and she sucked in a wavering breath.

"Daet, how badly does it hurt?" Sadie asked, leaning over her father.

"Pills . . ." he murmured.

"What?" Sadie looked up at Elijah.

"He said he missed his pills," Elijah said. "I don't know where they are, though."

Sadie did, and she dashed upstairs to fetch them. They were in the nightstand on her father's side of her parents' bed. Rosmanda met Sadie on the stairs, her arms filled with folded towels, and they came back down together. Sadie got a glass of water, and after Daet swallowed a pill, Rosmanda started wrapping him in towels.

"No—" Daet pushed the towels off. "I can't breathe . . ."

Rosmanda planted herself next to their father, and Sadie moved toward the door where Elijah stood, his arms crossed over his chest and his expression as stormy as the weather outside.

"He'll be okay," Elijah said quietly, and she realized in a grateful rush that that was exactly what she needed to hear.

"What happened?" she asked, glancing up at him.

"He encouraged me to take Hadassah home from singing and then clutched his chest," Elijah said wryly. "A nice combination."

Sadie looked out the broad window, but she couldn't see much past the driving rain. The ambulance would take a few minutes.

"You shouldn't have let him come with you today," Sadie said.

"Yah?" Elijah shot her an annoyed look. "And how was I supposed to stop him?"

They were scared and irritable, and arguing about who should have stopped her daet from checking on his own herd of cattle was a waste of both time and breath.

"I don't know," she conceded, and she shifted her weight toward him without even thinking and felt her arm press up against his muscular torso. She was about to move away again when she felt his hand press gently into the small of her back, out of view of her sister, who was bent over Daet, and Elijah held her in place with the comfort of his touch.

She closed her eyes, a surge of longing, regret, and anxiety flooding through her body. Whenever times were hardest lately—when she wasn't thinking straight—she found herself gravitating toward this man, looking for comfort, strength . . . as if he could give her anything for the long term!

But Elijah was also *here*. And sometimes she got so tired of being the strong one. Even with Mervin, she'd had to be the woman who stood on her own two feet, because while he'd been an honorable husband, he certainly hadn't been offering unspoken support like this. . . . She couldn't get used to this. It would only make their inevitable good-bye harder.

In the distance, the wail of an ambulance siren pierced through the rattle of rain and Sadie straightened, pulling away from Elijah's warm touch. From the window, Sadie could see Mamm's wagon turn back into the drive, and she pulled the horses up short, then dismounted from the wagon and headed back toward the road. Rural addresses could be difficult for emergency personnel to locate, and since they didn't have a phone to clarify their whereabouts, they relied upon more direct means.

"The ambulance is almost here, Daet," Sadie said, crossing the room and moving closer to the window. Her back was cold where Elijah's touch had been. It felt like an eternity, but was probably only a couple of minutes before the ambulance turned into the drive and two EMTs hopped out of the back of the vehicle. Mamm let them in the side door, and they tramped into the house. The next few minutes were a blur. The EMTs, a man and a woman, worked quickly. They inserted an IV into Daet's arm before loading him onto a stretcher and swiftly wheeled him back toward the door. Sadie and her sister followed, and they watched as the EMTs lifted Daet into the back of the ambulance and Mamm climbed up with him, clutching his free hand.

"I'll call the neighbor when there's news," Mamm called over her shoulder, and then the doors slammed shut. The siren came on and the ambulance wheels crunched over the gravel as it pulled down the drive.

Sadie stood on the grass looking in the direction the ambulance had disappeared, feeling like she was floating inside of her own body. The rain pelted down on her, soaking into her dress and dripping down her limbs. Tears filled her chest, but they did not fall. Her mind was spinning. They'd known Daet was sick, but they'd never expected this. He was taking it easy. He was taking his pills . . . one missed pill shouldn't result in this, should it? The medication was supposed to help! Daet was a healthy man who led an active life. All the Amish men were.

Elijah moved in beside her, and his hand brushed hers ever so gently.

"What do we do now?" Rosmanda asked from inside the open door, and Sadie startled, then turned. Had her sister seen that? She stepped away from Elijah.

"We do the chores," Sadie decided. "You take care of the house, and I'll go milk the cow. But first, check on Sammie for me. He's probably woken up from all the noise."

"I can't do everything in here," Rosmanda complained.

"I thought you said you were ready for a home of your own," Sadie said woodenly. "Prove me wrong, Rosie."

Sadie didn't have the energy to talk her sister into the work. Rosmanda was sixteen, had successfully broken up a couple so that she could have the man, and she balked at a little housework? Maybe it was time she faced the reality of being a wife.

Sadie shielded her eyes from the rain and looked over at Elijah. There was no point in getting dry now, anyway. Elijah fell into place beside her as she trudged toward the barn.

"I don't need help," Sadie said. The rain was starting to let up now, and Sadie shivered as a cool wind hit her wet skin.

"Didn't say you did," Elijah replied. "But I'm pretty sure your father just had a heart attack in front of me. Ever occur to you that *I* might want the company?"

"Oh . . ." She hadn't thought of the shock he'd just had, and she shot him an apologetic smile. He was just as wet as she was, and the work needed to be finished tonight. But the thought of going into that barn with Elijah Fisher again was still unnerving. Her body responded to him too readily, and he was the only man who'd ever been able to do that to her.

She hadn't been kissed like that in her marriage. Not once.

Elijah had awoken her like he had when she was a teenager. She'd always filed that experience away as youthful passion, impossible to repeat in her adult years, but Elijah had proven her wrong, and that left her off balance. She didn't have the luxury of playing that game—she was a widow and a mother, and that kind of dalliance could ruin her reputation for life . . . all for a few heart-pounding kisses.

"Is it . . . wise?" she asked, feeling the heat rise in her cheeks, because she was remembering the feeling of his tight muscles under her fingertips as his lips had come down onto hers. She was remembering how deftly he'd pulled her against his body, and how hungrily she'd longed for more than even that . . .

"Is what wise?" Elijah asked. "You mean, will I behave myself?"

"Something like that." Actually, she was more worried about herself. If she told Elijah to stop, he would. He hadn't pushed himself on her yesterday. She'd had every chance to walk away, but his mouth on hers had fired her up more than she wanted him to know. He had no right to make her feel that way—to ruin whatever sensible future might be ahead of her.

"Sadie." His voice was deep and warm, and she looked over at him to find his dark gaze enveloping her. "If you want me to keep my distance, I will. If you want me to."

"What do you mean, if I want you to?" she retorted.

"I mean that you kissed me back." There was a tingle of heat in his voice, and she licked her lips.

"I . . . did," she admitted reluctantly.

"And if you were to want me to kiss you again—just to prove my point—I couldn't turn you down now, could I? That would just be rude."

He was teasing her now, and her cheeks flushed hot.

Now it was like they were kids again, and he was needling like only he knew how. "Oh, stop it, Elijah!"

He laughed softly. "I'll behave, Sadie. Okay?"

Maybe she *wanted* a pious and earnest man. Maybe she preferred that to the way Elijah churned up her insides into a hot mush, because that kind of passion wouldn't last, and she needed a man who could be a good Amish father to her little boy and to the children that would come later. She needed a man who was respected in the community, and frankly, Elijah was neither of those things.

The rain lessened to a drizzle, then stopped completely as they reached the barn door. He held it open for her, but as she stepped inside, she glanced up at him to find those dark eyes fixed on her with a look so intense her breath caught. The door slammed behind them, and she realized in a rush that they were very much in private.

"I'm sure Daet will be fine once he gets to the hospital," Sadie said, stopping at the sink to thoroughly wash her hands. "All we can do is wait, really. But I heard him telling Mamm that he felt fine, which was obviously a lie, but if he feels well enough to try to make her feel better . . ."

She was rambling now, and Elijah leaned against a rung while she grabbed a milking stool and a metal pail, watching her in silence.

"And doing some housework on her own is good for Rosmanda," Sadie prattled on. "Let her see how very unready she is for marriage and responsibility!"

"Sure."

She headed across the barn toward the milking stall, and Elijah followed.

"Do you want a hand?" he asked.

"I told you before I didn't need help," she replied, but the truth was that she didn't dare accept his help. Work kept a distance between them of at least a cow's width. She sat down on the milking stool and prepared to clean the udder. From where she sat, she couldn't see Elijah, and maybe that was better.

"Sadie, look—all joking aside, I'm sorry about yesterday."

She exhaled a slow breath and rested her head against the cow's side. "Me, too."

"The thing is, I know I'm not the guy for you," he went on. "I don't want to be your little mistake."

A mistake—yes, that's what it had been, from the very start. She'd been in awe of him because he was older and had that glitter in his eye when he looked at her—in a way that no other boy had since, either. But maybe that was for the best. Look where he'd ended up—the bad boy to the end.

"I'm as much to blame," she replied, her voice feeling thick in her throat. "I could have stopped you. I should have. Next time, I will."

"Good. Tell me off. Smack me."

Did he mean that? Had he wanted her to put a stop to it yesterday, and she'd failed to be the stronger of them? She was the solidly Amish woman, and that should count for something when dealing with Elijah.

"The thing is, I feel . . ." He moved around to the other side of the cow so that she could see him, and dropped his gaze. "I feel the same way I've always felt for you. I thought it would go away over time, and it didn't. But that's not your fault. This wasn't . . . planned."

Sadie finished cleaning the udder, and adjusted the bucket underneath the cow. Then she started to squeeze and milk hissed into the pail. It was easier to focus on the jets of milk than it was to look at Elijah and see all those conflicted emotions flitting across his rugged features.

"I need some space," he said. "I need to think. We both know I'm not staying—"

"Are you quitting?" she asked hesitantly.

"I will, once he's back and ready to find someone to replace me. I'm not going to leave you in a lurch. I know who the work would fall to."

To her. Of course. And she appreciated him trying to protect her from that.

"Do you need space from me, too?" she asked after a moment.

"Yah. I think I do."

She nodded, her fingers continuing to work without her even needing to think about it. His words sank deep into her heart, and they hurt more than she'd thought they would. He needed to get his feelings in order, and so did she. So why wasn't she feeling any relief?

"Let me finish up here," Sadie said. "If you have other work you have to do . . ."

"Yah, I'll get to it." He straightened. "I'm sorry, Sadie."

Elijah tapped the rail in a wordless farewell, and she listened to the fall of his boots as he walked away. When the door banged shut, she heaved a shaky sigh.

Elijah Fisher had always made her feel like the most beautiful girl in the room, and she would miss that. But he needed his own life, and so did she. Maybe this time together was a good thing—forcing them to face reality together. When he did leave the farm, maybe she could finally get the good-bye she'd craved all those years ago and put him in the past where he belonged.

Chapter Seventeen

When Sadie finished the milking, she trudged back to the house with the pail of milk, covered with a clean cloth. She had to walk carefully so that it wouldn't spill. Her damp dress felt heavy and clung to her arms and legs, and there was a streak of dirt up the side. Drying it would not be enough. She'd have to scrub it in the tub by hand and hang it outside to dry, or she wouldn't have enough dresses to get to the next washing day.

The evening was warm, the clouds having passed, and the sun beamed down on her, dispelling the earlier chill. Everything smelled like fresh earth, and the birds were twittering in the trees. Just like everything was normal . . .

She clomped up the stairs and let herself into the side door. The faint smells of cooking met her, and she inhaled deeply. She was hungrier than she'd realized. Sadie put the milk in the corner until she could deal with it, and shot her sister a tired smile.

"I'm back," she said.

Sammie was awake from his nap, chattering at his aunt who stood in the center of the kitchen. His flaxen curls were rumpled from sleep, but that was the only sign that he'd ever slowed down. Rosmanda stared down at him, mildly panicked.

"What's the matter?" Sadie asked as she pulled off her shoes.

"I can't think. He just keeps talking!" Rosmanda said. "I've got scalloped potatoes and sausages, but I didn't get lettuce for a salad, and—"

"Rosie, it's fine," Sadie said. "Children chatter. Can you imagine Mamm with all seven of us?" She smiled, and Rosmanda didn't seem to see the humor. "Have you heard from the neighbor yet?"

"No," Rosie said.

Sadie nodded. "Mamm will call when there is news. She won't call for nothing—it's a drive down the road for the neighbors every time she does."

"I know," Rosmanda replied.

"Let me go up and get changed, and then I'll give you a hand, okay?"

Sadie didn't wait for an answer. She gave her son a kiss on the top of his head and gratefully went upstairs to peel her sodden dress from her body and get into something clean and dry. When she came back down, Sammie was quiet at the table, eating an apple.

"It's harder than it looks, isn't it?" Sadie asked. She pulled a bucket of string beans from the bottom of the refrigerator and grabbed a paring knife to start clipping their ends.

"That doesn't mean I can't do it," Rosmanda replied. "Mamm did—"

"Mamm was raised to be married early. You weren't. No one forced you to be ready. Don't blame yourself for it."

Rosmanda flattened her lips. "I'm still going to ask Daet to baptize me early."

All for Jonathan.

"Why?" Sadie asked. "Jonathan knows how old you are.

You're not ready for marriage yet. If he loves you, as you say, he'll wait."

Rosmanda shook her head. "He's ready for a family now."

And Rosmanda wasn't an adult yet! But Sadie couldn't say that. Instead she said, "When I spoke with Mary Beiler, she was certain of his love, too."

"She shouldn't be," Rosmanda retorted.

"She told me the same thing you did." Sadie's knife clipped through the ends as she dropped trimmed beans into a pot. "She said that she knew he loved her by the way he held her and kissed her."

Rosie was silent.

"He was doing the same things with Mary," Sadie clarified, just in case her sister needed it spelled out. Sadie looked over to find tears misting Rosmanda's eyes.

"I'm sorry," Sadie added.

"I still love him," Rosmanda said, her voice tight.

"But can you trust him?" Sadie asked. "You feel rushed to get baptized and want to skip your Rumspringa so that you can be eligible to marry him. Do you think he would wait, if he had to?"

"Yes! But *I* don't want to wait!" her sister shot back. "We love each other, and you're trying to ruin this for me—"

"I'm trying to give you something to think about!" Sadie slammed the pot down on the counter. "This is a young man who has lied to his fiancée, lied to her family, and snuck around behind her back so smoothly that she never suspected a thing! If he could do it to Mary, he could do it to you!"

"He wouldn't." Rosmanda shot her sister an arch look. "He broke up with her, didn't he?"

"Let's say that Daet agrees and allows you to be married next year. What if things go wrong in your marriage?" Sadie asked. "What if tragedy strikes? What if you lose a baby? What if you're put on bed rest and can't take care of his physical needs? Will you be so secure in his loyalty then? Or will he do the same thing he did to Mary and start looking around for a better option?"

"I know what we feel for each other, and I trust him."

Daet had been taken to the hospital, and Rosmanda was still determined to follow through on her plan to marry this boy. Why must everything fall on them at once? There was going to be no arguing her sister out of this—not overtly, at least. Rosmanda might argue until she was blue, but when she was alone, she'd do some thinking. It was the best Sadie could hope for, because forcing the two of them apart wouldn't work. If Rosmanda was to be saved from Jonathan Yoder, it would have to be Rosmanda who lost interest first. Otherwise, Sadie could almost guarantee that she'd be comforting her sister with a broken heart before the year was out. Leopards didn't change their spots, and men didn't tend to improve for the love of a good woman.

Advice she should keep front and center for herself, too, for that matter.

"Passion doesn't make up for philandering, Rosie," Sadie said softly. "It doesn't make up for a great many things."

"Did you have passion with Mervin?" Rosie asked pointedly.

Sadie sighed. Should she continue to hide this, or use the truth to help her sister? "No," she admitted. "I didn't."

"And didn't you wish you did?" Rosmanda asked earnestly.

"Yes!" Tears filled Sadie's eyes. "Every day, I longed for it. But being married to Mervin was still better than being married to a man who I couldn't trust. I *could* trust Mervin. He might not have lit any fires in me, but he was loyal and honest. If he'd lived, I'd have found a way to make my peace with it."

"So you're advising me to find a Mervin?" Rosmanda's mouth turned down.

"Not at all," Sadie replied. "I'm advising you to find a Mervin whose kisses turn you to mush. That's what I'm going to be looking for. Because without integrity, Rosie, you're heading for heartbreak."

Outside, an engine growled up the drive, and Sadie and Rosmanda exchanged a wide-eyed look. They didn't get visitors in vehicles, so this must be news about Daet. Sadie went to the door and opened it, spotting the neighbor's car. Sammie came to look, too, peering outside with the mild curiosity of a small child.

"There must be news," Sadie said, suddenly breathless. She scooped her son in her arms and headed outside. In a few brisk strides, she crossed the scrub grass and gravel to where Ethel Carmichael was getting out of the car.

"Ethel!" Sadie said. "Did Mamm call you?"

"Yes," the older woman said with a sympathetic nod. "Your father is stable, but he'll be in the hospital for a few days. She asked that you bring a few things for him—his Bible, a razor to shave his lip, his slippers . . ." She handed over a piece of paper. "I wrote it all down. They haven't assigned him a room yet. Your mother says to ask at reception."

"Thank you." Sadie tried to swallow a lump in her throat. "We appreciate this so much."

"What are neighbors for?" Ethel smiled gently. "Do you have a way to get into town, dear? I can give you a ride, but I have to come back early. I can't drive after dark. I'm a hazard on the road—"

"It's alright," Sadie said quickly. "We'll take the buggy."

"You're sure?" Ethel sighed. "Alright, then. If I can help you in any way, you let me know."

Sadie nodded, and Ethel got back into her car. It was an offer based in kindness, but they would turn to the Amish community now. They accepted aid from their Englisher neighbors in an emergency, but not as a habit. Too much Englisher influence was never acceptable. They meant well, but they meddled and talked, always asking questions and sharing their own ways of doing things, as if any kind of change would ever be acceptable to the Amish. So they were a complication best avoided.

Sadie turned back toward the house and spotted Elijah striding across the backyard toward her.

"Was there news?" he asked, his gaze sliding past her to the car turning onto the road.

She nodded. "Daet will be alright, but he has to stay for a few days. Mamm is asking that we bring him some toiletries and his Bible."

Elijah's expression fell in relief. "Good . . . very good. Is the neighbor driving you, or—"

"No, she can't do it," Sadie replied.

"Then I'll take you in my buggy," Elijah said. "I'm finished with the chores, anyway. We can drive past my place so I can change, and then I'll take you straight into town."

Sadie felt a wave of relief. There were times in a woman's life when she needed a man's protection, or at the very least, his assistance. The farthest she'd driven was to the market on the outskirts of town, and the prospect of driving all the way through town with all the automobile traffic this close to dusk was daunting.

"Thank you, Elijah," she said, hitching Sammie higher up onto her hip. "But come eat first. Rosie's worked hard on dinner."

And Elijah had worked hard on the farm. He'd be hungry, too. They all were. Sadie would leave Samuel with his aunt, and she'd be able to see her father . . .

Elijah's gentle touch slid across the small of her back as they headed toward the side door. She shivered at his touch.

He'd need to stop that. Caring as he meant to be, she had to forget the way her body responded to him.

As she'd so eloquently told her sister, passion wasn't enough.

Elijah barely tasted the food as they ate as quickly as possible. He waited for a few minutes while Sadie said her good-byes to her little boy, and Samuel sobbed piteously for his mother as they left the house. Her son wasn't dealing well with his mother's absences, it seemed, and he'd had enough.

Samuel's wails stabbed a place in Elijah's heart that he'd never experienced feelings in before. It was something like Absolom's description of his daughter's newborn cries—he wanted to fix it, to soothe those tears somehow. . . . The realization was unsettling. He wasn't supposed to be getting attached to Sammie, either.

"I'll be back, sugar," Sadie said softly. "I always come back, don't I? Don't worry. Be good for Auntie."

And just for a moment, Elijah was reminded of Sharon's promises to little Chase that she'd come back. Chase had more experience with a mother's absence than Samuel did, and, in a flash, he saw the difference between the boys. One cried when his heart was breaking, and the other turned to the TV. The boy who cried knew his mother would answer. Samuel would likely never fully appreciate how blessed he was to have a devoted mother like Sadie. It was easy to take such basic things for granted. When Elijah got back to the city, maybe he could put a little more effort into giving Chase some stability, too. That boy needed more attention than he'd been getting—maybe even more so since his tears had dried up long ago.

Elijah let Sadie say her last good-byes with her son while he headed out and hitched up his buggy. When Sadie emerged from the house, they drove the twenty minutes to his parents' house where Elijah changed his clothes and filled his parents in on what had happened. By the time they were on the road again, jiggling toward town, the sun had sunk lower in the sky, and shadows stretched out like lazy cats on the road ahead of them. There weren't any other buggies on the road, providing them with relative privacy, at least from anyone they knew in the Amish community. Elijah looked over at Sadie, who sat in silence.

Some cattle lay in the field chewing their cud, and Elijah let his gaze move over the landscape. This was something that he didn't get to do at the Englisher pace—just enjoy a beautiful scene. Life couldn't move any faster than this for the Amish, and he and Sadie eased into the rhythm. She was too far away from him, though. He knew he was supposed to be more careful, but there was something about this evening—the urgency of the trip, the timing, all they'd been through recently—that stripped his resolve.

Elijah reached over and took her hand in his. Her fingers were cool, and when he squeezed, she squeezed his hand back. This time on her family's farm was supposed to make a good-bye easier, but it didn't seem to be working out that way. She was no longer the teenager he'd fallen for all those years ago. She was now a grown woman with spirit and determination, and he realized that he'd managed to fall for her all over again—a whole lot more deeply this time.

And he'd have to say good-bye this time, too.

She blinked, dark lashes touching her cheeks, and before he could think better of it, he slid his arms around her and lowered his lips onto hers. She moved closer into his arms as his lips seared over hers, and all he could think about was how right this felt—how much he longed to hold her like this every day, to come home to her at night and pull her even closer in the warmth of their own bed . . .

He pulled back and shot her a rueful smile.

"I thought you were keeping your distance from me," Sadie said quietly.

"Yeah." He cast her a wry smile. "I will. Later."

Elijah kept his arm around her, and she closed the last few inches between them, her arm pressed against his side, her legs angled against his thigh. It was a relief to have her close, and he let out a breath that he hadn't even realized he was holding. She tipped her head against his shoulder, and he rested his cheek against the warm top of her head.

"Elijah, we can't keep doing this." Her voice trembled, and he looked down in alarm at the tears misting her eyes. "This . . . the kissing, the cuddling up . . ."

She straightened.

"I'm sorry—" He pulled his arm back, and his chest ached at the sudden distance between them. "I just . . ." Words couldn't encompass all that he felt. His heart was full of throbbing emotion.

"We know better," she whispered.

"Apparently not," he muttered. "All I want is to kiss you again, hold you closer—"

"Elijah, it isn't right," she burst out. "We aren't courting—are we? This is crossing lines we were never intended to cross!"

"You know what isn't right?" he retorted. "Pretending that there isn't anything between us—that isn't right. Hiding our feelings—for each other, about your brother, pretending we're tougher than we are. None of that is right! What am I supposed to do? Pretend I'm not in love with you? Why?"

"You're in love with me?" Her voice trembled and she stared up at him.

Elijah shut his eyes, wishing he could take the words back. But what good would it do?

"Yah," he admitted miserably. "I've been in love with you for years, Sadie. You've got to know that."

He turned toward her, and she searched his face with agonizing directness.

"That was a long time ago . . ." she began.

"I'm not talking about back then," he replied. "I mean, I loved you back then, but I was seventeen. I didn't know much about life, or about the world. I'm talking about now, Sadie. I thought if I saw you here in Morinville, I'd be able to let you go, that I'd see how the real woman didn't match up to the girl in my fantasy, and I'd be able to get over you."

"It didn't work," she said sadly.

"No. Not even a little bit. I tried to keep my head, but I fell for you all over again. This isn't about what we used to be, this is about how I feel about you now—the woman in front of me."

"Love isn't about warm feelings—" she started.

"Stop that!" he barked. "Sadie, love is all about warm feelings. Duty and obligation are about doing the right thing, but love—love is this, Sadie. *This!* This miserable mess of longing and desire. And between us, it may very well be unrequited, but this is love! And what's the point of all that obligation and duty if you don't love someone so much that you can't keep your hands off them?"

Sadie gripped the front of his shirt and pulled his mouth over hers once more. She kissed him with such bittersweet longing that Elijah felt like his heart would burst.

When she released him and their lips finally parted, he leaned his head against hers with a sigh.

"If you had any idea how I feel about you, how much self-control it takes to rein me in when I'm with you, you wouldn't go kissing me like that."

He wasn't thinking about her virtue, or her reputation right now. He was focused on closing that distance between them, because pretending they felt anything other than desperate longing seemed like a worse sin.

"Elijah, stay in Morinville. Don't go back," Sadie said,

and there was no flirtation or teasing in her voice, just that agonizing directness he'd learned to associate with her.

He realized in a rush that he wished he could—that this could be enough for him, that he could be released from his sense of obligation to her brother in Chicago. But nothing had changed. He couldn't erase the last nine years, forget everything he'd worked for with Absolom. He couldn't pretend that an Amish life could be enough, that he could trust this community again. He'd seen too much to be able to settle back into Morinville again.

"Sadie, if it were just a matter of sacrifice, I'd do it," he said bitterly. "I'd live in poverty for you. I'd cross oceans for you. But if I stayed here, I'd get hardened over time, and more and more angry at the rules that held me back. Staying in Morinville wouldn't change who I am at heart. You never did want what I could offer you, and you wouldn't like me quite so much if I stayed. I can guarantee that."

"I'm being selfish right now," she admitted, then swallowed hard. "I'm not thinking about what Samuel needs in a daet, or what I need for a husband who will grow old with me . . . I'm just not ready to give you up. That's horrible, isn't it?"

"Not unless you came with me to Chicago—"

"Are you really asking that of me?" she asked dully.

"No." He shut his eyes and let out a wavering sigh. "I just wish there were a middle ground, but there isn't when it comes to the Amish life. I'm not ready to give you up, either, but I'm not sure we have much choice."

The narrow path. The Amish life took sacrifice, but so did being true to himself. Sadie was the one he'd missed when he lay in his bed at night in Chicago, listening to traffic and longing for home. Hers was the face that rose in his mind when Englisher girls would try to flirt with him, and when he came back to Morinville, she was the first one he asked his parents about.

She'd been his first love, all those years ago, and while he'd never been mature enough to do much of anything about it, she'd stuck in his heart somewhere that couldn't be erased. She'd somehow seeped into his bones, and just having her close enough to feel the warmth of her arm against his was soothing to him on a heartbeat level.

If it really were possible to carve that pound of flesh from his own body in order to fit back into the Amish life, he would do it. But even as a teen, he hadn't belonged—not fully. His heart belonged to Sadie, but he couldn't promise her his future. No matter how deeply he longed to do so . . .

"I love you, but it's not enough, is it?" he asked dismally.

"No." Her voice caught. "It never was. We shouldn't have let ourselves do this—"

"No, I'm not going to live with regrets," he said fiercely. "I wish I could be more to you, I wish my heart was enough, but I won't pretend my life would have been better without you in it. You've been my lifeline, Sadie, the heroine in my hopes and dreams. You'll always have a piece of me. That's not going to change."

Sadie didn't answer, but he could feel her tremble next to him, and he slid his arm around her once more as her tears bled into his shirt sleeve. They were both giving up more than they'd ever imagined possible. But it had never been theirs to begin with. Whatever kept developing between them every time they came together—it was impossible to maintain. But not a sin. He'd never concede to that.

Elijah had read somewhere that a man only ever loved once, and the rest of his life was spent trying to find another love just like it. He suddenly understood what that meant. He couldn't have Sadie—it was an impossibility. But no woman would measure up to her, either.

He'd found his one love, and the rest of his life would be in its shadow. Maybe he just had to accept that fact.

* * *

Morinville Hospital was located at the far west end of town, and Elijah guided the horses through the streets, ignoring the curious Englisher stares of the people walking the sidewalk in shorts and T-shirts. He looked foreign to them—utterly different—but a few weeks ago, he'd have been able to blend in with them easily enough. Anger surged up inside of him tonight as he flicked the reins, urging the horses to pick up their pace. He was a man. Wasn't that what he'd been trying to convince Sadie of since he'd arrived back in Morinville? And now all he wanted to do was smash those stupid cell phone cameras that were pointed at his buggy as if he were a zoo animal performing for their entertainment. He was a *man*, and his heart felt like it was shredded within his chest.

The parking lot had buggy parking, as did most buildings in these parts. And after Elijah had tied up the horses with a feed bag each, he helped Sadie down from the buggy.

"Your father wouldn't approve of us, either," he said, attempting to sound lighter than he felt. It didn't work.

"And with his heart problems right now, my daet needs me, too," Sadie said, pulling her hand out of his grip. "I don't get to follow my feelings, Elijah. I have to make the right choice and trust that my feelings will follow me. It's all I've got left."

Maybe she was right. As they headed to the hospital's front doors, a warm breeze swept around Elijah like an embrace. He'd spent so many years loving a girl he knew he couldn't have—maybe it was time to put his feelings aside for duty and obligation. That was what she'd be doing, after all . . .

As they walked into the hospital, they saw several signs pointing to the emergency room in one direction, radiology in another. There was a desk to the left, and Elijah led the way.

"Can I help you?" a bespectacled nurse asked.

"My father came here in an ambulance." Sadie looked around as if hoping to spot him.

"His name is Benjamin Graber," Elijah provided. "He came in with chest pain."

The nurse clacked on her keyboard for a moment, then nodded. "Yes, here we are. He's upstairs on the third floor in cardiology. Room 1005. The elevator is just over there—" The nurse pointed with her pen, and Elijah caught Sadie's hand, dragging her along with him. It might be the last chance he'd have to hold her hand, and he wasn't going to waste it.

Elijah punched the elevator button, and he kept her hand tight in his. Sadie's cool touch was holding him up, too.

The elevator door opened and they stepped inside. Elijah punched the number three, and they waited while several other people crowded inside before the door shut and it started to move. When they reached the third floor, Elijah put a hand in the small of Sadie's back and nudged her forward as they squeezed past the other passengers and out into a fluorescent-lit hallway. Everything smelled of antiseptic, as sterile and bland as his life was to become without Sadie in it. Her hand brushed against his, and he fanned out his fingers, catching hers, and he knew that he'd have to quit the job on her father's farm. Now that they'd admitted to their feelings, said it out loud, he could feel the end. There'd be no more pretending.

Elijah spotted some rooms with prominent numbers that were moving in the right direction.

999, 1001, 1003 . . .

"One thousand and five," Elijah said. "Just over there."

And Sadie pulled her hand from his. She looked up at him, sadness welling in her eyes, then the door to room

1005 opened, and Sarah Graber appeared in the doorway. She spotted them immediately and walked briskly in their direction. When she reached them, she clasped Sadie in a hug.

"How is Daet?" Sadie asked, turning away from him.

"It was a heart attack," Sarah said. "Not a bad one, though, thank God. It could have been worse."

"Can we see him?" Sadie looked toward the room.

"Of course," Sarah said. "He'll be glad to see you. He keeps asking to go home, but they say he has to stay for a few days to rest. Maybe you can help talk him into it."

For the first time, Sarah included Elijah in her glance, and Elijah dropped his gaze. He'd have to deal with his own heartbreak later—away from the prying eyes of Sadie's family. Right now, he didn't want any of them to guess at what he really felt. It would only add insult to injury.

The hospital room was dim, the blinds shut against the lowering light outside. The bishop looked gray still, his eyes closed and his beard scraggly against the white hospital gown. He looked older and embarrassingly exposed without his straw hat on his head and his black suspenders. The bishop opened his eyes as they ventured farther into the room.

"Sadie . . ." he said with a wan smile. "Tell your mother I'm better off resting at home."

"I'm going to side with whatever the doctors say," Sadie replied, moving forward and taking her father's hand. "We need you better, Daet."

Perhaps it was the excess of emotion in her voice, but the bishop shook his head slowly, then his gaze slipped past his daughter to Elijah. He met Elijah's gaze for a moment, then pursed his lips. "Did you bring me my Bible?"

"Yes." Elijah held a cloth bag at his side. "Along with the other things you asked for. Right here."

"They say the food here is terrible," the bishop said,

turning back to his daughter. "I'll need some good cooking when I get home."

"You'll need some heart-healthy cooking," Sarah countered.

"Bah!" The bishop made a face. "What use is food if it doesn't have some lard or butter in it?"

Elijah smiled faintly. The bishop was teasing the women, distracting them with cooking plans so they couldn't focus on the severity of his condition. They talked for a few more minutes, and the bag of personal items was shown to the bishop. He solemnly approved, and requested that his Bible be left out beside him.

"Even if I dwell in the uttermost parts of the sea . . ." the bishop murmured. "Even there His hand will guide me."

Elijah could sympathize with the bishop's frightening experience, but the Englisher world wasn't akin to the "uttermost parts of the sea." Elijah was one of them now—even though he looked mostly Amish in his suspenders and straw hat. They weren't any different from each other, the Englishers and the Amish. They were all just doing their best to live a good life, to find meaning.

"Our patient needs sleep," a nurse said, coming into the room with a brisk smile. "So, I'll have to ask you to say your good-byes until morning."

"I'm much better off at home," the bishop said hopefully.

"You are much better off with medical supervision," the nurse quipped back. "Don't worry, Mr. Graber. We'll take good care of you."

When was the last time that the bishop had been called Mister? He didn't seem inclined to correct her, and the older man heaved a sigh. "How did you get here, Sadie?"

"Elijah drove us in his buggy," Sadie said, glancing back at Elijah for the first time, and she met his gaze sadly. The bishop's gaze flickered between Sadie and Elijah.

"I'll stay here with you, Benjamin," Sarah said, sinking into the chair next to his bed.

"No." The bishop sighed and shook his head. "I'll be fine. Don't worry about me. Go back home with Sadie and the Fisher boy."

The Fisher boy. That was certainly a change in how the bishop spoke about him. Or perhaps that was how the older man referred to him when he wasn't around. Whatever the case, something silent passed between the bishop and his wife, and she nodded curtly.

"Come, Sadie, Elijah. We'd best get home before it's too late."

Sadie and her mother took turns bending to hug the older man, and when they all turned toward the door, his weak voice rose a little louder.

"Elijah Fisher, if you would stay just a moment." There it was—the authority of the churchman. Elijah let the women leave ahead of him, and he moved back to the side of the bed.

"Yes, Bishop?" he said.

"I think it would be best if you found other employment," he said gruffly, and Elijah looked down at the bishop in surprise.

"Have I done something to upset you?" he asked uneasily.

"I just think it would be best," the bishop replied evenly. "For everyone."

For Sadie. He'd sensed something. Elijah sighed. He'd been meaning to do this anyway, but the bishop wasn't going to let him waffle about it.

"Alright," Elijah said. "I understand."

Elijah walked numbly toward the door, and when he stepped out into the hallway, the nurse pulled the door shut with a solid *thunk*.

"We'll see you tomorrow," the nurse said cheerily. "Good night."

Sadie and Sarah were eyeing Elijah questioningly, but it was Sadie who asked, "What did Daet want?"

"I'm fired," Elijah said, meeting her gaze.

"You're what?" Sadie's face blanched. They weren't ready to let go of each other, but it was time. The bishop was right.

"It's fine," Elijah replied.

With her mother next to him, he didn't dare touch Sadie, and they walked together as a group to the elevator. The bishop could see how Elijah felt about his daughter. It might be impossible for them to give in to the longing they shared, but Elijah's heart wasn't going to recover so smoothly. Perhaps the bishop was a little wiser than Elijah liked to think.

He was right. It was time to move on. This was over.

Chapter Eighteen

That night, Sadie sobbed into her pillow, her tears dampening the sheets as her son slept peacefully in his own little bed. She cried until she was dry, and then she lay awake staring out the window at the little patch of stars she could see beyond the creaking branches of the old oak tree. She tried to remind herself of every logical reason for suppressing her heart when it came to Elijah, and while she knew she'd made the right choice, somehow it didn't hurt any less.

She knew what she needed—a husband she could count on to keep their little family firmly in the faith. She needed a man who shared her vision for the future—one that included all those rules and obligations that chafed at Elijah so much. Her son needed a father who would give him the reassurance he'd need to stay Amish, too. If she foolishly followed her heart, what would become of her son? She *knew* all the reasons to tread carefully. So why was it so difficult to take her own advice—the very same advice she'd been giving to Rosmanda?

Sadie didn't remember when she fell asleep, but when she awoke the next morning, her eyes fluttered open, and she reached a hand out to touch her son's back . . . but he wasn't there. Sadie sat up in bed, her gaze flying around the room and landing on Samuel's little, sleeping form—in his own bed.

She rubbed a hand over her eyes. Was that childhood phase of coming to his mother at night over? If she'd known that the other night was the last one he'd crawl up next to her, maybe she'd have snuggled him a little closer. It was strange how slowly Samuel's years could crawl by, and then in a blink, he was suddenly bigger, older, needing her a little bit less. It only went to confirm that she'd made the right decision last night. She had a son to consider, too, and love wasn't always enough—at least not this time.

Sadie pushed back her covers and reached for her dress. She dressed quickly and pinned everything together by feel. In a matter of minutes, her hair was combed and she had her kapp in place, the strings tied. She took one last look at her sleeping son, then she stepped quietly from her bedroom.

Mamm came out of her room at the same time that Sadie did, and when Sadie moved toward Rosmanda's door, Mamm shook her head.

"Let her sleep," Mamm whispered. "I wanted to talk to you."

Sadie's heart sank. Had Mamm noticed more than she'd let on during that silent drive back from the hospital?

Mamm led the way downstairs into the kitchen, and Sadie hoped that her mother wouldn't ask her too many questions about Elijah. She'd made the right choice—the one her parents would approve of—and talking about it would only bring back the tears. She'd rather get to work and drown her heartache in chores.

"Sadie, I'm worried about your sister," Mamm said quietly. "I know that she's been sidetracked with a boy, which is all very normal at her age, but I've heard some rumors, and I want you to tell me what you know."

Sadie's stomach clenched. "Rumors?" Had it gone so far, already?

"Well, perhaps not rumors exactly. I know some things because of your father's position . . ."

"Mamm, Rosmanda thinks she's in love with Jonathan Yoder," Sadie said with a sigh.

"So, she's the one to break them up . . ." Mamm breathed. "Are you sure?"

"She's determined to marry him herself," Sadie replied with a weak shrug. "And yes, I've told her all the reasons why she's being an idiot."

Mamm smiled wanly. "I would expect as much." Then Mamm sobered. "So when Jonathan broke up with Mary, it was for our Rosmanda?"

"Rosie seems to think so," Sadie replied.

Mamm sighed. "I don't want to lose another child to the Englishers, Sadie."

Sadie nodded, silent. She could understand that fear. She carried a similar one. But how was a mother supposed to guide her child through the labyrinth of choices?

"She wants to marry him right away," Sadie said. "She wants to skip her Rumspringa completely."

"She can't," Mamm replied with a shake of her head.

"That's what I told her," Sadie said.

"I'm glad it's confirmed," Mamm said. "At least I know how to talk to her now."

As easy as that? Mamm had this in hand? Sadie wished she felt so confident with her own child. Love wasn't about warm feelings, but Elijah was right—what was duty and devotion without it? But a son could break his mother's heart just as efficiently as the wrong husband could break his wife's. Perhaps she was chasing something different from a warm feeling—to avoid heartbreak at the hands of the men she loved. All her caution hadn't helped a bit when it came to Elijah.

That morning, the community arrived to do chores, mend fences, do the work that had been falling behind the last few months. The women helped cook so that everyone could eat, but Elijah did not come. Sadie watched for him, marking each buggy as it arrived, but Elijah's buggy never showed, and she felt a wave of disappointment so strong that it nearly buckled her. But she understood. It was time for them both to forge ahead alone. Seeing him again would only make this hurt more. One thing she was sure of—she had no perspective right now. She was no better than her sister, coasting on a wave of emotion. It was no way to make life choices.

Sadie knew why Elijah was keeping away, and she could see that it was for the best for both of them, but her chest ached nonetheless, and she felt filled to the brim with tears that wouldn't drain away no matter how hard she cried into her pillow at night.

Two days later, Daet returned from the hospital. Mamm and Rosmanda went to fetch him this time, and Sadie stayed home with her son, quietly fixing dinner and cleaning house with her little boy at her heels until everyone arrived back home.

Everything felt more stable with Daet around. He had several bottles of medication now, and a firm doctor's order that he not only slow down, but find someone else to take over his workload. Daet promised to hire three new employees, all part time so Daet could stagger their shifts to cover as much work as possible. Daet would go out and supervise when he felt well enough, but Mamm had gotten more forceful in her commands, and Daet was required to rest. There would be no more "pushing it." In most ways, it felt like life had gone back to normal—Daet was back, and Elijah was gone.

And Rosmanda was furious with Sadie for having told Mamm her secrets.

"Rosie," Sadie sighed. "I'm sorry. You'll forgive me eventually."

"No, you aren't sorry," Rosmanda snapped. "Jonathan has stayed away, and it's because of you. Mamm threatened him with the elders."

"Well, now he'll have Daet to deal with," Sadie replied. "And if he's serious about you—"

"He doesn't love her," Rosmanda hissed. "I know that. He told me himself that he was very distant and proper with Mary. He treated her like a *sister*. He just couldn't see himself as a husband to her. So their breaking up isn't my fault! Would you have him locked into an unhappy marriage just because he made a mistake in proposing to her? They were not married yet, Sadie. Those vows were *not* said. He had every right to back out if he wanted to. I know what he was feeling for me, but you won't believe me. So why do I bother talking?"

Rosmanda had a very good point about a couple having the chance to cancel a wedding before the vows were said. It was better to walk away than to marry the wrong person in haste. His cheating on the first girl, however, spoke volumes about his character. If Sadie could move on after Elijah, then Rosie could move on after Jonathan.

"I love him!" Tears rose in Rosmanda's eyes. "And I will never forgive you, and I will never get over this!"

"Rosie, you're nearly grown up now," Sadie said quietly. "And as a mature member of this community, there will be times that you give up what you want for the greater good. I have been forced to do the same thing more often than you realize. I suggest you calm down and watch Jonathan Yoder. See what he does. He's just come against an obstacle. How a man deals with something in his path says a great deal about him. Will he find an honorable way to make you his, or will he simply walk away?"

And as she said the words, an image of Elijah burned in her heart. She'd been held in strong arms recently, too. She'd been kissed, and she'd declared her love for a man who was all wrong for her. . . . Sometimes, a woman had to set her feelings aside.

"And if he stays true to me?" Rosmanda demanded.

"Then when you are of age, I will support the marriage," Sadie replied.

"You mean that?" Her younger sister sounded breathless. "You aren't just saying that?"

"No, I mean it. If he stays true to you, I won't have any power to stop that wedding, Rosie. You'll be eighteen. But Rose . . ." Sadie sighed. "Your Rumspringa . . . don't go too far with Jonathan. You don't want to end up pregnant and ruin your chance at an honorable wedding."

"Of course." Rosmanda smiled for the first time. "I'm not that stupid."

Except so many of these "stupid" choices weren't made with a logical mind—they were made in the heat of the moment, when logic was turned upside down and all that seemed to matter was love. Sadie had shared some passionate kisses, too.

Daet ambled into the kitchen and smiled at his daughters absently. "Would one of you make me a tea?"

"Sure, Daet." Sadie got the kettle and filled it at the sink.

"I'll be reading banns at church next Sunday," Daet said conversationally.

"Whose?" Sadie and Rosmanda both turned at the same time. Daet regarded them calmly, then pursed his lips.

"Jonathan Yoder and Mary Beiler," he replied.

"No, Daet," Rosmanda said with a shake of her head. "They broke up. It's been called off. Did Mamm not tell you?"

"I stayed more informed than you might like to think,"

Daet said. "The wedding was called off, but then they discovered that Mary was pregnant."

Sadie stared at her father, aghast. "Pregnant?"

"It seems so." Her father nodded. "So there will definitely be a wedding—and quickly."

"But—" Rosmanda's eyes filled with tears. "But he said . . ."

"I'm not sure what he told you," Daet replied evenly. "But he got that Beiler girl pregnant, and he'll do the right thing by her or be shunned. There's no in between."

"He said he didn't love her . . ." Rosmanda's voice wavered. "He said . . . he didn't even kiss her—"

"He did a far sight more than that, Rosmanda," Daet said with a grimace, and Rosmanda's face crumpled into heaving, shaking sobs. Sadie started toward her sister, but Daet waved her off and pushed himself to his feet. He pulled his youngest daughter into his arms and held her firmly, rocking her slowly back and forth, his cheek pressed against her hair while Rosmanda wept.

"Now, now, Rosie," Daet said softly. "Now, now . . ."

Rosie sniffled and pulled back. "But you don't understand, Daet. He told me that he loved me, not her. He said she was like a sister to him. He said—"

"Now, Rosie," Daet said, putting his hands on her shoulders and looking into her red-rimmed eyes. "I'm going to tell you something that I want you to understand. Not every man is honest, sweet girl. Some are bare-faced liars. And if it means getting a husband's right for free, many a young man will lie his heart out. Unfortunately, you found a liar in Jonathan Yoder, and he'll pay for that. He's going to marry the Beiler girl—the elders will make sure of it." He paused. "You didn't let him—"

"No, Daet!" Rosie's face tinged pink, and then another tear trickled down her cheek.

Daet wiped her tears with the pad of his thumb. "You're

a beautiful girl, and you'll be married with a home of your own before I know it. But this home—with your Mamm and I—this will always be yours. Even after you're married. Do you hear me?"

Outside the house, an engine rumbled up the drive, and Sadie slipped away from her father and sister, and headed into the mudroom to open the side door to check who was in their drive. She felt wrung out, emotionally spent, and while she knew that her sister needed emotional support right now, she was glad that her parents could provide it. Sadie had been through enough. She pushed open the door and looked outside. Her breath stuck in her throat.

"Oh my God . . ." Sadie croaked, the words echoing like a curse. Her heart stuttered and did a quickstep to catch up. She didn't know the car, but she knew that driver!

"Who is it?" Rosie came up behind Sadie, and both women watched as Absolom opened the driver's side door and stepped out of the vehicle, slamming it behind him. Then he opened the back door, bent down and disappeared inside.

A little hand pressed against the back of Sadie's leg, and Sadie bent down to take Samuel's hand in hers. What was Absolom doing here? Was he finally home, at long last?

"Mamm?" Sammie said, sensing her shock, perhaps. He clutched her hand in a vise grip, then leaned out to get a better look.

"Absolom!" Rosmanda gasped. "It's Absolom! Mamm, Daet!"

Absolom emerged from the vehicle with a baby's car seat in one hand and little Chase coming up behind. Sadie looked back at her father to see him standing ramrod straight, his face as white as a sheet.

"Daet, are you okay?"

"Is it really him?" Daet breathed.

"Yah, Daet. It's him."

Daet didn't move an inch. He stood there, one hand over his chest, and the other on the doorframe. Absolom was here with the children, but Sharon was nowhere in sight.

Elijah stood in his father's little shop, tapping a pen against his hand as he waited for a customer. There had been two this morning—but only one order. Fisher Fencing wasn't exactly booming.

The shop was a clapboard affair on the far end of Uber Street in Morinville. All the barbed wire weaving happened on site.

"It's done," Daet said. "The Graber order is ready for delivery. Will you drop it by tonight?"

"I, uh—" Elijah winced. "Daet, he fired me, remember?"

"Yes, and you're delivering his order—working with your daet. There's no shame in a family business, son."

"I know you're working hard, and no one can fault that, Daet, but this business won't last. You have to know that. It's why you asked me to come back—" Elijah stopped when his father's face fell. "Look, I don't mean to be negative, but we have to face facts. If you're going to have a business that can compete, then something will have to change."

"And you have an idea," his father said bitterly.

"I've learned a few things with the Englishers." Elijah leaned forward. "I know Amish aim to keep their businesses small and manageable, but making the actual barbed wire—you're at the bottom of the ladder here. You need to be thinking bigger. A lot of people with acreages, or with hobby farms, have no idea what they're doing. On top of which, serious farmers are busy. When do they have time to install their own fencing?"

"So you suggest I add installation," his father concluded.

"No, I'm thinking bigger than that, too." Elijah rubbed

a hand over his chin. "This is the idea that Absolom and I are working with in the city. We're starting a business doing landscaping and snow removal. But it'll be more than that—we'll be the whole solution. Now, Daet, you know fencing inside and out. I suggest that you become a consultant, a planner. You would go to the location, give an estimate on how much fencing will be needed, the type of fencing that would be best, and locate the best materials for the job at the lowest price. You could even offer installation service—all at a price—and when you walk away, the fencing is complete and the farmer or Englisher acreage owner hasn't had to deal with any of the bother."

"And this would make money?" His father squinted at him.

"There is one thing I learned from the Englishers, and it's that they respect us Amish when it comes to farming and crafts. An Amish-made fence—that would be worth something to a fair number of people in this county."

"No." His father shook his head decisively. "I don't like it."

"Daet, you aren't listening . . ."

"No, you aren't listening!" His father's voice rose to a thunder. "My father made fencing with his own two hands, as did his father before him. And he learned from his father-in-law, who brought him into the business. And before that man is a whole line of fence-making Amish. Tradition, my boy! Tradition!"

"And that's all you care about, isn't it?" Elijah's voice undercut his father's. "Tradition—the Amish way. Even when your teenage son left, you clung to tradition . . ."

"I *gave you* tradition!" his father retorted. "What did you want me to do? I gave you everything I had!"

And his father couldn't be faulted there. He'd done his best to support the family, but when things got complicated, his father leaned back on the faith . . . as if a collection of rules could fix what had gone wrong in his son.

"You could have come after me," Elijah said. "You could have come to see where I lived."

Silence stretched between them, and his father slowly shook his head. "The bishop said—"

"Blast the bishop!" Elijah snapped. "The bishop said . . . and you were willing to risk your son based on the opinion of one man?"

"Watch your language," his father said, then sighed. "It wasn't only the bishop. What of the Ordnung? The traditions of generations past have guided us for good reason."

Elijah felt that old rage simmering up inside of him. "I didn't want the wisdom of the ages, Daet. I needed my father."

"I had no answers!" his father said, his voice rising in frustration.

"I didn't ask for solutions, Daet. I need you! That's what I hated about this community. The rules, rules, rules . . . they weren't what was inside of me, Daet. Rules weren't *enough*."

Elijah heaved a sigh and walked to the window, watching the cars creep along the street, stuck behind a buggy.

"And was Chicago enough?" his father demanded.

"It might be." With more work. With some luck. If the business took off.

"Let's start again. Stay for a little while. Help me implement your ideas."

Elijah rubbed his hands over his face. "I can't, Daet. I'm starting a business with Absolom, and he's counting on me. I couldn't count on this community to come after me, but damn it, Daet, *I'm* better than that." Even if his own father wasn't. Even if the bishop wasn't. Elijah could choose to be a bigger man. "I can't do this—be happy here, like this."

"And you can be happy without *her*?" his father asked, ignoring his language this time.

Elijah hadn't even mentioned Sadie, but he hadn't exactly been hiding his feelings, either. Was it common knowledge in Morinville at this point—that he was in love with a woman who knew she deserved better? "No, I can't be happy without her, but I can't change who I am, either."

"I wanted to come see you, son," his father said quietly.

"But the rules held you back," Elijah concluded. "And the bishop. You went against any fatherly instinct you had to obey that man, and you let me go. This is the community I'm supposed to trust? The very traditions that held you and me apart?"

Tears misted his father's eyes. "Yes."

"How?" Elijah demanded. "Because you taught me a lesson? Because I now know you can hold out until I buckle? Is that it?"

"Because you're one of us," his father said quietly. "We all doubt. We all get scared. Doubt and fear don't change who you are, son. You'll have to make your peace with that, either here with us, or out there with the Englishers. You can't get away from who you are."

Who he was . . . Elijah was the kind of man who liked a risk and a jump—and cruelly enough, no matter how desperately he longed to fly, he landed in that lonesome no-man's-land between his Amish heritage and the Englisher world. Even so, Elijah wasn't the kind of man who turned his back on his family. He wasn't the kind of man who chose tradition over the people he loved. Regulations didn't rule him.

But even if Elijah made his peace with his own demons, it wouldn't change what Sadie needed in a husband—tradition! Even if he stayed, he'd be forced to watch her move on with another man who'd never love her half well enough. Or worse . . . he'd watch her marry a man who would adore her as she deserved, and he'd have the distinct agony of witnessing it. He loved her, and if nine years hadn't cured him of it, nothing would. He was an interloper, a man stuck between two worlds, not Amish enough for Sadie and not Englisher enough, either.

"I'll deliver the fencing," Elijah said, and he held out his hand for the handwritten receipt.

"Son, I do love you," his father said gruffly. "I'm sorry— I thought I was doing what was best . . ."

"Yah, Daet, I know."

Tradition fueled his father's work; it drove the Amish community. They chose tradition because it held them back, it trimmed their wings, it dug in deep. Tradition told them how to live, what to choose, and what had value. Careful thought and cautious steps—that's how the Amish moved forward.

And yet his father was right—he'd never be happy without Sadie. Forgetting her wasn't even an option. His heart belonged to her whether she wanted it or not. He *was* Amish, born and raised. Elijah wasn't like the other Amish men, but maybe Elijah offered something that tradition could not . . .

Maybe there was still a way.

Chapter Nineteen

Sadie's heart leapt in her chest as Mamm came around the side of the house with a handful of beets in her hands. Mamm stopped, stared, and then tears welled in her eyes. She dropped the produce and ran toward her son.

"Absolom!" Tears rolled down her cheeks, and she wrapped her arms around his neck, kissing his cheek over and over before she released him and looked into the car seat.

"That's Sarah," Absolom said. "And this, here, is Chase."

The little boy stared up at them, his eyes round and filled with heartbreak. Chase was here without his mother—the mother Chase assured her would come back. *She always comes back.* Where was she now? Dread wormed its way up Sadie's stomach. Something was wrong—very wrong.

Daet came out and there were more introductions, but a wagon turned into the drive, the horses clopping steadily toward them. She recognized Elijah immediately, and she squeezed Samuel's hand a little tighter.

She hadn't seen Elijah since that night when they'd both said too much, and now he was here—driving a pair of draft horses that pulled a flat wagon, a load in the back that she couldn't make out. She didn't know why he was here, but she was grateful for his arrival all the same. There was something about Elijah that steadied her when she was off balance, and she had to curb the urge to run down the drive toward him.

They'd have to stop that—the slipping into each other's arms so easily. They were like magnets, always seeming to clap back together again, and it wouldn't do—her heart couldn't take any more of this, and she had a son who needed her, too.

Samuel tugged free of Sadie's hand and trotted toward Chase—as he would. Samuel didn't get to see other children that often, so a little boy about his own age was a rare treat. Daet glanced up at the approaching wagon, and Sadie strode down the steps and put her hand on her father's arm as she passed him.

"I'll see what he wants," she said.

As if that was her only reason to be heading toward him . . . but the family didn't need to know about their unrequited feelings for each other. This would be her own personal grief, and she'd get over it privately, as she'd done before.

"Hi," Elijah said as she came up beside the wagon. His gaze moved between Absolom and Sadie. "What's happening?"

"I don't know, exactly," Sadie said. "My brother just arrived with the kids."

"And Sharon?" Elijah swung down to the ground and reached for her hand—something he seemed to do without thinking. Sadie pulled her hand back. Holding hands every time she saw him wouldn't make this any easier. Elijah's face colored. "Sorry."

Sadie took a step back and looked toward her family. "I have no idea where Sharon is. . . . You don't think—"

"He can't return without her," Elijah said with a shrug. "I mean, unless she left him, but the kids . . ."

"Yah. That's my thought. If the children are here, then this is just a visit."

A wave of sadness washed over her, and she heaved a sigh. Just a visit meant that in a matter of days, her brother would be shunned, and this would be the last time he saw his family. This would be one last, agonizing good-bye.

"Why are you here?" Sadie asked, glancing at the back of the wagon. A tarp covered something large and round.

"I'm delivering barbed-wire fencing," Elijah said.

"So you're working with your daet?" She squinted up at him. "After all, I mean."

"Yah." He nodded quickly. "Until I go back. . . . Sadie, I've missed you."

Sadie swallowed as her throat tightened with emotion. "We'll get used to it. I did before."

Anyone could endure grief. Over time it lessened, and one learned to carry around the burden of it a little more easily. She'd learned to carry that aching loneliness when Absolom and Elijah disappeared, and she'd shouldered the grief of her husband's death. She could endure this, too . . . if she could just find her balance underneath it.

Sadie watched as Daet shook Absolom's hand, his lined face awash in emotion. After nine years of longing to see him again, her parents were finally able to touch their son. She could only imagine what they were feeling right now.

"Come on, then," Sadie said. "You might as well come in. You're as much a part of this as anyone."

It was better to see where things stood, because she couldn't cling to any more useless hope.

"Let's get you all inside," Mamm said, broadening her gaze to include Elijah this time. "Come on, now. This is something to celebrate!"

Everyone went inside, and there was a jumble of chatter and commotion while Mamm brought out shoofly pie.

Rosmanda made lemonade, and Sadie stared at her brother in silence.

Was he back? Was this a homecoming? Or was it something else? There was sadness in her brother's eyes that Sadie couldn't dismiss. She bent over the car seat, fumbled with the clasps, then lifted tiny Sarah into her arms. The baby wriggled and snuggled into the crook of her arm, and Sadie looked down into that infant face—a little older already—and wondered if this would be the last time she'd hold her niece.

Chase edged closer to Samuel, and the boys regarded each other solemnly. They weren't cousins in the traditional sense, but they were connected to each other.

"Where's your TV?" Chase asked.

Samuel blinked, confused. He wouldn't even know what a television was.

"There is no TV here, Chase," Sadie said, crouching down next to him with Sarah tipped up onto her shoulder. "Here we have cows and horses, and barns and fields . . . but no TV."

"Oh . . ." Chase looked around. "Where's the cows?"

"Outside."

"I've never seen a cow."

That statement might have shocked Sadie before she'd seen her brother's life in the city, but it didn't surprise her now. Chase likely had never left the city.

"Then you're in for a treat. We'll show you some while you're here," Sadie said with a reassuring smile. "Where's your mamm?"

"Mommy," he corrected her, and then Chase's lower lip quivered, and his face crumpled into tears. Sadie stood up, and since Elijah was the closest one to her, she passed the infant into his strong arms, then gathered Chase into hers. Chase pulled his knees up to fit all of himself onto her lap, closing himself into a ball as he sobbed into her shoulder, his entire body shaking with the force of his grief.

"Chase?" she whispered. "Chase, what's happened?"

But he was too young to explain, if he even knew. She'd cared for nieces and nephews for years before she had Samuel, so she knew a child's cry, and she'd never heard a sob so deep and guttural as this one. Sadie stayed crouched on the ground with the boy in her arms, and she stared at her brother in horror. "Absolom . . ."

Her brother looked toward her at the sound of Chase's crying. "You okay, buddy?" her brother asked, then he shrugged helplessly. "Maybe it's been a long day."

This had nothing to do with a child's exhaustion. This was deeper . . .

"I asked him where his mother is," Sadie said. "And his heart broke. Absolom, where is Sharon?"

Silence settled over the kitchen, and Absolom shifted uncomfortably in his seat. Elijah rocked back and forth in an instinctual rhythm with the infant in his arms, but the rest of the family was as still as ice. All eyes were on Absolom.

"She—uh—went out with some friends. . . . At least I thought that was where she was going. Later, I found a note she'd left." Absolom's chin trembled, and he swallowed hard. "The note said that it was too much. She couldn't take it anymore. She said she hated the kind of mother she was, and she just wanted—"

Her brother didn't finish, and he looked toward his mother pleadingly. He'd come back for help—Sadie could see it in his eyes.

"When we were there?" Sadie asked.

"No, she came back that time." Absolom's agonized gaze flickered toward her. "It was a few days later. In the note, she asked if I'd take the kids. I kept it, in case there was any legal trouble."

"She left her children?" Sadie said, switching to German to spare Chase, but her eyes welled with tears. "She left them behind?"

"Yah." Absolom sucked in a shaky breath. "She left us all. That's why I'm here. I need help."

Elijah felt pinned to the spot by the slight weight of the baby girl in his arms, and his heart slammed in his chest. Sharon had left her children? It was too horrible to wrap his head around in just a moment, and he absently patted the baby's diapered rump as the reality of the situation sank in. Sharon—his friend who had watched hours of television with him, clued him in on how things worked in the Englisher world . . . Sharon, the one who had loved Elijah in spite of all their differences, who'd sat up with them both late into the night listening to them talk about their families, their heartbreak, their anger . . .

She'd just left?

"Doesn't this . . . Sharon . . . have family?" Bishop Graber asked.

"No." Elijah answered for Absolom this time. "She was raised in what's called the foster system. She had no parents, and once she turned eighteen, she was on her own."

She understood loneliness as well as they did—she'd just had a lifetime to get used to it.

"No family . . ." Sarah shook her head slowly. "So you've come home, then?" She turned to Absolom with a faint smile. "You'll raise your children here—as Amish."

"No." Absolom cleared his throat. "I can't, Mamm. I'm sorry. I want the kids to have a safe and happy childhood—

I want them to swim in the creek and climb trees. I want Chase to see cows, finally! But I can't stay here—"

"Why not?" the bishop boomed, rising to his feet. "What holds you back from coming home now?"

"Me!" Absolom raked his fingers through his hair. "I'm not the same, Daet! I can't settle back into this life! The world is so much bigger than this . . . and I can't just leave Sharon behind. She's going to hate herself for having done this—I know her. I've got to find her."

Absolom's voice trailed off, and they were left in silence. Absolom was in love with Sharon, and he couldn't just turn that off, either. Elijah understood his friend's heartbreak better than anyone. Sometimes a woman could lodge so deeply into a man's heart that he simply couldn't move on without her.

"Then how do you suggest we help you?" Sarah asked desperately, and Absolom understood her panic. They lived a simple life right here in Morinville. They never traveled more than ten miles in either direction. What could they even offer him?

"Take care of my kids, Mamm," Absolom said quietly. "Until I can find their mother again. Elijah and I will start up our business, and that will give us more financial stability. Then I can take them back again and provide for them properly. But that building isn't a safe place for little kids. And the daycares I could afford—I don't think they're safe, either. I can't do it alone. I need someone to help me out, Mamm. Please."

"No . . ." she whispered. "Son, you have to come back—" Her voice shook. "In two days, the community votes on your shunning. . . . If you leave these children here, and you come back shunned—what would they see?"

"Shunning!" Absolom's voice rose in desperation.

"You've refused our counsel, chosen life outside of God's will," the bishop said woodenly. "If I don't offer you up to community justice in the same way any other son would be, then I am worse than a hypocrite."

"You won't help me . . ." Absolom breathed. "Even now."

But a thought had started to turn in Elijah's mind. Tradition was powerful and demanding, but perhaps Elijah could offer something that tradition could not—a way out.

"Bishop Graber," Elijah said and adjusted the baby in his arms. "If Absolom were shunned and had no food, we would be permitted to feed him."

"Yah." The bishop frowned. "But you could not sit with him while he ate."

"And if Absolom were shunned and we came across him wounded in the road, we could bring him back to our own land and nurse him back to health."

"Yah." The bishop's frown deepened. "But once he was well, you'd be required to turn your back once more."

"Even if Absolom is shunned, he could visit his children—have some time alone with them. The children wouldn't be Amish—not in the strictest sense—and not until they were adults and could choose through baptism."

"We could . . ." Sarah's breath grew shallow and hopeful.

"No!" the bishop roared.

Little Sarah started to cry. Elijah adjusted the baby up against his shoulder, leaning his cheek next to her downy head.

"You are my son, Absolom—" Tears welled in the bishop's eyes. "But I cannot bend for you anymore. If you don't come back home, confess your sin, and rejoin our community—" A tear slipped down the weathered face of the old bishop. "If you don't come home properly, then I cannot make the consequences of your bad choices any easier for you to bear. You chose the Englisher life, and you discovered just how much you gave up when you made that choice. You either come home fully and completely, or nothing. These children will not be raised in this house without you."

The baby's cries subsided with Elijah's rocking, and he looked down at Chase sitting on Sadie's lap. His large eyes were fixed on Elijah in heartbroken confusion. This conversation was in German, a language he didn't know, but Chase seemed to sense the import of the words, if not the meaning.

Elijah had known Chase since he was a toddler, and this boy's little heart couldn't take any more rejection . . . and neither could Elijah's. He knew what it was like to be cast aside, to feel like an outsider no matter where he went. He knew what it felt like to have his community turn their back on him, to have his own father choose a church over him. He'd never outrun that aching part of his heart, and it was very possible that he'd never fully heal from that betrayal with the English, either. He'd have to find his peace with it all, and maybe he could find some meaning by making a difference in the lives of two children—giving them the acceptance he'd missed.

"The children won't be raised in this house," Elijah said slowly. "We must respect that. But they could be raised in mine—"

All eyes swept toward Elijah, and he looked down at the infant in his arms. So small, so fragile, and already being cast out. He knew that he was letting his friend down in one way, but he could make it up with this offer.

"Absolom, I know we said we'd open that business together, but what if I stayed here? What if I took the kids and loved them like my own until you could come for them? I won't have Chase rejected again. I'll raise him. I'll love him like my own. And I'll raise this little girl, too."

"How?" the bishop demanded. "You're a single man!"

"My mamm will help me. She'd never turn away helpless

children. She'll be glad to have some kinner in the house again."

Heaven knew she might not ever get grandchildren from him.

Absolom rubbed a hand over his face, his shoulders seeming to deflate. "I don't make enough to raise them. I'd keep them with me if I could, but if I knew they were safe, and if I could visit them—"

Elijah turned to the bishop. He was their spiritual leader. As much as Elijah wanted to do right by his friend, he could not do so without the bishop's blessing.

"Please, Bishop Graber," Elijah said quietly. "I am asking your permission to accept these children into my home. I will raise them as Amish, and I will make it my life's duty and sole goal to give them the faith of my forefathers. I'm not family, but I'm Absolom's friend. I want to do right by Absolom, and by you. If you'll allow it."

The bishop was silent, and he turned toward Sarah, his eyes searching her face for answers.

"Mamm?" he murmured. "What do you say?"

Sarah nodded slowly. "You will maintain the community's respect for standing by what is right and true. You'll spare them seeing any weakness from you, and you won't be the cause of any weaker member to stumble." She reached out and took his weathered hand in hers. "And the kinner could be safe and loved with the Fishers."

"What about my shunning?" Absolom asked quietly.

"That is up to the community, my son," the bishop said, his voice tight with emotion. "The community will speak. That is out of my hands."

Absolom crossed the room and eased the baby out of Elijah's arms. He looked down into his daughter's face, and tears spilled down his cheeks.

"I will visit, little one," he whispered hoarsely. "I'll love you always, and I promise to visit just as often as I can . . ."

Sadie rose to her feet with the boy in her arms, his short legs wrapped around her waist. Samuel stood at her side, his eyes wide and his blond curls rumpled. Elijah had just taken on a family—and chosen to stay. His heart hammered in his chest, and he searched his own emotions, looking for a sign that he was making a miserable mistake. Would he regret this—staying here—if it meant that Sadie still married another man? The Amish life ran deep, and there could be pain in that plunge. Not everyone chose an Amish life out of religious certainty—at least Elijah hadn't. He'd always question, but maybe he could repay his friend a little bit. Maybe he wouldn't ever be a wealthy man, but he could make a difference for two little children who needed to be chosen just once.

"Thank you, Elijah," Absolom said, tears in his voice. "I don't know how I can repay you—"

"Just come home . . . someday," Elijah pleaded. "Find a way to come home."

Elijah had found his way home, and as he looked down at Sadie beside him, her gentle gaze met his. He loved her . . . oh, how he loved her. She'd been his plumb line and his foundation for years, even when he was away. And she'd continue to be, even if she married a man more deserving than he was.

Sometimes the way home hurt more than the road that led away, because instead of spreading wider, it carved down deeper. There was nothing easy about the narrow path, but looking at these children, Elijah knew he was making the right choice.

They needed him, and he would need this community to support him in this new role. His faith wasn't based on certainty—it was supported by hope and a sense that the God who required the narrow path of the Amish could accept his wayward heart, too.

Chapter Twenty

The sun had already set as Sadie walked with her brother to his car. Back inside the house, Samuel was already in bed. Mamm gathered up some cloth diapers and baby girl clothes for little Sarah while Chase dozed off on Elijah's lap. The children's lives would never be the same, and they would discover that bit by bit. She pitied them—especially Chase—whose faith in everyone would be shaken now that his mother had broken her promise to always come back. How did a child recover from that?

Sadie crossed her arms against the chill in the air, and she eyed her brother sadly.

"Are you sure you can't stay? Even for a little while?"

Absolom shook his head. "I love all of this, I do—" He looked around at the house, the familiar old tree in the front, the buggy barn beside them . . . "But Sadie, I'm too different now. I can't just walk away from everything I'm learning. I really think I can make something of myself—more than just a road worker. I'm going to go start my own business."

An Englisher life. She swallowed hard. "And the kinner?"

"I'll visit them," he replied with a small smile. "Even if

I'm shunned. They can't take my kids away from me. There are laws against that. So they can stand with their backs to me all they like—I'm visiting my kids."

Sadie smiled mistily. "If I'm forced to stand with my back to you, I'm going to cross my fingers behind my back so that you know I'm saying hello."

"My sister, the rebel?" He raised an eyebrow. "I'm not sure I believe this."

Tears welled in Sadie's eyes. "I'm going to miss you, Absolom."

He nodded. "Me, too."

Sadie licked her lips. "I'll get married again. You have to promise to hate my next husband less."

"If you promise to marry a man worthy of you," her brother shot back, and they exchanged a wobbly smile.

"Is there any chance you might come back—for good?" she asked.

Absolom was silent for a moment, his gaze trained on the house behind her. Then he said, "I don't believe what the church teaches, and that's big. I used to believe it, so there was no problem in that respect. My issue was with Daet and his demands of us. . . . I'm glad I got to see him again, but I can't pretend to believe something I no longer believe, or just go through the motions."

"For the children?" she asked hesitantly.

"I'll get an education—that's for the kids," he said. "And a better job, and live in a safer part of town. That's for them, too. I'll find their mother, and I'll remind her about the woman I know she is . . . but I won't fake belief for my kids. They need to see better from me than that."

It was impossible now—as she'd suspected. Once someone left, they changed in elemental ways . . . the secret was to never leave to begin with. Was that it? And her heart clenched a little tighter. It was her deepest maternal fear.

"And for all that," her brother went on, his voice thick with emotion, "they're still my parents, Sadie. But no one comes back for theology."

Sadie fell silent, her mind working over it all. The church was central to the Amish life, and they believed that there was no salvation outside of it. Not for those who were born to it, at least. So when children left, parents wrote long letters explaining the church's position, defending the reasons for the narrow path they walked. What better reason to return than for eternal salvation? They couldn't imagine their child viewing faith differently—the Amish weren't exposed to religious differences.

But Absolom had changed so much—she could see it. The old arguments fell impotent. If he did come back, it wouldn't be for theological argument, but because he loved them. . . . If he ever came back, it would be for *them*.

Sadie wrapped her arms around her brother's neck and hugged him tight.

"Come home as soon as you can, Absolom," she whispered shakily. "We miss you so much."

Her brother hugged her back just as fiercely, and then he let her go.

"Keep an eye on Chase and Sarah, okay?" he said, blinking and pressing his lips flat to hold back the tears. "Bring Chase to the creek—I think he'd really like it. He needs to catch fish and balance on rocks . . . and Sarah likes the old hymns. I used to sing them to her at night when everyone else was asleep, so I know that will comfort her. Maybe it will remind her of me."

"You'll be back to visit them soon," she said firmly. "And I'll keep close tabs on them. That's a promise."

"Thank you. I'd better go. It only gets harder."

Sadie nodded, and Absolom pulled open the car door and got inside. The engine rumbled to life, and Sadie watched as the car turned around and headed back down the drive. She stood there for several minutes after the red taillights had disappeared, the cool evening breeze billowing her dress in front of her.

Life had been simpler before she'd gotten a glimpse of her brother's life with the Englishers. There had been the right way and the wrong way . . . there had been the narrow path and the road to perdition. And while she had no desire to live apart from her Amish upbringing, the Englisher world seemed that much more daunting, because it no longer appeared to be composed of aimless, chaotic sinners. She could see how easy it was for a disillusioned Amish boy to go Mennonite . . .

She'd been so afraid of Samuel growing up with too permissive of a father, without the structure to keep him Amish, that she'd forgotten what would draw him home again. It was love—that was the invisible thread that wove them all together. Samuel needed what Chase and baby Sarah needed—parents who loved them as deeply and widely as the human heart could stretch.

Sadie heard the house door open behind her, and she turned to see Elijah on the porch.

"Sadie, I need to bring the kids back to my place," Elijah said. "Would you help me? I can drive you back after my mother has them settled, if that's okay."

If only her father hadn't drawn the line at caring for Absolom's children. She should be the one tucking them in, and waking up at night to give little Sarah her bottle. She could have opened her heart to these children . . .

"Yes, of course," Sadie said, wiping an errant tear from her cheek. "You hitch up the horses, and I'll get the children ready to go."

* * *

Elijah held the reins loosely in his hands, the peacefulness of the drive home settling in around him. He was staying . . . the choice he'd made in the Grabers' kitchen was starting to feel suddenly real. He knew this was the right thing to do, but it certainly wouldn't be easy.

The draft horses knew the way home, and Elijah looked over at Sadie, who sat with the baby in one arm and her other arm around Chase, who had drifted off to sleep against her side.

"What were you thinking?" Sadie asked with a soft laugh.

"It was when your father told Absolom no, that he would do nothing to help him unless he came home and repented," Elijah said. "I couldn't let the children face that kind of rejection. It was wrong. I had to set it right."

"You're taking on two children, Elijah."

"Yah. It seems so, but I owed your brother. He needed someone he could count on. Besides, there would be no changing your daet, or mine, so I decided to be the difference for someone else."

The stars twinkled in the dark sky. An orange moon hung low on the horizon, large and luminous. He'd pull Sadie close if they didn't have a four-year-old between them and a baby in her arms. . . . He wasn't supposed to be thinking about those things with Sadie anymore— he was trying to have self-restraint in that respect. But he couldn't help it. There was something about the moonlight reflecting off her pale skin, the way her eyes glittered when she glanced over at him, and the tender way she cradled the children. . . . It made the rest of their problems seem far away.

"You think you can do this alone?" she asked after a moment.

"I don't have much choice, do I?" He flicked the reins.

He looked over at her, and those glittering blue eyes were fixed on him. She was beautiful, and just close enough for him to . . . he leaned over and brushed his lips with hers. "I promise I'll stop kissing you . . . starting tomorrow."

"Tomorrow?" She laughed softly.

"Always tomorrow. I can't face it today." He smiled into her eyes, then straightened.

"I talked to my brother before he left, and I realized something," she said.

"Yah?"

"The thing that pulled him back wasn't theology or agreement with the Amish ways. He's tugged back because he loves us, and we love him. If he ever finds a way to make a life here, it will be for that love."

Love . . . it could be the sweetest of experiences, and the most painful.

"I'll never stop loving you, you know," he said quietly.

What did it matter if he was changing? It wouldn't be enough to turn him into a solemn farmer. He'd only be more of himself, and like his daet had said, if he pretended to be otherwise, he couldn't keep it up.

Sadie's hand touched his arm. "You need a wife to help you, Elijah," she said quietly.

"I need *you*, Sadie." The words came out before he could help himself, and he sighed. "But if I'm not the man for you, then I'll muddle along on my own. But don't toy with me. When I say I love you, I mean that with more depth than you might imagine. I'll never be a stern and pious farmer, Sadie. I can only be myself—the man I am with all the experiences that have formed me. But I can offer something that no one else can . . ."

"What's that?" she whispered.

"I'd cross oceans for you, Sadie. And I'd cross oceans for

our children, too. My daet obeyed your father's orders like a good Amish man. And while a rebellious husband might not be what you want, if Samuel went English, Sadie, I'd go after him. The bishop's orders be damned. I wouldn't sit around writing letters—I'd go bring him home. Love is action—isn't that what you say?"

Tears welled in her eyes. "Absolom said he wouldn't come back for religion anyway. . . . He'd come back for family."

"I could be that family, Sadie." Elijah reached over and ran a finger over hers. "I'm not the kind of man who's afraid of the Englisher world, or of oceans to cross. But I am daunted by the thought of a life without you. I want to be yours, and I want you to be mine. Anything less is misery."

"I want that, too."

Elijah's heart hammered in his chest, but if she was saying what he thought she was saying, then she needed his full attention. He reined in the horses at the side of the road. They were alone, the only sound that of a far-off owl. He turned toward her, and slid an arm behind her back. Chase shifted in his sleep, and Sadie patted the child gently, lulling him back into slumber.

"Marry me, Sadie," Elijah whispered. "If you're saying I could be enough for you . . . I'm not going to be like Mervin or some somber church elder. I'm going to be me—but I can love you and Samuel with all my heart. I'll take care of you. I'll take you both to the creek." He smiled tenderly. "Would you be a mamm to these two until Absolom can come for them? I know it's a lot to ask—"

"Loving them? That's not much to ask of me," she whispered. "That's the easy part."

"Then marry me. Please. Be mine, and I'll spend the rest

of my life convincing you that I was the best choice you ever made."

Sadie's eyes glistened. "You'll have to go speak with my father, you know. You'll have to ask his permission."

Elijah chuckled softly. "I can handle that. But the wedding will have to happen soon, Sadie. I don't want to put this off until next year. I want to marry you this fall— whether or not there's enough celery."

Sadie nodded, teary eyes fixed on his. "I'll marry you the first Tuesday my father will agree to."

"Good enough." Elijah leaned carefully over the child between them, and his lips came down onto hers. Sadie's eyes fluttered shut. When he pulled back, he added, "Sadie Fisher. I always did like the sound of that."

Her cheeks colored. "Well, you did tell me to marry a man who could kiss me breathless."

He shot her a grin. "And I stand by that. When we get the children settled with my mamm, I'll drive you home and make good on it."

Sadie laughed softly. "Promise?"

Elijah picked up the reins again and gave them a flick. The horses started moving once more, and he looked over the rolling pasture at the round full moon. He'd marry her on a Tuesday, and every day after for the rest of his life, he'd love her with everything he had. If a loyal heart was enough, she'd have all of his.

And he realized as the horses slowed at an intersection, ready to turn onto the road where he lived, that he'd finally found home. Today, he'd vowed to be a husband and a father, and instead of panicking, with her simple "yes," his heart had settled. Home was in the heart of the one woman he'd loved since he was a boy and she was a girl, and all he could think about was holding her hand.

The Amish life was deep and narrow, but for once he wasn't afraid of that plunge—his love ran deeper still. He'd be the difference for the children, and for Sadie, too. He'd love her like she deserved to be loved, and every night when he pulled her close in his arms, he'd remind her just how loved she was.

That beautiful Tuesday could not come quickly enough.

Epilogue

Elijah was baptized the first weekend in September, and the very next Tuesday, Jonathan and Mary were married. Mary's dress was let out to be a little looser than was typical, and it effectively hid her early pregnancy, although everyone knew at that point. The Morinville Amish community might be conservative, but they were also discrete, and since the couple were getting married, it was graciously overlooked. Babies were blessings—always. As for Jonathan and Mary's marriage, well, time would tell. They'd have to make the best of it. The community was also pragmatic.

In late October, Sadie and Elijah were married. The day started at four o'clock in the morning like any other—with chores to be done, and food to be cooked. Frost sparkled on the grass and crept up the fence posts—the chill of autumn bringing with it the promise of a long and cozy winter for a newlywed couple.

And then the flurry of activity began. Sadie had made her own wedding dress—this time a pale purple. She wanted it to be different from her first wedding, because this time she was marrying the man who filled her heart. Was he a risk? No, she realized. He wasn't. He was the safest choice she'd ever made because he loved her with heart and soul.

They were married outdoors, the guests seated on the Sunday service benches, and the blazing yellows and oranges of the leaves filled Sadie's heart with joy as she stood before her family and friends, facing the man who would be her husband.

"Will you support each other all your lives, respecting each other as God directs?" her father asked solemnly. "Will you cling to each other and no other, and stand by each other no matter what hard times may befall you?"

They responded with "We will," and Bishop Graber smiled tenderly at his daughter.

"Then I bless you as God blessed Abraham and Sarah, Isaac and Rebecca, Jacob and Rachel. May your marriage be filled with love."

It was done—they were wed!

The ceremony was much longer, of course. Sadie and Elijah sat down in chairs set a respectable twelve inches apart in a pool of warm autumn sunlight, and the married men and fathers took turns speaking about the joys and blessings of marriage. The minister preached a lengthy sermon, and Sadie could hardly even hear it, because seated next to her was her husband—he was well and truly her own—and she was so filled with happiness that she could focus on nothing else.

There would be a reception to follow, with tables set out on the lawn, matchmaking games for the single people, and much laughter and fun. And then later that evening, Sadie and Elijah would retire to her bedroom upstairs in her parents' home. Samuel and Chase would have a "sleep-over" with her parents. Rosmanda would care for baby Sarah, which was good practice for a girl who still believed she was ready for married life, regardless of everything she'd been through lately. Married life for Sadie and Elijah would begin with exactly one night of privacy.

It was how all marriages started—in the home of the bride's family—and the Graber house would be filled with children once more. They would be with her parents until spring, when Elijah and Sadie would set up house together for the first time. As for privacy—it would have to be stolen as everyone else looked away and pretended not to notice when they slipped off together . . . making Sadie's moments with her husband all the more exciting.

But as Sadie sat on that straight-backed chair, with Elijah at her side and the sermon floating around her with a swirl of autumn leaves, her thoughts were for her brand new family, including the three children they'd be raising together. Chase was already learning to do chores, and his tantrums had ceased without one spanking. Little Sarah was growing chubby and alert, and everyone loved caring for a new baby.

They were hers, this family stitched together with love.

The sermon drew to a close, and everyone bowed for prayer. Elijah slid his warm hand over hers, and her eyes popped back open. He shot her that boyish grin of his. He wasn't supposed to be touching her yet, and she couldn't help the smile that came to her lips.

Her husband, Elijah, a rebel to the last.

Connect with

Us

Visit us online at
KensingtonBooks.com
to read more from your favorite authors, see books
by series, view reading group guides, and more.

Join us on social media

for sneak peeks, chances to win books and prize packs,
and to share your thoughts with other readers.

**facebook.com/kensingtonpublishing
twitter.com/kensingtonbooks**

Tell us what you think!

To share your thoughts, submit a review,
or sign up for our eNewsletters, please visit:
KensingtonBooks.com/TellUs.

Romantic Suspense from
Lisa Jackson